Paul J. Newell w[illegible] an unsettlingly long ti[illegible]vel was *The Turnin*[illegible]ost unanimously as rea[illegible] of friends and family to coerce into buying it, he decided it was time to write another book. And, after a few more drinks and a couple of years off, he immediately set the cognitive wheels in motion. *Altered States* is the product of that motion.

ALSO BY PAUL J. NEWELL

The Turning

Altered States

Paul J. Newell

appian
publishing

Published by Appian Publishing

www.appianpublishing.com

First published in Great Britain by Appian Publishing 2010

www.pauljnewell.com

1 3 5 7 9 0 8 6 4 2

ISBN 978-0-9552245-2-2

Printed and bound in Great Britain by
J F Print Ltd, Yeovil, Somerset.

To Mum and Dad, with love.

With wholehearted thanks to Reina and Sam, for their tireless involvement, and without whom this book would exist only in a much poorer form, if at all. Thanks also to all of my other early proofreaders/sufferers whose keen eyes were gratefully received, and duly returned. And thanks to all of my friends and family who kept me sane despite my constant whinging and cantankerous ways.

In a more unwitting capacity, many great individuals contributed to the genesis of this book and I would like to acknowledge some of the *most* great here. First and foremost the Ming-bearded mind-botherer himself, Derren Brown, who provided the inspiration for this book in the first place, and indeed much brilliant material to draw upon. Additionally, of the many other influential items in my research the most significant include: the various early works of Richard Bandler & John Grinder; the superb Freakonomics by Steven D. Levitt & Stephen J. Dubner; a certain *New Yorker* article by Malcolm Gladwell; the moving *Independent* article and photography of Jason P. Howe; and, of course, the words and wisdom of Milton H. Erickson. See my website for more details if you so desire, but do please check out their splendid offerings.

- PJN

The greatest challenge in life is knowing what you want from it.

- Aaron Braunn

Author's Note

This story is fiction. However, historical references to names, events, dates and research studies are accurate. The science used in this book is real. Theories based on this science are those of the author ... and might just be true as well.

Prologue

A sick seventeen-year-old boy lays in his bed unable to move. He overhears three men talking to his mother in the next room. The three men are doctors. They tell his mother that her son will be dead by morning. The boy is infuriated. Not that he is going to die but that anyone could tell a mother that her son will be dead by morning.

A few moments later his mother steps into the room with an expression as serene as she is able, masking her deep despair.

The boy is paralysed with polio and he can barely speak, but he asks his mother to move his dresser; to push it up against his bed at an angle. She thinks he is delirious, but she is keen to comply with her son's last wishes and sets about moving the dresser. The boy issues further instructions to move the dresser back and forth, until he is satisfied. His mother does not understand why, and he does not tell her.

Finally, he is pleased. By virtue of the mirror on the dresser at its new angle, the boy can see through the doorway of his bedroom to the west-facing window of the next room.

This was his desire. To see the sun set one last time. Now he could fade with the daylight.

When the sunset comes he sees it across the whole sky. He doesn't see the tree or the fence or the boulder in its way. He knows they are there, but he stares at the sunset so intently that his mind blocks everything else out.

When the sun has set the boy loses consciousness.

But three days later, contrary to the doctors' prognosis, he wakes.

For months he lays in his bed, unable to move anything but his eyeballs. With nothing to do but watch and think. Over these months he gains a unique understanding of the human mind.

An understanding from which the world would learn.

An understanding by which the world would be healed.

The boy's name was **Milton H. Erickson** *(1901-80)*.

PART ONE

Branded Alive

One

My Moment

Ten years ago I died.

Okay, so I didn't actually die, but as far as the rest of the world was concerned, I ceased to exist.

And right now I was ceasing to exist in a hot tub, in San Diego, sucking on a strawberry daiquiri. Doesn't sound so bad, I admit. But there are a lot of things you don't know right now.

For the last few months I had been staying at this generic apartment complex – sorry, unique residential community. I like these places. They are pleasant, in a fake kind of way. Everything was just-so: the buildings perfectly maintained; the grounds litter-free; the vegetation neatly manicured and far greener than the climate would normally permit. It was like living in an artist's impression.

Occasionally, I paid a visit to the communal bathing area, but only at night. During the day it was way too busy with people sitting around looking at the swimming pool – seemingly content with bathing solely in its reflection.

Dotted around the pool were a number of hot tubs nestled under ornamental palm trees, and these offered a far more popular method of getting wet. I know they are massively decadent and a downright crime against the environment, but I appeased my guilt by reminding myself that they are also really warm and bubbly. Besides, I had bigger guilt issues to deal with in my life right now and this was my one method of escapism, of lubricating my ruminations.

As the bubbles jostled across my skin I leaned my head back and watched the breeze rustle through the broad leaves above. It reminded me of being a kid, when I used to imagine the wind as invisible giants brushing through the tress. That was how I explained it to myself back then. Explanations were so much easier to come by when you could invoke the service of invisible giants and the like.

Unfortunately, this night I had to conjure explanations without reference to a single mythical entity. And, moreover, I had to do so in the double-sized hot tub – the others being either out-of-order or occupied by canoodling couples. This presented the very real danger of interruption by outside parties, and sure enough my space was duly invaded by a bunch of drunken twenty-somethings. The male contingent were trainee pilots at the Navy base downtown. They were oozing so much charisma that a slick was beginning to form on the water. The girls of the party – Navy groupies presumably – lapped up all the macho bravado with flirtatious giggles. I did my best to be my super-sociable self but suddenly felt strangely insecure about my inability to land a helicopter on a boat.

Eventually, their beers ran dry, and the Navy crew all sloped off back to one-or-other's apartment to smoke some dope. All but one girl, who returned with a tall jug of the aforementioned strawberry-based cocktail, apparently drawn to my quirky English accent.

We chatted for a while about nothing in particular and it was, well, nice. Simple as that. And if it had been any other day, that might have meant something. It might have led somewhere. But today there were a lot more elements to the equation. And I soon realised it was only going to balance one way.

I made my excuses to the hot-tub-girl and climbed out of the water. She gave an affronted shrug and plodded off into the darkness, leaving nothing behind but a set of evaporating footprints. But that didn't matter. She was never going to register in my world. Not today. Instead she was consigned to the long list of fleeting blips that littered my personal timeline.

As I stood there, dripping wet and motionless, staring into the night sky, the words of the news clipping I'd read earlier that day replayed in my mind.

> **A forty-two-year-old man was arrested today in New Meadows, Nevada, in connection with the death of Pearle Jenkins. The six-year-old girl died a year ago, reportedly from a rare viral infection. Police have released no further information as to what role the man is alleged to have played in the girl's death, but the arrest has aroused suspicion surrounding the circumstances of the incident...**

This was not something I would have chosen to know – not anymore. I had already mourned the passing of Pearle Jenkins once. And although I played no part in her death, in some ways the event itself marked the culmination of all the bad decisions I had made in my life. The point when all my mistakes had manifested into a personal demon that struck a shard of guilt to the core of my soul.

And that was my moment.

For some people, there will be a *moment.* A moment that will define their life. A moment that every event before will unconsciously lead toward; and every event thereafter will be moulded by.

That was *my* moment.

It took me to a new dark place in my life. It took me to the edge of a million-gallon vat of whiskey that I was all ready to drown myself in.

Only recently had I allowed a glint of light to seep back in. Only recently had I felt ready to accept the fact that there was no mystery to obsess about; no answers to find. I was ready to think about the next step in my life.

But with this news the darkness came flooding back in like an unstoppable tide. I had no choice. I could not leave this behind – I could never outrun it.

I packed a few things into my rental Pontiac and started the six-hour drive to New Meadows.

Two

Forge Ahead

A man stood at the corner of the street, one foot flat against the wall behind him. His skin was pale and tired and was framed by a shock of unkempt hair. He took out a cigarette and a rip-off Zippo lighter, and brought them together in a motion long-since committed to muscle-memory.

And then he waited.

For a client.

Or a killer.

He was one of the nameless, faceless thousands who felt there was no other route than this one, his chosen career path; though the statistics did not make for an inviting set of Terms & Conditions. Over the next four years he could expect to be arrested seven times, suffer three serious non-fatal injuries and stand a one-in-four chance of being killed.

For all this he would earn less than the minimum wage, spend most of his days in the stairwell of a condemned building, and continue living with his mum on the sixteenth floor of a community housing project high-rise. Such were the attributes of his glittering occupation.

He was a rank-and-file dealer at the bottom of a very

large pyramid. He wasn't even a proper member of a gang yet. He just paid his dues for protection and the right to sell on their turf. There was none of the glamour others associated with his trade. Only hard labour, high risk and poverty.

So why did he do it? Why does anyone do it?

Dreams.

He knew how the guys at the top lived. These were the men who engendered respect and wielded power; the ones with the girls and the cars and the diamonds.

Looking up at these superstars of the underworld made many youths understandably star-struck. They were lured like the children of Hamelin.

These stars were where the dealer's sights were set. Pretty soon he hoped to earn a place as a foot-soldier in the gang, where he would still earn next-to-nothing, but crucially he would no longer be at the bottom of a very large pyramid; he would be *one step up* ... from the bottom of a very large pyramid. And that was what it was all about, climbing the ladder.

It was no different than the young woman who abandons her career and moves to Hollywood to wait on tables; doing the photo-shoots and bit-part auditions, holding out for her big break in the movies. The chances of making it were tiny, the risks were huge, but the incentives were astronomical.

And we all operate by incentives.

A man approached the dealer on the street. A new man; one the dealer didn't recognise.

'S'up?' the stranger said with an upward nod of the head. 'Yo holdin' any threads?'

'Aff. What tags yo chasin'?'

'Blood ticket?'

'Firm. Holdin' blues-uncut n tees-white. Intro?'

'Aff. Hit me wit' a midi-tee, stat.'

Brand-slang was what they called it. No-one was fluent. That was the point. It was a language that you could never pin down. It morphed over time; never persisting long enough for anyone to really know it, for meaning to ever stick. That was just one necessity for avoiding the law.

The dealer pulled out the requested item and handed it over.

'How green?'

'Two Jacks', ma'.'

As the money was changing hands neither of them noticed the black Mercedes roll up across the street; a tinted window gliding down silently. The first shot went through the dealer's upper arm, the second through his chest. Then the car was gone.

The client had been thrown to the floor uninjured. He acted quickly, pouncing to the aid of the victim as he punched nine-one-one into his phone. He knew that at the first sound of sirens he would have to make his move. He couldn't afford to be seen here.

Blood bubbled up through the client's fingers relentlessly as he pressed his hands down on the dealer's chest wound. Then he noticed that blood was pumping out of his back too – the hole went straight through.

As the crimson pool he knelt in grew larger, Detective Conner Alvisa glanced at the holdall lying beside him, its red-splattered contents now worthless.

What a frustratingly crazy world, he thought, that so much blood should be spilt over this...

Over a bag of t-shirts and jeans.

• • • • •

The 'rug trade' was the term coined by the media to describe the trade in fake branded textiles. There were no rugs of course, mainly shirts and jeans and the like, but the term had a nice familiar ring to it which sat neatly in the front-page headlines.

The story of the rug trade began over a decade before in New Zealand with a seemingly unrelated incident. A musician and recreational drug user was enjoying himself at a house-party when he was unfortunate enough to witness the horrific and public suicide of a friend high on meth. The musician had already lost one family member to drugs and this episode finally made him determined to kick his own habit for good. He began to experiment with legal alternatives, and he even sought out a professor of neuropharmacology to tutor him and aid in his search. Eventually, from papers published in the States, he identified a compound called benzylpiperazine, or BZP. It acted like methamphetamine but was non-addictive and carried an extremely low risk of overdose or death. What was more, it was a legal substance in most countries. The musician went on to set up a multi-million dollar company selling legal highs.

This development was what turned the tide against illegal street drugs across the world. And it wasn't just BZP; there was a massive selection of psychoactive substances designed to mimic the effect of pretty much every illegal drug on the street. Stimulants, opiates, hallucinogens – whatever your taste you could buy it online; you could even buy some at the grocery store.

All this meant that over time the bottom fell out of the illegal drug market and suddenly there were a lot of underworld dealers with nothing much to deal.

The attention of some wily dealers turned from white powder to white cotton, from Brazil to China. They realised that if you could manufacture an item for a dollar in China which had a street value of fifty in the West, then there was some serious money to be made. It was all about stitching in the right label.

The counterfeit goods market had been around as long as there had been goods to counterfeit, but this all happened at a time when intellectual property rights were big news. Record labels and movie companies were losing millions to illegal downloads and fake discs and they were putting massive pressure on world governments to do something about it. And the governments responded. Suddenly, protecting the profits of multinational corporations seemed to become the number one priority for the law.

So these two events collided. The counterfeit fashion industry gained the regimented structure and firepower of former drugs gangs; and the law enforcers gained a huge resource boost and impetus to shut the industry down. The result, predictably, was a mess. A bloody mess. And it got no messier than on the streets of New Meadows.

• • • • •

It was early evening when Conner Alvisa got back to the station. Only a few people milled about the large open-plan office. He was pleased to see Mila still at her desk. He knew that when someone died all over you, it was good to have someone to bitch to about it. Mila swivelled her chair to face Conner as if she'd been awaiting his return.

‘How’d it go with your new guy?’ she asked.

Conner held up his blood-stained cuffs.

‘Oh no. Please tell me he has some left,’ she said, regarding the blood.

‘Not a lot. And it’s not very warm now.’

‘Oh god, I’m sorry.’ She hesitated for a moment. ‘Kind of makes this harder to tell you then.’

‘What?’

She hesitated even longer. ‘Maybe sit down first.’

‘*That* bad?’ Conner slumped himself at his desk. ‘Go on, shoot. Make my day.’

‘Bigby’s been arrested.’

‘What?!’ Conner immediately stood up again and moved over to Mila’s screen displaying the arrest report.

‘*Murder*?’ he exclaimed with genuine confusion and leaned in to read the detail. ‘Six-year-old girl, twelve months ago? What the f–’ He held himself back from barking any profane rhetoric at Mila. ‘Is he in?’ he asked instead and marched off without awaiting a response.

‘Don’t...!’ Mila called after him hopelessly.

Conner was heading for the office of Chief of Detectives, William McCarthy. When he got there he burst in unannounced.

‘How could you let them arrest Bigby?’

McCarthy stood up to defend himself.

‘*Let* them? It was a federal thing. I didn’t even know about it till it was too late. Hell, I still don’t know anything.’

‘But, Jesus, we’ve been tracking this guy for eight months.’

‘Well, you don’t need to anymore. He’s banged up.’

‘Yeah, for the wrong crime. We had a chance to pull a whole network down here.’

‘I know; I know. What can I do? My hands are tied.’

‘Well, they might just as well be nailed to your desk,’ Conner fired as his parting shot. He stormed out and whistled past Mila who was standing outside.

‘That wasn’t fair, Conner,’ she said in pursuit.

‘Well ... life isn’t.’

Bigby wasn’t a dealer. He was a supplier. Or, at least, he was a go-between, a runner. It took six months of investigation just to find out his real name – nobody was stupid enough to use their own name in this game. He was called Jackson Burch, hence his dealer name, Bigby – ‘Big B’.

The investigation hadn’t uncovered enough solid evidence to pin anything on Bigby. But then, they didn’t want to arrest him anyway. He connected people. He was far more useful outside, doing his job. He could take them higher.

‘Where do we go from here?’ Mila asked.

Conner had calmed a little.

‘Home,’ he said with a resigned nod, and walked away.

Home would be dark and empty. It was always empty, but all the more so on days when you had seen someone die; when you had let someone’s life bubble through your fingers. It was a stark reminder that your own life was bubbling away too, just at a slower pace.

Conner knew he would be making a detour on the way back home that day.

He found Crystal Seth skulking behind a cheap hotel; one of his favourite skulking spots. The two men briefly exchanged pseudo-pleasantries, before Conner handed over some cash in exchange for three grams of kratom extract. Kratom is harvested from the leaves of a tree native to south-east Asia, and offers an energising and euphoric effect similar to opiates. You can buy kratom products in any of the specialist shops in the area. But some people are not so keen to be seen buying drugs, legal or otherwise, in the same way that some people are not so keen to be spotted visiting a sex shop. As such, there is a small niche market of street-trading legal highs.

Plus, rumour had it that Crystal Seth pepped up his wares a little. Conner wasn't sure exactly what Crystal Seth did to his products but the effect was real enough, and he knew it could only be *slightly* illegal. Certainly nothing compared to selling fake Levis on the street. Conner had been governed by the force for so long that he failed to see the irony in this sentiment.

What Conner also failed to see was that the gear he bought from Crystal Seth was identical to what he could have bought from a store around the corner at a far more reasonable price. The extra kick was purely placebo; a false high created by the thrill of obtaining drugs from a dodgy guy in a back alley; rendered even more potent by the fact that Conner was a cop.

After a muggy walk home Conner stepped into his apartment and checked the fridge. There was nothing in it that constituted food but there was three-quarters of a pint of milk, two days out-of-date. He unscrewed the lid and sniffed at the neck. Concluding that it wouldn't kill him, he poured it into a glass and added the three grams of recently purchased powder and two spoons of honey, before whisking it briskly with a fork.

In the lounge he placed the glass on the coffee table and moved over to the mantelpiece, boasting two photographs in matching aluminium frames. It wouldn't take a detective to determine that this was the mark of a woman's touch. But the layer of dust upon them revealed that the touch had not alighted here for quite some time. Fittingly, therefore, one of the pictures was of his wife and their son. It was taken when his son was about four, when he still had fair hair. That was about a year before they – well *she* – walked out on him. Conner gets to see his son every other week now, for the weekend. He gets to see his wife every other week too, for the passing of their timeshare progeny across the threshold and back.

The other picture on the mantelpiece was of his parents. He didn't see them as much as he should either. He always felt a pang of guilt when he thought about his parents, though he wasn't sure why exactly. It was as if he hadn't yet made enough of his life to justify the sacrifices they made to have him. Or something like that.

What he did know was that all of the people staring at him should be a larger part of his life than they were, and that one day he might get around to doing something about that.

He ran a finger down the face of his wife and smiled at her. Then he turned both pictures face down; turned away four pairs of disapproving eyes so they could no longer scrutinise him.

Slumped in the sofa he held the glass of milky-cocktail for a moment. Milk seemed such an innocent drink to be taking drugs with, albeit legal ones. It felt oxymoronic, but he didn't let it trouble him for too long. He necked the drink, laid back and let euphoria wash away another day.

Three

Bailing Out

I had come to New Meadows to meet an alleged murderer. There are a lot of people in New Meadows who might make you contemplate murder – if only in an idle musing fashion. Though it is not the kind of place I would wish to vacation in for the sake of idle musing. In fact, not even if my life, wealth or sexual health depended upon it. The beautiful rolling fields promised by such a pretty place-name are realised only by the endless green baize of gaming tables that stretch as far as the eye can see. Smoking is still legal here so as-far-as-the-eye-can-see is about fourteen feet, because as smoking enclaves around the globe get fewer and smaller, so the smoke gets denser and denser.

New Meadows is a border town that started life as a filling station in 1924. Now it's a gambling haven. It's fair to say that for all the things New Meadows is, meadowy it is not. To the best of my knowledge, the town has never nurtured the existence of a single blade of grass, rabid rodent or, in fact, any organism not sufficiently evolved to comprehend the rules of craps – and then lose their money playing it. Coincidentally, I have never evolved sufficiently to comprehend the rules of craps, which may have something to do with me being English. But, then, by the time I arrived in New Meadows it was the small hours of the morning and the only thing I felt sufficiently evolved to do was sleep.

As it turned out, I couldn't even do that very well, and I awoke the next morning to a fuzzy head. For a while I attempted to hide from the day and all that it represented, but the day was on top form and found me almost immediately, cowering under a hotel duvet. I peeled open my eyes and tilted my head toward the clock on the bedside table. The clock was partially obscured by the photo I had propped against it the night before. I reached out for it and stared into it once more. A habit I'd almost shaken until the previous day.

The picture was of a young girl on a sunny day – Pearle. A bob of fair hair bounced beside her face and a mischievous smile played on her lips. I drifted away to a better time; an imaginary time. I'd never met the girl, but at that moment I was with her. Her smile infectiously spread to my own face and I was at peace. Just for a moment.

The ability to enter altered states of consciousness is a powerful ability of the human mind. One that is very much under-utilised. Few people realise that our daily lives are littered with experiences of altered states – you don't need to be hypnotised or intoxicated. If you have ever arrived at work with no recollection of the journey in, then you experienced an altered state – a kind of 'autopilot' altered state. Or if you've walked out of a cinema after watching a superhero movie and felt invincible then this too was an altered state – a superdelusion state maybe.

My altered state was more meditative; pondering the questions surrounding Pearle's short life, for what seemed like the millionth time.

Since I first learned of her existence in this world.

Since her exit from it.

It was her mother who told me. The memory was still crisp in my mind. Still raw.

I remember standing at the entrance to the hospital ward, people scuffing past me clutching bunches of flowers and bowls of fruit and selections of magazines. I hadn't brought anything. What do you bring a woman you abandoned almost a decade before? I'm not sure a bunch of grapes and a copy of Cosmo really makes up for much.

Most people associate hospitals with some bad experience in their past: a childhood injury, an elderly relative passing away. I was no exception.

The time that passed as I dallied at the doorway was time I could ill afford. I knew I could not spend too long there. So I put procrastination to one side and set out on the journey to her bed, back to her side. Reality would insist that the ward was full of people, but to me there was no one else. There was just me and her, and the distance between us, which was less now than it had been for a long, long time. Every footstep echoed with meaning, as clearly as if I were tap-dancing in a vacant cathedral.

Then the dancing stopped.

There she was. I could picture my face at that moment, an ambiguous mix of emotions. Despite the circumstances I couldn't suppress a brief moment of undiluted excitement at seeing her again. Excitement which soon faded.

'Aaron?' she said in the faintest of whispers. The lump in my throat was so thick all I could do was nod as

I took her hand. And then she delivered those words that had hounded me ever since.

'She had your eyes, Aaron,' she whispered as her own eyes gently closed. The last words shared with a grieving mother ... with the only person who ever really understood me.

She was talking about Pearle, her daughter, who had died from a rare viral infection three days before. It was such an unusual condition that it had made the newspapers. Only in a minor bottom-of-page-fifteen kind of way, but that was enough to trigger the alert that brought me here.

The infection that took Pearle was claiming her mother's life force too as I stood beside her, running those words over in my mind, s*he had your eyes*. Pearle was not my daughter, so what kind of sense did it make?

Most people would not have paid such heed to these words. She was slipping in and out of consciousness at the time, prone to what doctors call confabulation: the filling of gaps in one's memory with fabrications believed to be fact. I know all about this. But, hell, if there was one thing I knew more about, it was *her*, the woman lying before me.

I had been out of her life for a long time, but that day, she saw me, and I mean she *saw* me, she *recognised* me. And those words were no idle ramblings of an ill mind. They weren't entirely lucid, but with every fibre of her body she felt that they represented the single most important fact I needed to know.

I didn't know why, and in the months that followed I tried to come to terms with the fact that I never would know why; that I never would make amends for letting her down so badly.

As her eyes closed there was the hint of a proud smile about them.

I could not smile.

I could only cry.

From that moment on I carried an unwavering belief that Pearle was the answer to a lot of things as far as my life was concerned – maybe everything. I had little evidence to support this hypothesis, but then I didn't really know what the questions were.

Pearle was my very own forty-two.

On occasion I worried that it was just my need for something to cling to, something to obsess about. I couldn't deny that I needed such a thing, since I had left behind all the substance of my life.

I don't get to interact with the world much these days, not on a personal level. I'm what you might call a low-key kind of guy. By low-key I mean that my parents don't even know I exist anymore. Funny how life goes full circle in some ways. As a kid I was pretty darn good at hide-and-seek. Today hide-and-seek was my day job. Mainly hide.

The reason for me hiding was nothing clichéd like there being people wanting to kill me. This may also be true but it was just a footnote in my story. The main reason was that I am, well, kind of special; I have certain abilities. And there were some people – powerful people – to whom I would be very useful. There was a time when I thought helping these people was the right thing to do, but then I changed my mind. That's when I had to bail out; to run away. That was a long time ago now.

At first you feel guilt at severing yourself from everyone you know, at absolving your responsibilities. Then after a while you actually start to believe you don't exist anymore. You walk the streets like an invisible man, with an unparalleled sense of liberation. It's quite exhilarating for a while.

But the exhilaration soon transitions to isolation; an isolation beyond which can never be imagined. Most people suffer loneliness at some point in their life. Anyone unlucky enough to be devoid of family or friends for a time. But to also have no enemies, no neighbours, no colleagues, no postman; to have no consistent figures in your life at all; is a terrifying experience. The meaning begins to ebb away from your world. People become nothing but automaton to you. That is a very dangerous place to be. When people become objects ... the world turns bad.

I didn't want the world to turn bad. Not if I could help it. So, in many ways, I felt I was clinging to the last shreds of sanity via the girl in that photo, because when looking at her I actually felt something inside – which was a rare experience for me these days. Or maybe that wasn't it. Maybe I just needed a stable figure in my life; and one thing you couldn't deny about Pearle was that she was very stable. She was six years old when the picture was taken – and she always will be now.

I shook myself from my reverie; I had a job to do. I needed to see a man in a prison. The man arrested in connection with Pearle's death. This was not as straightforward as it should be. Nothing ever is for me.

I'm something of an expert at laying low. I could write a book about it – though promotion may prove problematic. Specifically, I can impart that one particularly bad way of laying low is to walk into a city jail and visit a murderer; what with all the policemen, cameras, form-filling and so forth. So there was really only one alternative, and it was potentially a rather expensive one.

I pulled on some clothes, and grabbed the briefcase full of cash I always had handy for just such occasions.

I headed into town and then slipped off the main Strip. One block makes a big difference in New Meadows. Sneak behind its glitzy façade and you find the true depth and hue of its foundation. Ugly storage units, grimy offices, low-grade accommodation for the underpaid workers. It was virtually a different world. This was the real New Meadows. The rest was just a front. A crocodile smile.

As unwelcoming as it was, this was just the ambience I was seeking. I was heading for a bail-bondsman and I needed a distinctly back-street kind of outfit. A place that wouldn't ask too many questions. I also needed to be face-to-face. Calling 1800-GET-ME-OUT would not suffice.

The door tinkled as I walked in.

'Can I help you?' The question originated from a pale-looking man sitting behind a dishevelled desk. He seemed somewhat surprised at receiving any custom in person. The décor seemed quite surprised too. In fact, it seemed to have popped out for lunch. The ceiling was short of its full complement of polystyrene tiles, and most of those that remained bore the familiar brown stain of a leaky air-con unit. Loose cables trailed across the floor beneath furniture that was mostly fashioned from bare chipboard. A real classy joint.

'I'd like to post bail,' I stated succinctly.

There was a name plate on the man's desk. It wasn't a shiny brass affair. More of a grubby plastic fridge-magnet, propped up against a pot of pencils. As such it served the double purpose of clearly stating the name of its owner – one Kent Bradshaw – and of equally clearly stating that he was a loser. He was not a bad man, I could tell that; with a less than savoury employer most likely. In this respect I felt a twang of sympathy for him, and at some level felt bad about what I was about to do. But sometimes we have to do things that make us feel bad. Sometimes there is a greater need.

'Do take a seat,' Kent urged.

I didn't take a seat. I just gave him the particulars of my desired inmate, a man named Jackson Burch. The clerk tapped the details into the terminal in front of him, peering intently at the screen, flashing the occasional look of apparent confusion. Clerks in such mundane roles often strive to convey the impression that there is something extremely complex and unusual about entering the same half-dozen pieces of information they enter a hundred times a day. You can experience this phenomenon when checking-in for a flight. Despite the fact that the airline already has all of your details and has been expecting your arrival for the three weeks since you booked the ticket, the check-in clerk still appears utterly confused at your arrival and indeed your very existence in this world. It's a power thing – that is, trying to pretend they have some. Fortunately, at the end of Kent's taxing ordeal he still found the energy to speak.

'The bail is five-hundred thousand dollars. Our fee is ten per cent, payable in advance. How would you like to settle?'

I placed the briefcase I was carrying on the desk without saying a word.

'Okay,' he said, with a slight, incredulous inflection.

'And what will you be using as collateral against the balance?'

I pushed the briefcase forward six inches in a confident motion, and offered a dry smile.

Kent looked at me quizzically. 'You have half-a-million dollars in cash? ... In a briefcase? ... And you wish to use a bail bondsman?' he over-punctuated.

'Yes. I have five-hundred thousand dollars ... In a briefcase ... In one-hundred dollar bills ... And I'd like to use a bail bondsman,' I said with subtle mimicry. 'Is that a problem?'

'N-No,' the clerk stuttered. 'But you do know you can just go right up to the court with this money, yeah?'

The guy tilted his head. I tilted mine.

'And *you* know that some people place a very high price on anonymity. Right?' I leaned in a little. 'I trust you can respect that?'

By this point Kent would be thinking I was a mafia gangster wanting to knock off a witness, or someone with a similarly socially-unacceptable hobby. I figured he'd at least be smart enough to know that compliance was a good life-preserving tactic when dealing with such people.

Kent busied himself again at the keyboard with beads of sweat beginning to bristle on his forehead.

'How long will it take?' I enquired.

'Well, we'll have to count the money, of course.'

'Of course.'

'But assuming there is no problem, the bail will be wired straight from our account; and he should be out within three or four hours.'

'Excellent. I'll wait.' Finally, I took a seat. The guy was getting steadily more nervous. I can have this effect on people. When I want to.

A couple of hours later I got the nod from Kent.

'Everything's in order. The bail's been posted,' he announced with what looked akin to bladder-evacuating relief.

'Great,' I responded with an outstandingly cheerful smile which confused the hell out of the poor guy.

When it came to explaining to his boss why he'd mistaken a case of one-dollar bills for half-a-million bucks he'd be left with very few answers.

What can I say? I'm a very persuasive guy.

Four

Once Beaten

Conner was at his desk early. He always was. Detective work was the kind of work that followed you home; the kind of work that woke you up early in the morning to a mild state of anxiety. It was an occupational hazard and Conner accepted that.

He'd been attempting to tease meaning from the reports in front of him since 6.30am, but they were proving resistant to his best teasing tactics. So, when Mila arrived she was a welcome distraction, especially as she was escorting fresh bagels and coffee.

'Bagels?' Conner enquired. 'On a Thursday?' Friday, of course, was traditional bagel day.

'I thought that having breakfast *twice* this week might be good for you.'

'Hey, I have breakfast.'

'Yeah, not quite as many calories in a cigarette as you might think.' She plucked the bready contents from a brown paper bag. 'Cinnamon-and-Raisin or –' she peered at the second '– Shit-Loads-of-Seeds?'

Conner jabbed a key on his keyboard. 'Given that I'm already suffering a poppy-seed related F-key malfunction, I shall opt for the former, if that's okay. Thanks.'

Mila took a seat at her desk. 'What've you got there?' she enquired, nodding at the report in front of Conner.

Conner turned to her pensively. 'It's the ballistics report from the other day's shooting.'

'Something interesting?'

'I think so.' He thumbed through a couple of leaves of pre-amble to the last page of the report and handed it to Mila. 'According to this, the same gun that killed our dealer friend was used in another gang murder last week.'

'So?'

'So, that victim was on the *other* side.'

There are only two gangs in New Meadows worth knowing about. The first, Scrips, is a gang of primarily African-American members, which originally formed in Southern California as a splinter from the infamous LA gang, Crips. The gang grew and spread quickly. Within a few years of forming dozens of sets popped up in Southern California and eventually in the major cities of Nevada. In New Meadows, Scrips control the streets on the North side of the Strip. The South side of the Strip is owned by the only other gang worth worrying about in New Meadows: the notorious Hispanic street gang, Sanguins.

Tensions between the gangs are constantly high, and gang-related killings in the city are not uncommon. But over recent weeks there had been a conspicuous leap in attacks and the newspapers had been quick to mark this as the beginnings of turf war.

Mila assessed the facts offered to her by Conner. 'So what's troubling you?' she asked referring to the two killings. She was experienced enough to know that members of opposing gangs being killed by the same gun was not such an unlikely scenario. Assaults and killings within a gang were commonplace as a show of power and punishment when a member breaks the rules.

Also, competition between members of the same gang is very high. They are all vying for power and promotion. The kind of member that might pop off a member of a rival gang to earn some kudos, may just as likely kill a rival member of his own gang to remove the competition.

'What's troubling me,' Conner responded, 'is that neither of the killings seemed like an inside job. Both of them were drive-bys for a start.'

'Okay. Well maybe the guy who did the shooting last week was sensible enough to dump the weapon back on the black market and it ended up in the hands of the other side.'

Conner shook his head. 'Firepower is an important and expensive commodity. If guns do move around it would be within the gang. Besides, it would be quite a coincidence that the gun happened to be used the following week in a similar shooting.'

'Similar?'

'Yeah. The MO for the two crimes is virtually identical: fairly covert drive-by shooting; single shooter; single target. And, in fact, it's this MO that's troubling me the most.'

'Go on'

'Drive-bys are about making a statement to a rival gang. *Killing* anyone is almost secondary. It's about making a scene. Shed-load of shooters; lots of bangs; lots of screeching of tyres; and lots of people lying on the floor afterwards, perforated or otherwise. The murder I witnessed was too slick, too clinical. The fact that I'm sitting here now, covered in bagel crumbs, is testament to that.' He paused to brush some crumbs off his lap. 'In fact, if I didn't know better, I would say it was very much like a hit job.'

'A hit? But these were nobody bottom-of-the-pile rug dealers. Who's gonna pay to get them whacked?'

'I dunno.' Conner released a big sigh as he turned to gaze out of the window. 'Maybe the newspapers are having a slow time.'

'Yeah, or the city undertakers.'

'Ha, a hitman undertaker.' Conner smiled. 'I like that. That kind of makes sense.'

'Maybe in professional wrestling.'

'Well, New Meadows is just about as fake.'

'True.'

After another frustrating morning of exploring dead-end avenues, Conner spotted the familiar cocky gait of an assistant DA striding down the corridor outside the office. Dickens was his name and he might just represent Conner's last hope of gleaning some information about the Bigby arrest. Conner surged into the corridor with last-hope powered momentum.

'Hey, Dickie,' he called after the imposing figure.

Dickens turned around. He was four inches taller than Conner and about twenty pounds lighter. And his Thursday-suit was an order of magnitude more expensive than Conner's best suit would be when he got around to owning one.

'Mr Alvisa. Haven't seen you move this fast for a while. *Must* be important.'

'Always keen to see you, that's all,' Conner said with a wink as he motioned Dickens to one side of the corridor.

Cops and DAs share a special kind of relationship. No respect is present on either side of the equation but both are acutely aware of how much they depend on each other. The status quo is maintained with them both floating around in an atmosphere of mutual cooperative loathing.

'What do you know about the Jackson Burch arrest?' Conner asked in a hushed voice.

'Why? You interested in him?'

'No, just wanted to pester you.'

'You are excelling.'

'Thanks.' Conner flashed a ironic grin. 'So?'

'So, I know two things about the Burch hearing and that's all. One, I won't be the prosecuting attorney because they're bringing in a federal prosecutor from DC.'

'Figures.' That was expected but still a blow. It meant that the chances of blagging a look at the case notes just dropped from unlikely to non-existent. 'And the second thing?'

'That around –' he glanced at his watch '– two hours ago ... Jackson Burch was bailed out onto the street.'

'What? You're kidding?' Conner hadn't even considered this as a possibility. 'You got the details?'

'Of course,' Dickens said with an overplayed twang of sarcasm. 'I actively memorize all details of the court's proceedings just in case I can be of service to you.'

'Thanks. Appreciate it,' Conner concluded sarcastically and walked away to go look up the information himself.

A few moments later he was back at his desk studying the details of Bigby's bailer and bail-bondsman. A few minutes after that he concluded that whoever the bailer was he had used fake ID. No surprises there, which left only one course of action. He stood up purposefully, grabbing essentials from his desk.

'I'm off to visit a back-street bail-bondsman,' he announced to Mila. 'You coming?'

Mila was engrossed in something at her desk such that the words did not even register.

'Mila?'

She looked up this time. 'Sorry, what?'

'Back-street bail-bondsman questioning. Fancy it?

'Oh, umm, inviting offer, but I'll pass. Got some ... stuff to sort out here.'

'Okay.'

On his way out, Conner was pulled to one side by McCarthy.

'Listen,' the chief said, 'don't go sniffing around the Bigby arrest. I don't think it would be good for your health.'

'Why? What do you know?'

'Nothing, other than I've had federal heavies on my case giving me the same warning. I believe them. You should too. They don't want us messing around in this.'

'Sure.'

Conner nodded slowly and walked out. He didn't want to commit further because that would mean either lying or disobeying. The truth was that he was too personally invested in Bigby to drop out now, but he was damned if he was going to investigate on his own time. Cops in the movies may do their best work whilst suspended but he was rather fond of the pay cheque.

Conner tried his best not to curse his bad fortune regarding the Bigby release. He knew that such things just came with the territory of undercover investigation. With sensitive operations you can't go around shouting about them. You can't put little Post-it notes on people's desks – like in City Hall – saying 'If you know anything about this man please give Detective Alvisa a call on 555–etc.' Hence, things can happen outside one's sphere of knowledge. Like this.

In an ideal world Conner would have tailed Bigby from when the guy had been released. But Conner was a few hours behind the curve for that to be an option, so his only next shot was trying to figure out who bailed Bigby out. Presumably, bailer and bailee would be meeting up at some point and that would lead him back to Bigby.

As he walked along the street, he mulled over the scenario. The federal heavies come waltzing in; arrest a guy with some cock-and-bull murder story; slap gagging orders left, right and centre, like it's some issue of national security; and then? Then they grant the guy *bail*. Bail is virtually unheard of in murder cases and this was clearly no ordinary murder case. When did everything stop making sense?

When Conner arrived at the bail-bondsman's establishment he found the front office empty. He stepped in and looked around the shabby room. On a desk there was a computer screen showing a half-completed game of solitaire. Then he heard distant raised voices from the back of the building. He un-holstered his gun and made his way quickly but cautiously down a dimly-lit corridor. At the end was a closed office door. The din of voices was louder but he could make out no figures through the obfuscated glass in the door. He placed one hand on the handle and held his gun in readiness. Slowly, he turned the handle and held it for a moment to wait for a reaction. There was none. In a swift motion he swung the door away from himself and brought both hands to his gun. The room was empty. It was a boardroom of some kind with an oval desk in the centre. On the desk was an open briefcase with piles of dollar bills spewing from it, some of them onto the floor.

The raucous voices had now evolved into the unmistakable sounds of a man being repeatedly punched. Adjoining the office was a small kitchen area leading to the back yard. That was where the beating was taking place. Conner judged that only two people were involved and started to move quickly. By the time he was outside the larger and uglier of the two men was wielding a metal bar.

'Police!' Conner screamed. 'Drop it. Now!'

The bar-wielder stood motionless for a while, assessing the situation, slowly arriving at the inevitability of each of the possible outcomes. Eventually, he dropped his arm to his side, and then the bar to the floor. Whilst the big man was growing accustomed to the new balance of power, Conner called-in for uniformed back-up and a paramedic. As he did so, the guy on the floor spoke up weakly.

'No,' he rasped, 'I don't want to press charges.'

'I don't care,' Conner replied. He quickly assessed the man's physical condition. 'You need medical attention. And this guy needs to calm down. So, either way, both of you are getting some flashy-light action. Now, anyone care to tell me what the hell's going on here?'

Silence.

Silent submissive cowering from one; silent seething anger from the other.

'I'm not very happy about this, I'll have you know,' Conner pointed out to break the silence. 'I'm not supposed to be here. I only came for a quiet little chat and now I'm going to have to file a bloody report about it.' The two remained motionless. 'Well, this is nice. Whilst we're sharing, you might like to know that I came here to ask about a man called Jackson Burch.'

The angry guy's seething erupted vocally. 'That idiot –' pointing to the man on the floor '– lost me half-million bucks over him.'

'What do you mean?'

The man quickly regained control and composure. 'I'm not saying anything more till I've spoken to an attorney.'

'Great.' Conner rolled his eyes. He had to wait a while for the uniformed guys to turn up. He used these moments to arrive at the conclusion that there was no way his chief would not find out he was here, disobeying his orders. He figured that as he was already in deep enough shit it wouldn't make much difference if he kept digging. So he took a ride to the hospital with the battered guy – one Kent Bradshaw, who was employed as a clerk at the bail-bondman's office. The man doing the beating was his boss, and the altercation was over the bailing of Bigby. Apparently, the man who had bailed him had handed over a case of hundred-dollar bills that later on turned out to be a case of *one*-dollar bills. The case had only five thousand dollars in it when it should have had five-*hundred* thousand dollars.

'That's not a mistake you make easily,' Conner pointed out to the clerk.

'I know that. Especially when you know this is the result.' He pointed to his tumescent features. 'I can't explain it. I sat there and I counted every single note.'

'No chance of the case being switched?'

'No, I put the case straight in the safe afterwards. Besides, the notes in the case were the actual ones I counted because I marked the top note of each deck as I went through. It just defies logic. He must have been some kind of magician or something – I don't know.'

Conner attempted to garner an accurate description of the man.

'How old was this man?'

'Err, mid-thirties...'

'Okay.' Conner jotted it down.

'...to late-forties.'

'Riiight.' He amended his notes. 'Height?'

'Average.'

'Build?'

'Kind of ... medium.'

'Excellent. Hair?'

'Dark-slash-fair.'

'Slash bald?'

'Sorry?

'Never mind.'

Conner didn't dare to wish that the office had CCTV. By the state of the establishment it was quite remarkable that even the walls managed to perform their intended function, let alone any complicated surveillance equipment doing so. Besides, he knew this kind of outfit was designed to service a certain class of clientele, those who did not like their picture being taken.

Conner plodded his way back from the hospital. It

was a few miles home but he didn't mind the walk; he walked pretty much everywhere. Walking offered high-quality thinking time. Plus he found all other modes of transport in the city pretty much unbearable. Grid-locked roads. Crowded subways. Slimy taxi drivers.

After thirty minutes of walking and thinking, something finally struck him. It wasn't so much an idea; more of a ... bat.

Moments later he came to, slumped against a wall with a baseball bat thrust to the centre of his chest. At the other end of the bat was a small-framed individual wearing a kid's toy mask. Or maybe it was just a kid wearing a kid's mask. Through his haze he couldn't be sure.

He shivered slightly from shock and breathed heavily. His face had hit the wall on the way down and he felt a trickle of blood from just above his eyebrow begin its journey down his face, following the tracks of his tears. He had not yet mustered the energy for even an expletive before the bat-wielder spoke. The voice was disguised by a cheap synthesiser in the mask.

'Leave Bigby alone,' it said with tinny resonance that clawed at Conner's pounding head. 'Or things will get much worse. For you. For everyone.'

He was too sluggish to respond before a final prod from the bat signalled the departure of its owner. As he watched the figure walk away he realised that there was something odd about the walker's gait, but he couldn't place what it was. And he knew this wasn't the time to care.

Slowly and somewhat apprehensively, Conner reached up to examine the damage to the back of his head. Duly his fingers returned to rest before his eyes, and they were completely covered in ... nothing. In fact, the only fresh blood offered by his head was from the cut above his eye. Last time he checked, his skull wasn't made from titanium, which meant that the bat couldn't have been made from wood or *anything* hard. What kind of thug's weapon-of-choice is a rubber bat?

Another riddle that could wait. Getting home was his only immediate priority. He stumbled to the nearest busy street and hailed a cab.

At home he nursed a bump on his head, a cut over his eye, and what remained of his pride. He longed for someone else to be doing the nursing. He'd had a lot thrown at him in the last few days and it suddenly felt that in this game of dodge-ball that people called life, everyone else was standing on the other side of the court. He wanted someone to be on his side, for someone to just give a damn.

He placed the mantelpiece photographs face down once more and slumped back onto the sofa to begin rolling a salvia joint. The dried leaves of *Salvia divinorum* – literally 'sage of the seers' – act as an intense but short-lived hallucinogen. Most people don't get on with salvia. Many find it frightening. But paranoia was not an issue for Conner right now – he really *was* being persecuted.

The woman was slender, really slender, but she carried it well, so as not to appear at all skinny. Her hair was brilliant red; her skin translucent blue. And her edges were peculiarly well defined, as if they had been inked-in by a graphic-novel illustrator. Conner recognised her, though she had no face to speak of. As a large bee circled her body, the woman contorted rhythmically for a moment, in a motion that couldn't quite be described as a dance. Then she turned and walked away. Conner watched her hips sway distinctively as she passed effortlessly through the wall.

The effects tapered off only minutes after they had begun. Reality solidified around Conner once more and his thoughts snapped back to his assault a few hours earlier. Suddenly, it was so obvious what was distinctive about his assailant's gait.

He realised that the man in question was in fact ... a *wo*man. Further proof, if needed, that even a man concussed can maintain relatively clear focus when a woman's bottom is involved.

Yet another question. What kind of thug's gender-of-choice ... is female? – no offence.

One thing was certain. This was not the Feds. If they were in the business of sending out thugs to warn off nosey cops, then slim chicks with rubber bats would not be their style.

Surely?

Five

Taking a Life

In New Meadows, the only escape from the tacky, flashy, nastiness of the casinos is the undeniable class of the grungy themed bars and restaurants. I found myself in old-town, contrary to much sound advice, including the government health warnings on the road signs: *Warning: this neighbourhood may seriously damage your life.*

I was purposefully striding along, casually risking violent muggings as I did so, when the rain began to fall. Yeah, rain in a desert – such is my meteorological fortune. Luckily, I would be ducking into the next establishment, which looked like it was ready to welcome me with open gun barrels. Satori it was called, some has-been Japanese-themed café-bar. And in an impressive homage to the concept of irony, the sub-theme seemed to be water. It was everywhere. By design, rather than the result of some bad plumbing work, but gratuitous to say the least. But then, New Meadows is the definition of gratuity – and not the 15% kind.

I made my way to the bar, rather unnerved by the vivid orange carp looking up at me from beneath the glass floor. Occasionally, a column of water fell from the ceiling and disappeared into a hole in the ground. Hopefully, this was governed by some clever system designed to avoid the clientele, rather than hydrating them in a fashion they hadn't requested.

I pulled up a stool at the bar and mumbled a request of a beer at the Japanese-themed barmaid, who was about as oriental as a Big Mac. Shortly she slid a glass in my direction. The bar she slid it over yielded no exception to the watery theme. Water coursed through a cavity within it, along with tiny brightly-coloured fish no longer than a fingernail.

'It's free if you want to take it upstairs,' the barmaid said nodding toward a baroque iron staircase that spiralled around a column of tumbling water, leading to the mezzanine level.

I knew what she meant, and I wasn't in the mood.

'No,' I said. 'Thanks.'

As I sipped, I toyed with a photograph between my digits, idly staring through it. I allowed myself an indulgent moment of escape until the barmaid dispassionately flitted a cloth across the bar in front of me, and I was back in the room – back to reality. I allowed the sensations of the external environment to return to me one-by-one, and then I held the picture of Pearle up to the side of my face.

'Do *you* think she had my eyes?' I queried toward the barmaid. The woman looked rather perplexed at the question.

'Ummm,' was all she could muster.

'Never mind,' I said with a quick shake of my head, and placed the photo on the bar in front of me. Of course, this little charade was all for the benefit of the man sitting next to me.

That was why I was here, in New Meadows, in this bar. To sit next to this man, Jackson Burch, whoever he was. Instantly – if not slightly sooner – I knew I didn't like him. Five minutes later I knew I had to kill him. He was a bad man, you see. He'd done bad things. I could tell. That's the way it is with me. Not the killing part, but the knowing things, bad things, about people; the not liking people.

It's a drag.

In my periphery I saw the guy make the occasional sideways glance at the picture. I'd placed it slightly to one side – conspicuously closer to him. An invitation to steal a glimpse – not that he usually awaited invitation. He began to shuffle a little in his seat. I purposefully moved my attention away from the picture. Now we weren't sharing her. Now she was all his. Minutes passed and a tension grew between us that was beginning to condense on the bar top. Eventually, I broke the silence.

'Do you like her?' I asked.

The man didn't speak but threw me a look that betrayed a battery of inner thoughts and questionable desires.

'Do you *know* her?' I continued, analysing his every movement.

And then finally, 'Did you *kill* her?'

Unsurprisingly, that got a response out of him.

'Who the fuck are you to be asking questions?' he snapped with unsubtle hostility.

'I'm the guy who bailed your ass out of jail to ask you these questions,' I responded enigmatically, choosing not to match his aggression.

Burch sported an expression somewhere between

suspicion and confusion. 'Expensive questions,' he said. 'You know there are visiting hours, right?'

'I'm not a big fan of jails,' I said with a distasteful look, which I hoped would make him a little jittery. Mystery bail-touting benefactors in his world rarely have good intentions. I guess that was true of me too, although he could have done a lot worse. I mean, I wasn't *definitely* going to kill him.

I didn't need to say anything else now. It was probably beginning to dawn on his dullard mind that his future participation in this world might depend on his answers to the questions being put to him. He looked at the photo again, sliding it closer to himself.

'Is this the girl I'm supposed to have murdered?' he asked.

I nodded.

'Then no, I didn't.'

Normally, I would not be so direct. Normally, I'd be about as direct as a philandering politician. But when determining whether someone had committed a murder, there was no need for subtleties. When asked a question about an objective fact of such magnitude, it would be virtually impossible to react without revealing the truth, regardless of what you said. If, of course, the questioner knew what to look for.

I knew what to look for.

And the truth was ... he didn't kill Pearle; he didn't even know her. He didn't know my story or the people I had lost. He was not a player in that episode of my life. He was just unfortunate. Wrong place: here. Wrong time: now. Wrong guy: me – pissed (in the vernacular of either side of the Atlantic).

It wasn't the truth that I had wanted. It wasn't a truth

that got me any nearer to closure on this issue. I sighed and tapped the table with my fingers. Where did this leave me? It left me with a rather obvious question.

'If you didn't kill her, why have you been arrested?'

'I've been set up.'

'By whom?'

He shrugged. 'I wish I knew'.

I pondered this for a moment before asking, 'Why did you come to New Meadows?'

In response to the question Burch downed the last of his drink and motioned to leave. Surprisingly, it seemed, he hadn't come here for a spot of charity work.

'Doesn't it trouble you?' I said, without looking up.

The man paused. 'What?'

'That whoever set you up has done it so well that they've managed to convince the police?'

'Sure it does. Don't see what you're gonna do about it.'

'Listen, I don't care about you, it's true. But I want to know what happened to this girl. So I want to know who set you up. So I reckon that makes me about the only person who is gonna to do anything about it, yeah?'

'Or you could just be a cop.'

'So you were here with criminal intent?'

'I didn't say that.'

'Not directly,' I flashed a smile which verged all too close to cocky. So much for subtlety; I really should have known better. With that smile I knew I'd blown it. I wasn't going to get anything useful out of him now.

He narrowed his eyes. 'I need a piss,' he said and headed off toward the bathroom.

He wasn't the only one that needed relief. I was finding it increasingly difficult to remain affable with him. With every word I gleaned another morsel of information, beyond the word itself. And they were not tasty morsels. So whilst the liquid of his first few beers was exploring some Japanese-themed porcelain, there was only one thing left to decide.

Was I going to leave empty handed?

Or was I going to take a life?

I searched around in my jacket pockets and recovered a small cylindrical object. It contained a substance known as Necrovial, which is used for spiking drinks with a nasty kick. It does so in a virtually untraceable manner. It uses 'clever-nano-shit' to deliver a spike of insulin into the bloodstream. An overdose of insulin reduces the level of glucose in the blood to a point where the brain can no longer function. But being a substance found naturally in the body it is virtually impossible to detect as a cause of death.

Insulin has been used as a murder weapon almost since it was first used to treat diabetes in the 1920s. It says something about the world that the first mechanism devised for delivering insulin into the bloodstream orally was perfected by a government agency for the purpose of assassinating people rather than saving them.

Ethical debate aside, Necrovial is an extremely sophisticated method of killing, which can always come in handy for the odd spot of fatal imbibing. I 'acquired' a supply before I left the agency and as of yet haven't exploited it once. That was about to change. Maybe.

My best mate was making his way back from the bathroom. In his absence I had ordered him another shot of bourbon. I had also palmed a Necrovial capsule in my hand, in readiness for his unwelcome return. But before I could take that final step, I needed to elicit one final piece of information. This was going to be more difficult. This was where subtlety came in.

In his past he had been involved with the police with regard to his unhealthy interest in young girls. He'd done some real nasty things, and just standing near him made me feel dirty to the core. But that wasn't enough. It wasn't enough to award me the role of judge and jury. I needed to know something else. I needed to know whether he was going to do it again. Because knowing this fact, I reasoned, could conceivably make the act of killing him the right thing to do.

Uncovering this detail was not like asking someone if they had a blue car or whether they'd killed somebody, with objective definite answers. This was exposing hidden desires and future intent. He may not even know the answer himself consciously. But underneath it would be there – everything was.

Just as he was lifting his drink to his mouth I placed my hand over it and forcefully slammed it back to the bar. The action was intentionally incongruent and at odds with what little the guy knew of my behaviour so far. It would jar his comfortable mental state; cause his unconscious mind to stall for a moment. It's called a pattern interrupt – the disruption of an indivisible pattern of behaviour in an unanticipated way. It leaves a person with no program of what to do next. It leaves them looking for a way out, open to suggestion.

Looking the man squarely in the eye, I instantly began to speak with an unusual pace and tone.

'It's just that it's interesting to know ... why we do the things we do. And how sometimes we manage to *justify* to ourselves actions which we know at some level to be wrong. Like maybe we speed in a restricted zone, but we tell ourselves it's okay because it's really *late*; there's no one around. And we *know* the road well. It's like an *acquaintance*, so it's fine. It's fine to go *beyond the limit*.'

I placed particular emphasis on certain words and parts of words, prompting his subconscious to stitch together a subtextual meaning.

'So all the time, when we do these bad things, we are *prob*ing our minds, *penetrating* our thoughts, until we *touch* on a loop*hole* that will allow us to *do* these things we like and escape the immorality.'

As I continued to fold the massively layered suggestions into the metaphor Burch stood virtually motionless but responded with almost imperceptible twitches of affirmation.

'So there really is only one question left,' I stated in conclusion. 'Will you do it again?'

In an instant the man was composed and laughing at me foolishly.

'What *are* you talking about, man?' he jibed.

To anyone but a handful of people in the world, that was a perfect transition. The telltale micro-expression would have passed everyone else by unnoticed. But not me. Just for that split second it was written on his face as clearly as his five-o'clock shadow. And now that his misdemeanours were playing wholly on his conscious mind, all I need do was repeat the question – just to be sure.

'*Will* you do it again?'

This time he said nothing, just frowned at me as if I was a madman – spot on there I guess – and shook his head in confusion. But once again a tiny twitch of a face muscle belied his inner feelings. That was all I needed. I cracked open the fatal capsule that was nestled in my palm, then left the bar without wasting another word.

Within thirty-seconds of being in the street I knew exactly what I was going to do next and it started with me repeatedly kicking a nearby wall in frustration. I chose this symbolic gesture of head-banging rather than the real thing as it carried with it significantly less risk of cranial haemorrhaging. A good tip by anyone's standards.

Then I made my way back to the bar. Burch didn't have time to know what hit him. He was halfway towards the door by the scruff of his throat before he was going for his holster; at which point he noticed his gun sitting on the bar where I'd dumped it, getting further and further out of reach. The clientele didn't seem too perturbed at me dragging him out of the establishment, just slightly disappointed that it wasn't going to kick off inside for their own titillation.

He was still struggling to find his feet when we reached the street. I gave him a quick elbow to the face to pacify him and then shoved two fingers down his throat. The small quantity of vomit that didn't actually find its way up my sleeve splashed into the gutter. When he was done I dropped him to the ground.

'If you feel a bit faint in the next few hours,' I said, 'eat some chocolate.'

I crouched down close to his flushed face.

'Maybe reconsider your life choices – in case I'm ever back in this neighbourhood.' I stepped over him as he lay panting and shell-shocked in the gutter. As I walked away I added, 'And don't try to find me. I don't exist. Not in your world.'

Then I was gone into the darkness, like some

clandestine crime-fighter, dressed all in black, with bad-guy vomit up his arm.

Maybe it would change him. Probably not. But I proved to myself once again that I couldn't do it. Couldn't take a life on my own say-so. Whatever bad he had done and whatever bad he may do in the future. It just didn't feel right. I figured that was a healthy thing.

But now I was back to square one.

Almost.

Six

Truth or Care

Conner was delighted to awake to a generous helping of aches and pains. He took a peek in the bathroom mirror to find one of his eyes peeking back at him from the centre of dark swollen tissue. He decided not to go into work, figuring he was justified in calling an uncharacteristic sickie – at least for the morning. His physical injuries were not so bad, but his soul was battered and bruised, lying prostrate on the floor, and it wasn't planning on getting up anytime soon.

Conner set about doing nothing but slouching around in his favourite sweatpants, which was a mistake as it allowed his mind to set about doing way too much thinking. What he thought about began to trouble him quite severely, not that such an outcome to his thought processes surprised him anymore.

It was mid-morning before a distraction presented itself in the form of a long-overdue message from Mila. Although it did not query his whereabouts; it was merely a forwarded phone message from the office. Apparently, Kent Bradshaw, the clerk from the bail-bondsman's office, had tried to get hold of Conner, saying he needed to speak to him. Kent hadn't left a number, just a place and time to meet.

So his day off wasn't happening. But on the up side, he hadn't consumed anything but coffee and cigarettes since waking, so taking up the offer of a lunch date may prove wise.

When Conner arrived at the rendezvous café Kent was already there, sipping on a tall milky coffee. Conner opted for the healthy option: *black* coffee. And added a blueberry muffin to notch up the first of his five-a-day. He took a seat opposite the clerk, who settled his mug down onto its saucer with a nervous rattle.

'So what's up?' Conner enquired.

'Hey, someone beat you up too?'

'No, I just do this to look intimidating.'

Kent nodded as the sarcasm whistled merrily past him.

'So, why did you want to see me?' Conner asked again.

Kent glanced around the establishment, trying to pull off nonchalance, but landing squarely on shifty.

'What I tell you now didn't come from me, okay?' he offered in a hushed voice, leaning forward.

'Sure.'

'I don't want you visiting me or calling me up like we're old buddies, right? That wouldn't be good for my health.'

'That won't be a problem. I don't call anyone up like they're my buddy.' Conner began to peel his cup-shaped baked good from its wrapper. Everyone eats their muffins differently. Conner always ate his bottom up, saving the crispy sugary bit on the top till last.

Kent shuffled in his seat. He could learn a thing or two about nonchalance from his muffin-eating companion. 'How do I know I can I trust you?' he asked.

Conner leaned back in mild frustration. 'Look, *you* called *me* here to talk. I'd just as soon be at home watching daytime TV. So it's really your call.'

'Okay.' He sighed resignedly. 'So, last night, after I got home from the hospital –'

'Oh yes, sorry,' Conner interrupted with an overfull mouth. 'How are you feeling?'

'Quite sore, thanks. Anyway, so I'm at home and I get a phone call. Well, it's a call to the office, but they get diverted to my cell phone out-of-hours. And guess who it is?'

Conner shook his head. 'Columbo?'

'Who?'

'Never mind. Who was it?'

'It's only the guy who bailed out Burch, isn't it?'

'Really?' Conner got interested at this point – even stopped chewing for a moment. 'And what did he have to say?'

'Well, that's the odd thing. He goes and tells me where Burch is and suggests we go pick him up before he skips town.'

'Why?'

'Dunno. Doesn't make much sense.'

'So, what happened?'

'Well, I figured this might improve relations with my boss, so I call him up. And he sends a couple of heavies down to go get him.'

Conner frowned as he tried to process this information. He took a long drag of caffeine hoping it would help.

'So where is Burch now?'

'As far as I know he's in a lock-up in town, tied to a chair. They wanna make sure he gets to court for his hearing.'

'Understandably. Isn't that what you want too? Get your boss's bail money back?'

'Well, yes.'

'So, why are you telling me? Snitching on your boss for kidnapping ain't going to put you in his good books – if indeed he has any good books.'

'Because I don't trust these goons. I think this way he'll either end up missing or dead. I'd feel much more comfortable if the cops *happened* across the lock-up and took Burch in for his own protection. Besides, is it so hard to believe that some people actually prefer operating on the right side of the law?'

Conner shrugged in response. He generally finds it best to assume that they don't.

Kent continued. 'Look, I just want to see Burch get to court, and the more people with that aim the better. As soon as that money's back I'm outta this town.'

Conner contemplated these details as he finished off the last crumbs of his single-serving cake. Eventually, he gave a consenting nod.

'Give me the address of the lock-up. I'll sort it.'

Kent returned his coffee shakily to its saucer again and wrote the address on a scrap of paper. Conner motioned to leave then stopped himself.

'Have you talked to anyone else about this?'

'No.'

'*Any*one? Priest, wife, men in suits?'

'No. Do I look like the kind of man that would be religious ... or married?'

'It's the suits I'm worried about. Has anyone other than me come asking questions: about Burch, about who bailed him ... about me?'

'No.' He shook his head in the first confident motion Conner had observed.

'Okay. So it's my turn to trust you. But if I discover you're lying, rest assured I *will* come visiting. And you won't need to worry about me acting like your buddy. Far from it.'

Conner pegged Kent as way too weak and stupid to be trying something on – whatever *something* might be. So, he left. Unfortunately, the knowledge he left with deposited him squarely on the horns of a dilemma.

Being a cop he should do exactly what Kent expected him to do. Call in the boys in blue, rescue Bigby and keep him safe till court time. But the clerk had come to the wrong cop, because all Conner wanted was Bigby back on the street, doing his job, leading him to the big boys in the rug trade.

He needed to make some decisions but he didn't have much time. Worse, his mind returned to what had been troubling him earlier. It was troubling him more now that time had passed. He knew he had to resolve that issue first, before he could make any informed decision as to his next action. Who was he trying to kid? Any decision he made would be a long way from informed. If he could achieve anything above complete ignorance he'd be well chuffed.

There was only one thing for it. He had to go on a date.

That evening Conner waited for his guest in the Crown Liquor Saloon – the best of the seventeen so-called Irish bars in town. Having never left America he had no idea as to the bar's authenticity, but he liked it, and that was all that mattered. The exterior was exquisitely decorated with polychromatic tiles and stained glass. The interior was even more elaborate. Complex mosaics spilled across the entire floor. Every surface of the walls, fixtures and ceiling coalesced into what was effectively a single, highly-decorative wood-carving; as if the room had been whittled from the centre of a massive tree trunk. The altar-style bar-top that stretched the length of the establishment was made of a deep-red granite. And the whole place was lit by polished brass gas lamps. But the best feature of all were the carved wooden booths – or snugs as they called them – each with its own little door, originally designed to accommodate the more reserved patrons of a Victorian era.

It was indeed spectacular. It was also, of course, fake. A modern replica. A cheap imitation. The product of cold-blooded mimicry. The Crown had never hosted survivors of a potato famine any more serious than the kitchen running out of curly fries. But it didn't matter. Not to the kind of people that visited New Meadows. The quaintness seemed genuine enough. The Guinness tasted real enough. It more than fulfilled the needs of its clientele to feel in touch with their 'Irish roots' – the one-sixteenth of their genes that came from somewhere near Europe – and that sufficed.

It sufficed for Conner also. It was not one of Conner's dreams to visit a *real* Irish pub. It never really occurred to him. Trans-Atlantic travel was in fact very far from his thoughts as he sat at a table in the Crown, keeping a beer company, waiting for his guest to arrive. He was wearing his most recently washed jeans and his only remaining non-work shirt with a full complement of buttons. This constituted a noteworthy level of effort on

Conner's part, even if the result wasn't going to win any Best Groomed Male of the Year – or Bar – awards.

Mila, on the other hand, looked considerably more elegant, when she arrived. But women are good at that kind of thing: looking elegant. She walked over to Conner, took one look at him and broached the expected remark.

'What happened to *you*?'

'Long story,' he moaned. 'Drink?'

Conner procured a white wine from the bar and they settled down to study the menus. The fact that this exquisitely accurate homage to ale houses of old actually *had* menus didn't strike either of them as vaguely inconsistent. But that's progress for you.

Over their meal Conner told Mila about the events of the previous night and she made all the right noises of sympathy and dismay. Then they chatted about nothing work-related, which was somewhat of a rare occurrence. Conner began to realise that he didn't know as much about Mila as perhaps he should.

After the meal Mila finally asked the question that had been hanging there over their plates for sometime.

'So, what's this all about?'

'What?'

'Us. Here. Now. And don't give me an innocent look. It doesn't take a detective – which I *am,* by the way – to determine that this is an unusual turn of events; that something is up. So what is it?'

Conner conceded with a nod.

'Shall we adjourn,' he said, motioning to one of the booths. The booth in question was furnished with a battered leather sofa and a low wooden coffee table. They slumped back into the sofa and Conner produced a small package from his jacket.

'Before we do the *what's-up* thing, I want you to try something?' Conner unfolded a piece of paper to reveal two white pills.

Mila looked at them and recoiled slightly. 'Conner, you know I'm not into that stuff.'

'You drink alcohol don't you?'

'Yeah, so?'

'So, where's the difference? You can get *these* over the counter in a convenience store. Trust me, the chemicals in these have been subjected to far greater scrutiny than that banoffee pie you've just eaten.'

Mila was apprehensive. 'What do they do?'

'It's called EZB. It's designed as an end-of-evening calmer. Extends all the mellowing, relaxant qualities of alcohol without enhancing the bad ones. Even lessens the effects of a hangover.'

Mila pouted in consideration. 'If I do this will you tell me what's going on?'

'Deal.'

It wasn't strictly true that you could buy EZB – pronounced 'easy-be' with an American 'Zee' – over the counter. Not yet at least. Although it had gone through FDA accreditation and was awaiting final sign-off as safe for consumption. It was important for drug companies to take market control quickly after approval of a product, before rogue parties managed to synthesize the drug and start pumping out fakes. So, as it was close to a done deal the well-known drug company that held the patent for EZB had started the production lines rolling in the Far East. Consequently, a number of pills had seeped onto the grey market early. Conner had acquired his from Crystal Seth at quite an extortionate rate, but it would be worth it.

One effect that EZB had was to lower one's guard and diminish inhibitions; to make you feel more open and confident. Like when a person is drunk, they will say things that they'd never say when sober: will confide personal details that they would never have shared otherwise. EZB has this effect, only stronger. It's the closest thing there is to a truth serum.

Mila popped a pill and then popped the question again. 'So why are we here?'

Conner swallowed down his pill and followed it up with a deep breath. He looked straight ahead to avoid eye contact, because he knew it was easier that way. Words didn't come immediately. He managed a few false starts, opening and closing his mouth like a goldfish, but with no actual sounds. He tried shuffling around in his blocks a bit, to make sure he was comfortable. He wasn't. But he had to start sometime. Eventually, the words came out.

'One thing you might not know ... about guys,' he began, 'is that sometimes they need to be vulnerable. They need to be able to show weakness; to be afraid, or sad, or just tired. Culture dictates that they cannot do this very often. Not with strangers or workmates or children. Not even with friends. But with a partner they can. A partner can smooth his feathers, pat his head and say everything's going to be okay.'

Conner paused momentarily to steel himself.

'Since I've been on my own, since Lisa left, this is what I've missed the most. I didn't expect that, but it's true. And I've been so focused on work and my own problems, that I've felt like there's been no one looking out for me; no one I can be vulnerable with.'

He took a long draw on his drink and then continued.

'But then, suddenly, I realised something. When I didn't go into work this morning and I was sitting at home alone, I found myself *expecting* your call; actively *anticipating* it. I realised at that moment that all those mornings when I'd not been eating properly and bagels had appeared on my desk ... somebody had *made* them appear. And when I was down about something, somebody *knew* that I was down, somebody was there asking me if I was okay. I know this sounds bloody obvious but another thing about guys is that they can be fucking dumb sometimes.'

Conner looked up at Mila and laughed at his self-deprecation. She smiled back coyly. Then the seriousness seeped back into Conner's face. 'Anyway, it's bad enough that I didn't realise this sooner. But what's much worse is that I didn't reciprocate, even subconsciously.' He looked away ashamedly. 'I guess this makes me a pretty bad person. But the point is,' he locked eyes again, 'I'm truly sorry, Mila. This is the very least I can do to start making it up to you. And to say thanks for looking out for me.'

'Well,' Mila smiled with dewy eyes, 'you are welcome.' Her lips stayed parted as if more words were to come, but none arrived, and silence reigned for a while. There was a palpable tension in the air. Mila could not be fully aware as to why, but that would soon be rectified...

Conner formed a smile; a smile that a select few people in the world would call a Duchenne smile. He just knew it as fake. He fell quiet and focused on the pint glass he was rolling between his hands. He downed what remained of its contents and then placed it heavily on the table, before pulling himself up in the chair and ringing his empty hands together anxiously.

'The thing I don't understand, considering all this, considering what a great friend you have been to me all these months...'

'Yes?'

'The thing I don't get is...' – the thought was thundering through his mind like a runaway locomotive and there was no way he was going to stop it from vocalising – '...is why you attacked me last night?'

At this point Conner looked Mila in the eye and waited apprehensively for a reaction. Mila processed what Conner had said for a moment, before she truly grasped what he was asserting. Then her eyes widened in fury.

'Jesus! Is that what this is all about? You get me here; you fucking *drug* me with whatever this shit is; just to entertain some stupid hypothesis of yours? Is that it?'

Conner leapt to the defensive. 'But you didn't call. I –'

'You what? Assumed I already knew why you hadn't turned up at work?'

Conner looked sheepish as Mila continued to berate him.

'Did it ever occur to you that the reason I didn't call was because I actually thought you were big enough to look after yourself for a day? An opinion I may have to alter after this.'

'I'm sorry. I –'

'Stop! Don't even consider giving me the hard-done-by crap again. It only spreads so thin and you're real close to putting a hole through the bread.'

Mila turned away from Conner as if deciding her next

action: leave or stay. She arrived at her decision and turned back to him. Her tone was calmer now.

'Okay, you want the truth? You want the truth that's been staring you in the face all these months but which you've never seen because you spend all your time looking behind you?'

Conner nodded almost imperceptibly. Mila paused for a moment and her whole demeanour changed. Her shoulders dropped, her expression softened and then water began to well in her eyes. 'Here's the truth,' she said in a hushed voice. She took a deep breath and closed her eyes, as if steeling herself, and as she did so a tear seeped out. A couple more breaths and she was ready. She opened her eyes, leaned in and kissed Conner firmly on the lips. For a moment he did not react. Then he began to kiss her back but she pulled away.

In almost a whisper she spoke. 'There is your truth.' She turned away shyly. 'Of *course* I was worried about you today. But a girl gets embarrassed when she's made a fool of. When she chases a guy but doesn't get noticed. That's why I didn't call to find out where you were. I was desperately hanging on to what little dignity I had left.' She grabbed her coat from beside her. 'Now ... now it's all gone. Thanks.'

She stood and walked away in tears.

Conner stared forward, wide-eyed and motionless; and wondered just how much more spectacularly he could mess up his life if he *really* tried? Maybe he knew the answer.

He took out his gun from its holster. He released the clip, checked its contents and snapped it back home with a satisfying click – all in a single reflexive motion. He didn't *need* to check. He knew the status of his gun: fully loaded. It's just one of those things that an armed man does with his gun...

...when he knows he is about to use it.

Seven

Detextion

Hiding these days is a lot trickier than it used to be. Not that I've tried hiding in any previous time-period, but it's a considered deduction. Technology is to blame – though I hate to use that word. People like to 'blame' technology for a lot of things, whilst reheating their coffee in the microwave. On the whole, technology is pretty awesome. But it necessitates so many extra things to worry about when you're trying to lay low. Browsing the web is one of them. I'm not alluding to some Big Brother state here. I'm not suggesting that every word you type into a search engine is scrutinised by some government intelligence operative. It would be pointless. You would be amazed at the sheer volume of people searching for instructions on how to make biological weapons on an hourly basis. It would be a complete waste of time to assume that any of the searchers are any more of a threat to the nation than the average eleven-year-old kids from Dorset that they are. Just for the record, I'm not suggesting there is a disproportionate number of budding biological terrorists living in Dorset. It's just an example, to highlight the impossibility of filtering the few true evil-doers from the millions of simply-curious.

Nevertheless, you'd be naïve to think that your 'e-activity' is entirely anonymous and unmonitored. So, I can't be too careful. As an example of the lengths I have to go to, consider the problem of me wanting to keep tabs on anything – or anyone – known to be associated with me. Bearing in mind that the people I'm hiding from are very resourceful.

For this task I have a mechanism. I employ custom-written data-mining agents: harmless software viruses that replicate themselves across the net, sniffing out information of interest to me. They go to places far beyond the reach of your favourite search engine, sneaking past firewalls, proxies and gateways to reach potentially any resource hooked up to the internet. They can't defeat all security measures but they come pretty close. And being benign they survive longer than malicious viruses. But they don't go undetected forever. After a while virus scanners will learn their signature and kill them as soon as they are detected. So from time to time I have to release new ones.

An irksome but clearly necessary restriction of agents is that they can hold no detail pertaining to their owner, such as an email address or a phone number. So when they find stuff that might be of interest, they post snippets of information on public web forums containing innocuous code words that I can look out for. I can hit these forums along with the million other users that day and suddenly I'm a leaf hidden in a forest. This was the mechanism that alerted me to Pearle's death a year ago; and to Burch's arrest more recently.

This path to information that I must follow is not entirely undetectable; the trail is still there. But it adds enough layers of indirection to be good enough, for long enough. Long enough to finish up in whatever internet café I am visiting on that occasion and move on.

But it's not just the web where we leave our signature. You can barely take a piss these days without leaving your watermark in *the matrix*. Every step you take through life you leave behind an electronic breadcrumb trail for anyone to follow: hard disks, cell phones, credit cards, surveillance cameras. And this trail does not get gobbled up by the animals of the woods. It stays.

Considering how heavily the law enforcement agencies rely on these sources for their investigations, it's hard to imagine how detectives solved *any* crimes fifty years ago. Take away forensics too and I just don't know where they'd begin.

This e-trail everyone leaves behind is not an issue for the average person on the street. Only those who are particularly paranoid, or are a criminal, or just plain have something to hide. I have something to hide. Me. So it can be hard work sometimes.

But, today, technology was on *my* side. Today, *I* was the detective.

From my meeting with Jackson Burch earlier I learned that he had *not* been involved with Pearle Jenkins' death. He was quite confident on this issue – I could tell. Which unfortunately meant it was true. After all, he would have remembered. Worse still, he didn't even know Pearle, or her mother. He had been framed for the whole thing.

I really wasn't expecting this. People get framed for things all the time in TV shows. But it's really not that easy, especially considering all of the aforementioned techie stuff. It would only be possible by someone intimately acquainted with the details of the crime and the person being framed. Burch was quite nonplussed by the situation. He didn't seem to have a clue who this might be.

If I'd known beforehand that he was going to be so clueless, I wouldn't have made contact. But it was too late once I had. I couldn't really continue following him around. Plus, that's another thing that happens a lot on TV, which is logistically non-practical. Try it sometime.

There was one other thing I picked up from Burch. I got the impression he was in New Meadows for some shady activity. That he was here for some kind of deal. I couldn't conjure anything more than a hazy feeling about this though. I would like to know what he was up to and who he was up to it with, but at the end of the day I'm not actually a mind-reader, and he was in no mood to tell me.

So I figured I was pretty much done with him. After dumping him in the gutter I called up the bail bondsman and tipped him off, saying that his bailee was about to skip town. The bondsman was almost half-a-million dollars down so I knew he would do a good job of keeping the guy out of harm's way for a few days.

Of course, before I let him go I lifted his mobile phone from his jacket pocket. *This* would connect me to the rest of his life. Or so I hoped.

A few blocks down from where I left Burch I started scrutinising the phone. The first thing I learned was that the guy was a professional, or an obsessive compulsive. His phone was virtually clean. There was no data on it that might provide some kind of clue as to who he was: no names, notes, images or documents. There was nothing in his calendar either, which was a shame, but it was a long shot to expect him to be that dumb: '9am: Rob bank'. There weren't even any entries in the phone's contact list. Though this was quite standard practice for certain individuals who do dealings with other certain individuals.

What did impress me was how fastidious he was about deleting his text messages. There wasn't a single one, incoming or outgoing; which was a big disappointment. These little babies can be a gold mine of personal information.

The only bookkeeping he hadn't done that day was to clear his call register, so this was all I had to go on. I inspected the list. It showed that after leaving the jail he had made three outgoing calls. With no entries in the phone's contact list I had no names to go on, just the numbers. There was only one option. I stopped off at a pay phone and called each one up in turn.

The first number had an area code I didn't recognise. I tapped in the number and waited. The phone rang a few times before a woman answered. I asked for a random name, wrong number style, just to have a brief conversation with her. She was helpful and pleasant. She had a mature voice and I estimated her to be in her sixties or seventies. I came to the inspired conclusion that this was Burch's mother. Who would've guessed it? It seems even bad guys have mothers. Some are even nice to them.

The second number had a 562- area code, which meant something to me but I couldn't place it. I called the number up and it turned out to be a haulage company based at the Port of Long Beach, California. This was more useful than a natter with his mom, but I couldn't do anything with it just yet.

The final entry in the register showed the call had been about ten minutes in duration. I dialled the number. It rang for a while then cut through to an answer message. The owner was probably screening his calls; wasn't going to answer to an unknown caller. The message was short and the voice was that of a middle-aged man. It was gruff and gravelly like he'd smoked his body-weight in cigarettes since breakfast.

From my chat with Burch earlier I gathered he was in town for business, for some kind of deal, but I didn't know what. Being incarcerated wouldn't have been part of his plan so I knew that as soon as he was out he would have had to rearrange any meeting he'd set up. I was pretty sure gravel-tones was who he was supposed to be meeting. I just didn't know where or when. If he had missed the first appointment, then it would probably be soon. He may already be late. He may have been waiting for the guy at Satori where I'd met him. This was rotten luck. If I'd known all this at the time I wouldn't have approached him in the first place.

I needed to make contact with gravelly but I couldn't risk a conversation. I needed to elicit some information without setting off too many alarm bells. I tapped a text message in Burch's phone and fired it into the ether.

> Can't talk. Need
> more time. 10pm,
> Bar Satori?

Suggesting a new time was easy, but I couldn't just say 'same place' because I didn't know where that was. I had a punt at Satori. If I was right it would just seem like

I was confirming the location. If I was wrong I hoped the question mark would indicate I was suggesting a change of venue.

Assuming I heard back, 10pm would give me a couple of hours to freshen up and straighten my thoughts. To this end I headed back to my hotel du jour.

I spend a lot of time moving from hotel to hotel these days, which can involve significant context switches in a theme-crazed town like New Meadows.

The trouble with themes is that there are not so many of them – not so many that can be recognisably shammed at least. If you frequent the occasional fancy-dress party you'll know what I mean. The same tired old themes being recycled time-after-time. Hotels are no different.

The Edwardian, therefore, was a little refreshing. On the face of it, hundred-year-old England was a bit of an unusual choice of concept – much less scope for architecturally-challenging structures and gaudy interior design. I was born and raised in England so was no stranger to *actual* old buildings. Granted, The Edwardian was a little bit more plastic than the real thing, but it was a great deal more authentic than, say, the twenty-four storey igloo across the street, or the erection down the road that, shall we say, needs no further introduction.

The lobby of The Edwardian was all wood panelling, slender furniture and classical paintings hanging on the walls. There wasn't any neon in sight. It was quite strange. There was of course a handy casino, situated conveniently between the reception and the elevators. Those Edwardians did love their one-armed bandits.

Back in my room I ran a bath, complete with lavender oil and rose petals. Seriously, who do you think I am? No, it was a strictly straight-guy bath, with just two or three complimentary bottles of generic cleansing substance emptied into it to make it good and bubbly. The porcelain bath was in the centre of the room, freestanding on little cast-iron feet. The taps were nickel-plated with ceramic inlays on top saying *hot* and *cold*, beside each of which was one of my feet hanging over the edge. I've noticed that most baths are clearly not designed with adult humans in mind. Either that or they are not intended for lying down in, which just seems like a crazy design assumption from the start, but what do I know?

My right arm rested on the side of the bath to facilitate the clutching of a large tumbler of scotch. I don't really like scotch; it was just the most masculine drink I could think of to offset the effeminate leaning of my current pursuit. Trust me, I wouldn't dream of touching an Appletini until I'd gotten at least a couple of fist fights under my belt first.

I allowed myself to slip down a little into the warm water, just chilling-out, relaxing a little. Then suddenly there was an almighty ear-shattering sound, like someone in a china shop had gotten a little bored and set the gravity switch to Up.

So, herein lies some advice. When your phone is on vibrate, do *not* leave it on a porcelain toilet cistern, unless you *do* intend to wake the recently departed ... on the fourteenth floor.

I climbed back into the skin I had just jumped out of, shook the excess water from my hands and grabbed the phone. The message read:

10pm OK. Has to
be BlueJay. Be
there this time.

Game on.

Eight

Eye for an Eye

Conner arrived at the lock-up, on a dirty street on the east side of town. From the faded sign above the door it looked like it used to be a mechanic's workshop. The front consisted mostly of a closed metal shutter, large enough to drive a truck through. To the side of the shutter there was a door with a blacked-out window. The black-out paint showed fine scratches in places and when Conner brought his eye up close he could see a flickering light from behind. He turned his ear to the window and could just make out the muffled tones of the Friday night TV schedule.

Conner took out his gun and rapped the barrel on the shutter doors a few times. After a moment of nothing he tapped again, louder this time. If the babysitter inside was worth his fee he would know to ignore whoever was knocking. If he was religious he may also choose to pray for his visitor's disappearance. Conner knew this. But he wasn't going anywhere. He banged the shutters a third time just for luck, then on the fourth attempt moved to hitting on the window.

Finally, there was a reaction, of silence – the TV had been muted. Someone was coming to investigate. Conner took two paces back.

‘Who is it?’ a voice called from behind the glass.

‘Police,’ Conner replied with complete integrity – one of the last sincere statements he would be offering the man. ‘I suggest you open the door.’

Conner gave the man a moment to consider his option – singular. If he refused it would be obvious he was hiding something. If he complied it might turn out the nice policeman was just making a neighbourly visit. Or, at least, it would give the heavy a better chance to pop a swift bullet into the cop’s head if his hand was really forced.

Sure enough, after a moment, the door opened a crack. Conner took another pace back, not wanting to crowd the guy, fully aware of the bullet-in-the-head scenario. He held up his badge at arm’s length.

‘Officer?’ the guy said as sweet as his mother’s apple pie. ‘How can I help?’

‘You can help by staying calm and listening carefully to what I have to say. If you do, everything will be cool, and we can all go back to our Friday night entertainment. Okay?’

‘Okay.’ The hired-help was apprehensive, not quite sure what to make of the situation.

‘Good. First, I need you to know that I am mic’ed up to a radio.’ Conner lifted his coat to reveal a covert personal radio inside. ‘And round the corner there is a car with two cops in, listening right now. Got that?’

The thug at the door got twitchy but he didn’t make a move.

‘We know you are holding a man against his will. But this is your lucky night. You hit the bonus ball. I need to talk to him in connection with an unrelated case. And I can’t afford any fuss, you understand? All you have to do is go back to your goggle-box and keep on goggling, and in half-an-hour I'll be out of your hair and you'll never see this face again. Won't that be nice for you? Or ... we can do this the hard way?'

Once again Conner allowed a moment for the thick-skulled heavy to consider his options. Eventually, the door opened a little wider and Conner got his first good look at the man behind it. He was not a big man and Conner pegged him as good with a knife rather than good with his fists. He had a wide untrustworthy face, and a grade-one stubble from chin to scalp.

'Is there anyone else in there with you who you need to relay this information to?'

'No,' the man grunted.

Conner wanted to be sure there weren't any trigger-happy gun-touters around who didn't know the score; didn't know that anything they tried would be broadcast to the supposed cavalry.

Conner stepped into a greasy office which was virtually bare apart from a portable TV on a work surface, and a swivel chair. The man nodded to the door at the other end of the office, then resumed his TV-watching position.

'Turn it up,' Conner suggested as he walked past the happy viewer.

At the end of the office there were windows and a door looking out onto a large workshop area. Conner stepped through the door. The workshop was almost empty too, save for a few bits of old cars lying around: a dented fender, an exhaust back-box, a stack of bald tyres.

The few strip-lights above that remained operational cast a sallow pool of light into the room, successfully creating that *Eerie Chill* ambience that was so popular with thugs these days. The floor looked as though a thousand cars, living and dead, had deposited layer-upon-layer of grease, engine oil, gasoline and rubber upon it, leaving it with a grimy sheen.

And in the centre of the cavernous space was a lonely figure on a chair, tied to an upright steel stanchion. The figure was kitted out in a loose orange jumpsuit like those worn by convicts – which seemed like an odd touch to Conner – and had a hood over its head.

Conner was here alone. He had figured that he couldn't go to the police with what he knew because he wasn't supposed to know it. It would almost certainly end in his suspension from the force. Besides, he didn't really see what good that would do anyone. It may protect Bigby, but that was exactly what the thugs were trying to do anyway: protect him and keep him in one place.

What Conner really wanted was to bust Bigby out, because he was key to the rug trade investigation. He'd rather the guy was back on the street. But it was too late for that. Bigby was due in court in a little over forty-eight hours. If he found his way to the street either it would only be for a couple of days until he was back inside, or he would do a runner and skip bail. Besides, busting him out was way too risky. Conner hadn't gone that far off the rails yet.

So he'd figured his best option was to get in, get some info, and get out. That was the plan.

He walked towards the centre of the room, his footsteps echoing hollowly about the walls. When he was standing directly behind the orange-clad figure he made some suitably threatening noises with his firearm –

like *click*. Guns only make two noises: *click* and *bang*. The former is usually far more productive. The hooded head, which had been bowed forward, twitched at the sound.

'Right, I'm going to keep it simple because we haven't got much time. *You* haven't got much time.'

Conner walked around to stand in front of the man.

'Your life depends on how you answer the next three questions. Ready?'

The figure's head moved a little and there was a muffled sound. Conner knew that Bigby would be gagged and so didn't expect a verbal response just yet.

'Here we go. What is the real name of the man who bailed you? Why did he bail you? Where can I find him?'

Conner glanced back toward the office. The thug was not in sight. The glow from the TV still flickered onto the walls. He holstered his gun. Not something he liked doing in such a precarious situation but he needed both hands to lift the bottom of the hood and remove the gag. Bigby did not know who Conner was, of course. And Conner wanted it to stay that way. Didn't want the eyes of this rug dealer falling on his face.

He took a step forward, reached out toward the hood, then froze.

Something wasn't right.

Something his peripheral senses had clocked a moment before was suddenly ringing alarm bells.

He walked back behind the chair. The arms of the detainee were gaffer-taped together tightly at the wrists. He bent over to take a closer look at the hands ... then he jumped back.

'Fuck,' he expleted.

Suddenly, he was no longer in control. A moment ago he had all the information. He knew where he was. He knew the game. He knew the players. He was in the driving seat.

Now, he was not. Now, he was a passenger.

The person before him ... was not Bigby.

He didn't know the players any longer, and he didn't know the game. All bets were off.

For a moment he thought about just running like hell. Running away from this dark place. That way he might just stay alive. Might make it into the sodium glow of the streets outside. But however far he ran, he'd still be in the dark. And that wasn't good enough. Not any more.

He needed to see who the person was sitting in the chair. He needed that knowledge.

He knew that to see ... meant to be seen.

But that was a trade he was willing to make.

An eye for an eye.

He steeled himself for what he had to do. He planted his feet firmly, shoulder-width apart, facing the person before him. His heart was racing as if it knew something he didn't. As if it knew how this moment would change everything. He took a deep breath then reached out and lifted the hood.

And the face he saw made him jump in horror. Not that it was a horrific face – just unexpected.

It was, in fact, a pretty face. A *familiar* face.

It was Mila's.

Her head hung low and her eyelids were heavy to the point of being closed. Now he really had no idea what was going on. He'd seen her only a couple of hours before when she walked out of the Crown.

He was spooked – big time.

For the moment he left Mila. He rushed toward the office, pulling out his gun as he did so. The office was empty. The TV was blaring reruns of Friends, but *his* friend had gone. Conner burst through the door onto the street, looking quickly in every direction. A canoodling couple in the shadows jumped and scuttled away, but there was no one else.

His flight instinct kicked in aggressively. There was no time for reasoning. He had to get the hell away from here fast. Somewhere safe. *Then* he could think.

He ran back into the office and started rooting frantically through drawers for anything sharp. The place was abandoned and everything had been taken by the previous occupier.

'Damn it,' Conner exclaimed as he slammed the last drawer shut, but didn't hesitate before hammering the butt of his gun against the office window. It bounced off on the first attempt, but a second blow smashed straight through. He pulled the sleeve of his coat over his hand and picked up a long shard. Then he ran back to Mila and slashed through the tape around her wrists and ankles, with swift, precise motions.

He ripped the final piece of tape from her mouth and she flinched, but only a little.

'Mila, can you hear me?'

There was a groan but nothing else.

'Come on. We have to go.'

He put her arm around his shoulder and tried to get her to her feet, but she would take no weight. He had no time to teach a rag doll to walk so he slipped his right arm under her knees and lifted her up.

He staggered determinedly to the exit making a mental note to give up smoking the next day.

The street he stumbled onto was the kind of street that few pedestrians dared to venture down and hence even fewer taxis bothered to canvass.

Calling a cab would involve a frustrating conversation with directory inquiries just to get a number – or a visit to the seedy bar across the street with his dead-weight date. That would be followed by a frustrating call to a cab company. Followed by a frustrating wait for the cab to arrive. Conclusion: frustrating.

Stealing a car was an option, with just two minor drawbacks: one, Conner did not know how to steal a car; and, two, there were no cars in this neighbourhood worth stealing – presumably they already had been.

The occasional brave soul did risk their life driving down the street, being sure not to travel slow enough for any opportunistic thieves to whip off the hub-caps. So commandeering a willing citizen seemed like the only option.

Conner stepped into the road. The first two cars swerved around him and blasted their horns in an overly zealous fashion. He stepped further into the road and the next car screeched to a halt; its driver leaping out almost before the vehicle had come to a stop.

'What the fuck are you –'

'Shut it!' Conner said with such authority the driver was silenced immediately. 'I'm a police officer. Get me to the nearest street with a cab on it.'

The man opened the rear door of the saloon and helped Conner load Mila onto the back seat. Conner followed her in.

The car owner set off with a new sense of civic duty, not quite sure whether having a harassed policeman in the back seat meant he should rigidly adhere to the road laws or actively flout them. He judged correctly that now was not the time to ask the question, so decided to just take the middle road, as it were. He drove a couple of blocks – half-jumping one light and not-quite coming to a complete stop at a give-way – then took a right onto Fifth, where there would be cabs-a-plenty.

Taxis in New Meadows are rather like the hotels – flamboyant and largely impractical. Most of them are themed; a lot of them are stretched; far too many of them are pink with bunny-girls in the back; and one of them is a Lamborghini.

Conner managed to flag down a regular one: yellow in colour with an ethnically-minor driver boasting language skills just sufficient to *completely* misunderstand where you want to go. This would not be a problem for Conner. After he'd bundled his passenger from one car to the other – making a mental note to give up doughnuts the next day – he resorted to the modern day Lingua Franca, the emergent international language of capitalism.

'McDonald's,' he barked. The cabbie looked confused momentarily until Conner affirmed with a sharp, 'Drive!'; and the cab pulled confidently into the flow of traffic almost embedding itself into a gem-studded stretched Hummer full of GI Jane bachelorettes.

They had to drive almost two whole blocks to reach the nearest big yellow M. At the drive-thru Conner picked up a sweet black coffee and then issued his next globalised instruction to the driver:

'Holiday Inn.'

All the Holiday Inns were on the outskirts of town, so it didn't really matter which one. He just needed to be someplace else.

The coffee wasn't for him, it was for Mila. He assumed she had just been sedated. If so she should slowly start to lift out of her lethargy, and coffee would speed the process. It was a shame he didn't have any more uppers on him. Conner began to pop the lid of the coffee, which was a task impossible to achieve on firm standing without spilling half the cup's contents. In the back of a cab, crotch-scalding was a mandatory outcome. Fortunately, McDonald's heat their drive-thru coffee to the tepid heights of four-and-a-half degrees above body temperature for just this reason. After confirming this via a few splashes to his pants he put the lid back on and started feeding it to Mila through the lid-spout, whilst cradling the back of her lolling head with his other hand.

'Drink,' he said encouragingly. She made some kind of moaning-cum-gurgling sound in response which he took as a positive development from straight moaning.

After the coffee was drained he scoped their location and determined they were only about three miles from the nearest Holiday Inn – so it would take another mere twenty-five minutes to get there at their break-neck speed of stationary. He decided to phone ahead and make a reservation to minimize any lobby-based commotion on his arrival with old Ragdolly Anna beside him. Then, finally, he sat back and took a moment to contemplate his predicament.

He opened the car window a crack to get some air, but the air outside was warm and humid. He watched the people on the busy sidewalk pass by the window, and kind of wished it wasn't because they were travelling faster than he was.

Any one of them could be the enemy now. Someone was messing with him, but he didn't know who. It seemed unlikely in the extreme that it was some fun-loving Feds warning him to stay away from Bigby. Surely they would use official channels if they knew he was still digging around. It could be the bail-bondsman reaping some revenge for his clerk-beating fun being interrupted. But he'd have to be truly crazy to start kidnapping cops if he wanted to stay in business. Scariest of all, it could be one of the rug trading gangs. Maybe his cover had been blown by one of his informants. But they would have simply dispatched him by now. Subtle games are not their style.

Whoever it was knew a lot about him, which was scary. They knew his actions and they knew Mila. That was why he had to get somewhere neutral fast. Not his place, or Mila's. Even a hospital would be too risky right now.

Once in the hotel room, Conner stayed with Mila until she could accomplish the feats of sitting and monosyllabic discourse unaided.

'What happened?' he asked.

'Walking,' she said slowly with a slight slur. 'Man ... grab.' Then she clumsily mimed a syringe motion with her first two fingers and thumb against her upper arm. Conner inspected the puncture wound. She seemed to be livening up as time passed and he was confident that she had been injected with nothing more than a sedative.

'What else do you remember?'

'Sleep'. She shrugged and gave half a smile at the thought of slumber.

'I know,' he said compassionately, realising that Mila

would be providing little in the way of useful information given that she had been unconscious for the whole ordeal.

There was only one thing left. He had to pay a visit to Kent the clerk. He sighed heavily at the prospect. He guided Mila to the bed and pulled the duvet over her.

'Stay here and don't answer the door to anyone,' he instructed, though was fairly confident that such a task was way beyond her current abilities.

Conner thudded on Kent's apartment door. He'd buzzed a different apartment's number to get let into the building, just so he had the satisfaction of thudding on Kent's door. After a moment the door opened and the person behind it was dragged into the corridor by the lapels of his pin-striped pyjamas.

'Talk!' was all Conner said as he pushed him up against the wall.

'What?' the clerk whimpered.

'What do you mean what? It wasn't Burch in that lock-up.'

'Huh? Yes it was. Your guys picked him up a couple of hours back. I assumed you'd sent them.'

Conner loosened his grip.

'What?' he stated again – a sentiment he thought was worth reiterating. He let go of Kent. 'Stay there.'

Conner made some calls to confirm what Kent was saying. Sure enough, Bigby was back in custody.

Deep down Conner had known Kent would know nothing. He was a pawn just like Conner was.

He began making his way back to the Holiday Inn – on foot this time. All his ends were dead. There was nothing more he could do. His heart rate hadn't dropped below about one-eighty since he first popped a methamphetamine clone two hours ago. Now he was crashing big time.

Back in the hotel room, Mila was fast asleep and breathing normally. Conner grabbed the spare blanket from the wardrobe and collapsed onto the sofa. The multitude of aches across his body had merged into one holistic dull pain. But in a rare moment of positivity he counted this as a good thing. He had no idea who was messing with him, but he knew one thing: if they had wanted him dead, he would be dead by now. The fact that he could still feel pain was very reassuring. Reassuring enough to allow him to sleep.

Nine

Dressed to Sell

BlueJay was the trendiest and therefore most expensive place to hang out in town. I arrived in good time, to give me a chance to settle in. The two large bouncers on the door looked me up and down with suspicious eyes. I flashed my most opulent looking smile at them, which proved rather ineffectual so I flashed a fifty at them instead to marginally better results. I received half a nod from one of them that clearly articulated he would allow me to pass but that he was offended by my mere existence. I didn't argue. I respected the fact that his eyebrows alone were better communicators than most cab drivers around these parts. I stepped into a large atrium.

Let me take this opportunity to tell you about the retail phenomenon that is BlueJay. It is not a standard bar or restaurant. It is a whole new concept in the genre of ... well, there is no genre – that's the point. BlueJay is a cross between a bar, a restaurant and a clothes-store. The idea is that you get the chance to browse and buy the latest fashionable apparel whilst enjoying your food and drink – or waiting for it to arrive.

Items of clothing for sale are deposited about the place in a seemingly random, but actually extremely strategic, fashion. The staff are all dressed in purchasable garments too. And each time they nip out-back to fetch your curly fries they are preened and styled like catwalk models – which they mostly are. It is well understood that nothing will sell a product better than draping it over someone unfeasibly attractive, or draping someone unfeasible attractive over it – whichever is geometrically more plausible.

The clothes for sale are those brands deemed suitable for the clientele. Not the ridiculously expensive made-to-measure shit; just whatever are the coolest off-the-shelf brands at the time. The kind where someone on an average wage would only have to forgo a single week's pay for a pair of boxer shorts. That kind of level.

This concept of plying vain fashion victims with alcohol to the point of intoxication and then offering them the opportunity to buy overpriced branded items is genius; and you have to hand it to the smug marketing bastards who dreamt up the idea.

BlueJay, New Meadows, was the original, established only about five years ago. It proved so successful that there are now a couple of dozen stores open or opening across the major cities of America.

I made my way into the establishment, studying the environment and its denizens as I moved. At the tables some people watched foot-tall holograms of themselves meandering amongst beer glasses and plates of nachos, sporting the latest catwalk styles. This was a pretty nifty piece of kit new to this flagship BlueJay store, and was creating quite a stir with the punters. I noticed how the holograms all looked particularly more stunning – usually about seven or eight pounds more stunning – than their real-world counterparts, and decided that if I wished to try something on I'd use a method less open to silicon-minded interpretation.

I cut my way through the crowd, heading for the large circular bar at the centre of the room; the best place to take a reasonable stab at not looking too conspicuous by myself. The bar itself was rather like those you find at a sushi restaurant in that it had a conveyor belt running inside it. Only, instead of cold rice and raw fish, it proffered trendy urban kickers and neatly pleated chinos. You had to be real careful where you waved your credit card in these places.

I grabbed a stool at the bar and got myself a drink and some cigarettes. I don't actually smoke, by the way. Well, I do in the strictest sense of the word, in that I occasionally suck air through smouldering sticks of dried tobacco. But it's not through pursuit of pleasure, and that's the difference. And I'm not just some latent addict in denial. I genuinely hate the things. They make me feel nauseous, and that's not a sensation I wish to pay for. Nevertheless, I feel that my role and my associated image necessitates that I light up from time to time. Especially in places like New Meadows; especially when I'm on the hunt for bad guys. It just seems right.

BlueJay was getting busier with the evening crowd. I could hear them but I wasn't paying particular attention. My beer was company enough for the moment. As such, I was slightly irked, not to mention surprised, when a young semi-transparent lady rose up beside my beverage. An extension to their holographic mannequin technology I presumed.

'Hi,' she said in a song-like tone. She had a tight dark bob showing off large heart-shaped earrings and was dressed in a pink cat suit. 'Don't forget to treat your loved-one this Valentine day. Be sure to visit our promotional display in the West Wing to check out our exclusive designer range of lingerie from only the best names in ladies' fashion. Thank you for visiting and happy Valentine.' The six-inch saleswomen gave a theatrical wink and faded out classily with a slight wibble to her edges.

'Fuck off,' I said politely and brought the glass to my lips before any more bar-top peddlers decided to try their luck.

I took a second to reflect on my plan: scope out the place for my mark and then ... decide what to do next. Okay, maybe not a *whole* second. The plan was in quite a nascent form, but I didn't let its brevity trouble me.

BlueJay was large. It sprawled across two floors, with several bars and many different nooks for its clientele to hang out in. There were at least a couple of hundred people currently enjoying its services. This would make it impossible to study everyone, but overall it made things easier. I could blend in here whilst trying to identify the man Jackson Burch was supposed to be meeting. And if I didn't succeed, I could employ a far more fiendish method to determine which of the many revellers he was: I could text him and ask where he was sitting.

I scanned the local vicinity. Most people were in mixed groups or couples; most were late twenties/early thirties. I was happy to rule out all of these. Although, I wasn't really sure who I *was* looking for. Certainly a little older; say, in his forties. Maybe on his own but quite likely with one or two other guys. At least one of the other guys was liable to be large and thuggish. The main man though, I wasn't so sure about. He certainly didn't have a plum in his mouth, from his accent, but he insisted on meeting in BlueJay so he wasn't allergic to sophistication. Despite his gruff brogue he was likely to be quite a slick operator.

As I was studying the locals, my attention was drawn to

a mild hubbub which erupted next to me. Two guys took stools just around from where I was sitting, ushered there by an overly-hospitable gentleman wearing a black suit with a gold name badge on the lapel. I assumed the latter was the manager of BlueJay – or a senior employee of some kind anyway. He introduced the two men to one of the stunning female members of the bar staff, and encouraged her to ply them with free drinks. Then the manager left, all smiles and flattery. I checked out the two guys. One of them looked familiar but I couldn't place him. I hate that. I'm pretty good with faces. I remember lots of them, but I don't always know who they go with. I closed my eyes in concentration, tapping my fingers on the bar-top in an it's-on-the-tip-of-my-brain kind of way. Eventually, it returned to me. He was a pro-baseball player; a hitter for the local team. I had seen him on the news recently. I guess that counted him as a minor celebrity in these parts, deserved of free drinks for the honour of his patronage.

I didn't know the guy he was with. Maybe another team player, or his agent. I'm not really into these American sports. I know enough trivia to get me by in casual conversation with a native. Although, to be honest, you don't have to know much. Get talking to a guy who's into his sports and he'll do all the running.

The hitter was loud and obnoxious as might be expected of someone earning a house-a-week in endorsements alone. His companion was fielding the batter's every word with well-practised sycophancy. They were interesting subjects, it was true, but they weren't my men – so to speak. So I did my best to divert my attention away from them.

And I would have succeeded if it weren't for what happened next.

The manager returned with a woman who he introduced to the men; and all hope of keeping my mind on the job was lost. The woman was extremely distracting, but not in the way you are thinking. Not that she wasn't pretty, or whatever, but that's not the point.

That is a long way from the point.

She was tall and immaculately turned out. Everyone in here was smartly dressed, like they were moving on to classy nightclubs after. But she was dressed like she was moving on to a classy movie premiere after.

She was wearing a wine-coloured dress and black high heels. She had Latin features and coffee-coloured skin. Her dark hair was swept back revealing pixie-like ears, from which long slender earrings hung almost to her shoulders.

But all these superficial aesthetics were meaningless and irrelevant; rendered so by the magnitude of one single quality. A quality that she exhibited to the world with undiluted openness. Yet one the world did not care to notice.

No one knew how special she was. I was confident of this fact because there was only one person on this planet that could possibly understand the uniqueness of this woman; who could comprehend her significance.

And that person had just spat his drink across the bar-top.

But to understand why *she* was so special ... you have to know more about *me*.

You have to know who I am; where I came from.

You have to know what I can *do*.

I have to take you back to the very start. To where it all began.

You need to know who I am, where I came from.

And [illegible] to know what I can do.

PART TWO

Reading and Writing

Ten

Finding a Path

When I was a kid, growing up in England, I naturally assumed that I was going to be a superhero. It's a fairly natural belief for young boys. It is the only way to make sense of the world at that age. It just doesn't seem logical that you will grow up to be one of those normal adult creatures, with mundane things like cars and jobs and back pockets. Indeed, discovering that tea-towel capes are not sufficient for human flight is almost a rite of passage for young boys.

But, I wasn't *that* dumb. I knew I wasn't a superhero *yet* – not till I was at least sixteen. I hadn't put a great deal of thought into what my super power might be. Just so long as I was tough I wasn't too worried.

As the years went by I grew to suspect that life wasn't going to pan out quite as anticipated, which was a bit of an annoying revelation. But as with *most* childhood revelations there was a long period of uncertainty that dulled any pain that might ensue. The reality of my superhero future gradually drifted out of my consciousness, hitching a lift on Santa's sleigh.

Growing up, it seems, is just a whittling away of fantasies to the bones of everyday life; and the next phase of my whittling was that of super-delusions into more feasible aims. Feasible only in the sense that they were not prohibited by the laws of nature.

At the age of fourteen I decided I was going to be successful and maybe a little bit famous. I was either going to be an accomplished sports star, a wealthy entrepreneur or a respected academic. Some people choose singer, doctor, writer, et cetera, but these were my top three. I wasn't sure which one yet. I assumed this would just become apparent to me when the time was right.

Of course, it doesn't quite work like that. By about seventeen I figured this much out. To be the next great baseball player[1], I'd already left it about twelve years too late to start being any good at it. So, the first of my top three whistled past without me even getting a swing at it.

Strike one.

On starting university I quickly realised I wasn't going to be a world-famous scientist either. I'm quite a smart guy, but to be an academic you need to be quite, well, academic. I found my physics degree pretty easy, but it didn't turn me on – not beyond the five hours of labs and lectures a day. After that, I found other things to interest me. I'll let you decide if that was National Geographic supplements or national drinking competitions. Either way, no Nobel prize for physics heading my way.

Strike two.

Entrepreneur it had to be. That was my last shot. I

---

[1] In fact, it was actually *tennis* I wanted to excel at as a child, not having been exposed to American sports, but then the whole analogy breaks down so run with it.

had this mate at university. Well, not really a mate. He just hung around with us and we put up with him because we had an inkling he'd be useful to know one day. This proved to be the case in our second year, when he set up a bunch of adult web-cams in his halls of residence and enlisted local sixth-form schoolgirls to staff them. He made an absolute mint – and two girls pregnant. I'm not saying his particular display of business acumen was commendable, or indeed ethical, but it did show balls – on more than one count – and it made me realise I didn't have the tenacity to be a truly successful entrepreneur.

Strike three.

Out.

Time to worry. Incredibly, it was starting to look like I wasn't actually going to grow up to be a mega-rich superstar. It was starting to look like I was the kind of guy who wouldn't have a story to tell.

I have a story to tell.

My epiphany came in my third year at university, high on caffeine and checking out a girl in Starbucks.

But let me rewind briefly, because the path to this moment of clarity began the day before when I had been on the hunt for something in my room. Being a student and having only been in my current room for about three months – oh and not being a girl – about ninety per cent of my belongings were still in boxes under my bed. I dug one out in my search, and as I was rifling through its contents I came across an old book that I'd had since I was a kid. Now, I don't do superstition in general, but occasionally you can get caught up in one by accident. When you do, you can't escape it – and it has a very real effect. If you come to believe that you have a lucky pair of underpants then you will feel more confident wearing them, and be more likely to succeed at whatever it is you want to be lucky at doing in your underpants – umm, if you see what I mean. But on the flip side there is a much greater effect. If you *forget* your lucky underpants – or rabbit's foot, or horseshoe, or whatever – it will play on your mind so much that you *will* be less successful.

On a number of occasions this book that I'd rediscovered had helped me decide what path to take or helped me find answers to some question or other. Before you take me for some religious zealot, let me reassure you that this book is not the Bible or any other holy text. Although, maybe it could be offered as an atheist's scripture; a collection of secular teaching tales for the non-spiritual.

The world doesn't need gods, just guiding words.

Whatever it was, the idea got lodged in my mind that this book was a guiding mascot, and so for evermore I was stuck with it – like a set of bad lottery numbers. Heaven forbid I ever lose the damn thing.

I hadn't really paid any attention to it for ages. It was just an object in my life that I unconsciously transported from one place to another – like my bladder. On this occasion, for whatever reason, I paid it greater heed.

Its cover was dated, in a way that made you wonder if anyone twenty years ago had any aesthetic appreciation at all; like looking at photos of your parents in their youth. The cover was a sickly pale green, framed with garish blue and white triangles, and adorned with large blue lettering in a selection of ugly fonts.

The hand of fashion is indeed far-reaching. Not just hairstyles and clothes, but bathrooms and corporate logos and, yes, book covers. It made me wonder how I could look upon something with disgust today that a room full of designers twenty years before thought looked pretty swish.

Had *we* changed? Or had the *world*?

Anyway, I sat down and thumbed through the book. I stopped on a story and read the first paragraph. The tale immediately leapt back into my mind. It was about a boy dying from polio. He overhears doctors telling his mother that he will be dead by morning, and knowing this he gets his mother to manoeuvre the dresser in his bedroom such that via the mirror on top he would be able to see the sunset one last time. When the sunset comes he watches it so intently that all obstacles in its way are blanked out by his mind.

The message of this tale is that you must always have a goal. No matter what your situation, you must always have an aim. The fact that this was a true story made it all the more potent.

But there was *another* message – for me, at least. One that was far more important. For me, it was not the tale that was most pertinent, but who it was about. And, crucially, what he became. I knew a little about him, but soon I would realise I needed to know more.

It was all to become clear the next day, with the girl in the café, when thoughts of the story would return to me and coalesce in my mind; and change the direction of my life forever.

The café was pretty busy. I'd just acquired my over-priced beverage and was looking for a place to sit, worthy of the eat-in supplement. I made my way toward a small clearing at the far side of the room. At the same time a young woman did likewise from a different direction. There was an awkward moment of polite motionings until we eventually arranged ourselves about two small tables that were virtually touching.

I wasn't sure if this was one of those situations where it was acceptable to actually say something to another person. In most cases it seems to be a social faux pas to initiate unsolicited discourse with a stranger. This activity is considered the domain of weirdos and charity muggers.

Regardless, I was not endowed with sufficient social bravery to do so anyway. So I merely observed her in my periphery.

If you've ever spent time watching people in a coffee shop you'll have noticed that generally everyone comes prepared with a 'primary activity'. If they are not talking to someone, they will be tapping away at a laptop, or reading a book. No one ever just drinks coffee.

She was just drinking coffee.

She hadn't even stripped herself of coat and scarf. She was just cupping her beverage with both hands and staring out of the window – her eyes focused way into the distance.

It didn't take much skill to know that she was distracted. But there was so much I *didn't* know. Was she unhappy? Did she want company? Did she need help?

These were odd questions to be asking oneself, and the fact that I was asking them made me feel that at least some of the answers were yes. But I didn't know why I felt this. Maybe it was something about her demeanour – the way her body was angled slightly toward mine; the way she didn't busy herself with a 'primary activity'; the way she had placed her bags on the seat such that they slightly encroached on my space. I didn't know; it was just a gut feeling, and so I couldn't be sure.

I wondered whether, if I had been a cleverer man, I could have constructed a non-threatening way of establishing the details I sought. Then, maybe, if she was unhappy, I'd know what to say to make her feel better.

Being able to read people and manipulate people in this way was suddenly becoming very important to me. Manipulate is a word with such negative undertones, but unjustly so. When you pay someone a compliment you make them feel better. You've affected their mood, their state of being – you've manipulated them in a *good* way.

I sorely wished I had this skill at this moment. I felt that I could have helped this girl. At some level I could hear her crying out to me, but I wasn't sure enough. And as I couldn't be sure, I did the noble thing. I finished up my coffee and walked away. And I never saw her again.

About fifty yards down the street I became drenched in a sense of failure. I knew this was ridiculous. I had no responsibility toward this girl, whoever she was. Or did I? Should we all accept responsibility for whoever is in need? Maybe so.

But walking away is so much easier to do.

At that moment, I finally decided what the next step in my life was going to be. At that moment, my story began.

Eleven

Seeding Genius

Shortly after my coffee-induced epiphany I made my way to the campus library for a spot of research. This was exactly the second time I had visited the library in my university career to date. The first time was to shelter from the rain. It's true, libraries are not so frequented as they once were, even by students.

The great thing about the modern information landscape is that it is so incredibly easy to hone in on the very nugget of information you require, with virtually no physical or intellectual effort. This seems like a good thing, and mostly it is; but the downside comes when the aforementioned nugget of information equates to half a paragraph of a four-hundred page book. In such cases you tend to lose a spot of context – like three hundred and ninety-nine pages of context.

This pattern repeats itself throughout our lives. We are forever foregoing context, for a quick hit of concentrated information. Be it daily news or exam revision, espresso info is what we seek.

The result of this skim-reading is the continual erosion of our depth of knowledge, and indeed our personalities. We are, as a society, shallower now than we have ever been before in the history of our race. The quality of our TV is testament to this fact. We are all sound-bite and no substance.

Hence, this seemingly innocuous trip to the library was a noteworthy occurrence in my development. No longer was I going to skim the web for paraphrased titbits. I was actually going to study – I was going to learn something. I was going to read a text-book from page *one*. No, I was even going to read the preface bit that everyone skips. Note to authors: if you want someone to read a page, don't put Roman numerals at the bottom of it.

And from where did this new-found fervour originate? Over the previous few years I had grown despondent that I clearly hadn't become the genius I always assumed I'd grow into. I just didn't *have what it took*. And that irked me. I was irked by the unfairness at which genius is doled out. I didn't feel it fair that those born with a natural gift should be awarded wealth and acclaim for what amounted to little more than fortuity. Whilst us average Joes had to make do with our average remunerations.

Not that I saw any other way. I never found a solution to the inequality of the gene pool. If you think about it too hard you end up following the redbrick road to communism; and that road has never led to any solutions.

But as it turns out ... maybe we don't need any.

I was obsessed with genius for so long, but it had never occurred to me to *read* about it. Not until my epiphany episode in the café. After that I dug up some research on the topic, and it led me to an enlightening discovery. Enlightening to the extent that it should be on the school curriculum. No, it should be a school mantra, chanted in morning assembly.

As it is not a school mantra then now is your only chance. If you take nothing else from my story – if you never even get beyond page one hundred and twelve – then take this simple fact, and believe it...

Geniuses are *made* ... not born.

This is true. The quality we call genius – or extreme natural talent – arises not from innate gifts but from an interplay of the following three ingredients:

– *Average* natural ability;

– Quality instruction;

– And a mountain of hard work.

By way of example consider New York City's Hunter College Elementary School, which only accepts students with IQs in the top *one* percentile of the population, and boasts an average IQ that maybe only one in five thousand people exhibit. A study of graduates from this school showed that not *one* of them – none, zilch, zero, nada – went on to be superstars in any field.

Even Stephen Hawking himself – one of the greatest theoretical physicists of all time – was of only *middling* intelligence and achievement until his mid-twenties. Only at this point, when he grew obsessive about black holes, did he catch fire. It was the obsession that was key.

The truth is, the successful elite are rarely more gifted than the also-rans, but they almost invariably outworked them on the way up.

That's not to say that there are *no* natural prodigies out there, for there are. But the majority of our great masters, from Mozart to Einstein to whomever may be your sporting hero, made it to the top of their game more through hard work and good tutelage than through innate talent.

And what does this mean? It means something very profound. It means you can be who you want to be. *If* you are willing to put in the hours.

I was finally willing.

The salient points that I had missed until now were twofold:

– One: an individual can do remarkable things when they really put their mind to it;

– Two: if an individual wants to do remarkable things ... *they have to put their mind to it*!

The difference between these two points is subtle, but massively important.

It was now when it all came together, when I gained the unquestioning belief that this was an attainable goal: to understand people; to read them and to rewrite them. I had faith in this in a way I had never had in anything before.

This was not about winning poker or picking up girls – not entirely – it was about being ... well, superhuman, in a way. It was about walking down the street and knowing I had a 'skill'. And a worthy skill at that, not some arbitrary skill like hitting a ball into a hole with a metal stick.

I wasn't clear how my worthy skill was going to benefit mankind, but I knew it could. I knew it had the potential, and that was good enough for now.

Twelve

Learning to Read

I lost count of how many books I ploughed through when I began my learned journey. Dozens certainly, hundreds maybe. On topics as diverse as body language, face reading, cold reading, hypnotism, suggestion, cognitive therapy, even magic. I traced my way back through a trail of bibliographies to where the source of these topics began; quickly learning to avoid any modern books, which paraphrased and simplified and distilled until all meaningful content was lost.

I tracked down second-hand, out-of-print books, coming to associate the musty smell of aged pages with the kind of sincere knowledge that seemed all too scarce since commercialism had taken hold.

These tomes were home to a wealth of fascinating characters who, by rights, should be the icons and heroes of our age, but who have been all but forgotten. One such character I need to tell you about is a man named Silvan Tomkins.

But first I need to explain a pattern I noticed during the early phase of my studies. For it appeared to me that each advancement of human understanding to date had occurred in three stages: Prodigy, Professor, and Scholar.

The Prodigy is someone with such a natural insight that even she – for want of a gender neutral pronoun – does not know from where her skill or knowledge arises. She will be the first person to know something or the first to be able to do something. But her gift is so innate that she cannot put into words what she does such that others might learn. Her talent would disappear and be forgotten if it were not for who comes next.

The Professor will make it his life's work to painstakingly study the Prodigy and others like her, and over time may uncover the mechanisms at work, and may even learn to employ them himself. The Professor will be best placed to articulate the workings of which he studies.

And so then come the Scholars, who can learn at their leisure, standing on the shoulders of giants.

In the subject of face-reading I was the Scholar, still at kindergarten. Few would argue that a man called Paul Ekman took the role of Professor in this domain. And *he* would not argue that a remarkable man named Silvan Tomkins was the Prodigy.

Tomkins was born in Philadelphia in 1911, the son of a dentist from Russia. He was short, and slightly thick around the middle, with a wild mane of white hair and huge black-rimmed glasses. And he just may have been the best face reader there ever was.

He was a legendary talker. At the end of a cocktail party, fifteen people would sit, rapt, at Tomkins feet. Someone would say, 'One more question!'; and they would all sit there for another hour and a half, as Tomkins held forth on a diverse raft of topics that enfolded into one extended riff.

During the Depression, in the midst of his doctoral

studies at Harvard, he worked as a handicapper for a horse-racing syndicate, and was so successful that he lived lavishly on Manhattan's Upper East Side. He had a system for predicting how a horse would fare based on the horses standing either side of it, based on their emotional relationship. Some may call it a system, others say it was just a gift.

And when studying people, rather than horses, Tomkins' gift was even more profound. He could glean all manner of secrets from a person's face, beyond merely their emotion. It was said he could tell a man's crime from just looking at his mug shots.

Tomkins taught psychology at Princeton and Rutgers, and his writings showed an undeniable mark of brilliance: no one could understand them. He was a true Prodigy. He didn't understand his gift well enough to articulate it.

Fortunately, Tomkins had a profound effect on a young psychologist named Paul Ekman, who had long harboured an obsession with facial expressions. Ekman was working on the problem of whether human facial expressions were universal at the time of one particular encounter with Tomkins; one that Ekman would never forget.

Ekman showed video footage to Tomkins of two tribes from Papua New Guinea. All context had been removed from the film, only close-ups of faces remained, yet Tomkins was able to accurately describe the nature of the two tribes. Ekman was astounded. Playing the film in slow motion Tomkins showed Ekman exactly how he did it, pointing out the particular bulges and wrinkles in the faces.

That was when Ekman realized that he had no choice

but to create a complete taxonomy of human expressions. It was an awesome undertaking. First, from the structure of facial muscles, he defined forty-three atomic muscular movements – Action Units as he called them.

He and a colleague then spent no less than *seven years* cataloguing ten thousand possible Action-Unit combinations. Most of them turned out to be meaningless nonsense faces, but around three thousand did have meaning and amounted to a complete directory of facial emotions.

Crucially, what Ekman had established was that expressions were the products of evolution, *universally* recognised – even by members of the remotest tribes in the world. The face was part of a physiological system; and so the system could be learned.

All I had to do ... was learn it.

I began like Ekman did, sitting in a room for hours a day, watching clips of people laughing and shouting and crying; people that were sad or confused or scared; trying to see the connections between the face and the feelings. When Ekman started learning he soon assembled a videotape library which filled three rooms in his lab, and studied them to the point where he could look at a face and pick up a flicker of emotion that might last no more than a fraction of a second.

But watching clips of endless unknown faces was beginning to drive me insane. It was too dry, too flat. I needed real people. I began to talk to friends and strangers alike, trying to analyse their faces as I spoke to them. But I found myself concentrating so hard on their expressions that I was no longer listening to what they were saying. It was a mental juggling act and I kept dropping the balls. I got a lot of odd looks in those days.

I found talking within a group was the best strategy. I could sit back and study people's faces without having to worry too much about responding.

The key to reading faces is micro-expressions. These are the involuntary facial expressions that can reveal emotions not intended to be expressed. They often appear only fleetingly, before the conscious mind masks over them with an alternative message. Micro-expressions are the leaky tap through which our true emotions leak out.

At first it was impossible. I couldn't keep up. I couldn't spot the momentary glimpses of the all-important micro-expressions, before they vanished. It was frustrating. But I understood now that frustration was just one step along the path to any goal. Even failure is just a step along the path. It marked the line at which most people would come to a halt. It was the line where *I* would have given up before. But that was why I'd never achieved anything before. I knew now that all you had to do was step over the line and keep on walking – to pick a route and stick to it. This was my route – at all costs.

It was an arduous journey, there's no doubt, but slowly it started to come together. Slowly, it started to become natural, almost unconscious, to weave this new source of information into a meaning. Eventually, the face became more than just a face. It became an unmistakable narration to an individual's actions; a subtext to their words.

One day, I recalled an event from a couple of years before, which allowed something enlightening to dawn on me.

• • • • •

It was my first year at university. I was high on something extremely legitimate, and packing a stonking queen-high at the poker table. When I say poker table, I mean upturned crate in my room in halls.

The hand had gotten a little carried away, and by this point I figured that if I was going down then that queen was going down with me. The one in my hand, that is, not the guy facing me. I think he was straight. At least with respect to his sexual orientation – alas not with the quality of his cards.

So, there I was, admirably bluffing my way towards a substantial student debt, now holding a paltry pair of queens. The river had left three pretty little diamonds on the table between us, and my opponent had just gone all-in off the back of it. I stared into his eyes, trying desperately to determine whether he was holding a flush or a bluff, wishing that there was some way I could know.

And then some words escaped from my mouth, and I don't know where they came from.

'You're looking pretty flushed mate,' I said.

And with that I knew – he was bluffing. I didn't understand at the time; how the subtle ambiguity of my inspired statement had blind-sided his conscious mind, just long enough for a fleeting unconscious response to seep out. Nobody else spotted it. Very few people would, but I did – somehow.

• • • • •

I began to realize where all the hunches I'd had in my life had come from – like the one about the girl in the coffee shop. More profoundly, I began to realize that, in fact, I was not learning a new skill at all.

I was learning an *old* one.

I was reawakening a latent talent. It became so obvious. Before humans had mastered the spoken word, this *was* how we communicated. We *all* used to read faces. Now I could again.

And it felt ... good.

It felt ... empowering.

But power is not always a good thing. If only I'd known that at the time.

Thirteen

Reading for Others

Back in the mid-sixties Ekman and his team of psychologists in San Francisco devised a set of tests – as psychologists are wont to do – and set about finding individuals who had a reputation for being uncannily perceptive. The tests' purpose was to study people's ability to detect lies told by others. Subjects would sit in a darkened room and watch video footage of people who were either lying or telling the truth. All the subjects had to do was identify the fibbers. Simple.

The tests were given to policemen, customs officers, FBI officers, trial lawyers, psychotherapists and a bunch of other professionals who should have had a knack for spotting deception.

And their scores? Bang on fifty per cent. No better than chance.

This might have been disheartening if it weren't for the fact that every now and then, roughly one time in a thousand, someone walked into those labs and scored off the charts. Someone who could see something that nobody else could.

I read about the project with excitement. I knew I could have been the one in a thousand. That project had long-since ended. But after a little research I discovered that a couple of years ago an almost identical study had been initiated and was still being conducted by a team of researchers at the University of California, San Diego. They had been commissioned by the US government to develop training programs for law-enforcement agencies.

Just like most other young adults about to set foot in the real world, I was looking for some kind of validation. For most people the idea of validation is a fairly woolly concept, but for me it was black-and-white; it was a multiple choice exam waiting to be taken on the other side of the pond. I contacted the team in San Diego and said I wanted to take the test. Normally researchers have to go hunting for willing guinea pigs so they happily agreed; although, of course, their expenses budget did not run to transatlantic jet-setting.

I wasn't going to let money hold me back, so as soon as I graduated I scraped together enough cash from various bar jobs for a flight to the States. And there I was, in America, ready to be prodded and probed by be-sandaled boffins.

On my first day there I asked one of the psychologists how they normally identified people to test. He said that some were random but that others were invited in because they were thought to be gifted. He told me about one cop they had called up after a news report about him had been forwarded to them.

'He was out on patrol one night,' the researcher began, 'parked up in an area known for prostitution, when a guy starts to walk toward the patrol car. The cop opens the window and asks an innocuous question, then shoots the guy dead. His partner was like – *What the fuck did you just do?*'

'So you invited him to do the tests because he was crazy?' I asked.

'Not at all. It turned out that under the dead guy's trench coat there was a sawn-off shotgun ... oh *and* a makeshift flamethrower. He was mentally unstable and looking to torch the inside of a cop car – and the cop could see it in his face. No one else would've been able to see it, but he did.'

'Right,' I said, maybe with less awe than I was supposed to.

The technician looked at me with earnest eyes. 'No one has ever beaten his test scores.'

'Ooh,' I said slowly, making more effort this time.

Then, on my very first set of tests ... I knocked that cop's scores right out of the park.

All the boffins were terribly excited – it was cute. Me, I was just kind of satisfied. I'd come all this way just to prove what I already knew. I had validation now, but that was it. I didn't know what this meant; what I was going to do with my validity.

As it turned out, my lack of direction wasn't going to prove a problem for long. Somebody else was ready to set my heading for me. His name was Zack Bayliss. I got a call from him a couple of days after my first test and he made me an offer I couldn't refuse. US citizenship, good salary, company car. Even a 401K.

'A *gun*?' I queried, highlighting just how green I was.

'Err ... a 401K is pension plan.'

'Oh.'

On a twenty-one-year-old's scale of excitement, guns and pension plans fall at quite opposite extremes. However, for a recently graduated student, a salary – good or otherwise – falls pretty much at the same end of the scale as guns. Besides, this was *America.* Needless to say, I bit Mr Bayliss's metaphorical arm off.

Zack Bayliss was a deputy director of national intelligence, which meant he worked in the office that oversaw the activities of the sixteen members of the US intelligence community: CIA, NSA, FBI, DEA and all the other three-letter abbreviations that are so influential in the States. In simple terms Bayliss was a *really* important person. Not that I had any clue. And what I also didn't know at the time was that being contacted by him directly was very irregular. I never met him in person and rarely even spoke to him after that first call.

My initial training was in Arlington, Virginia, where all the clever stuff happens. I was put to use in a number of mundane ways: to observe interrogations, analyse surveillance footage, and sometimes just to watch news reels of foreign leaders.

Eventually, I was sent into the field, but I was always kept out of harm's way, holed up in a nearby van or hotel room. I didn't know at this stage that this was all a try-out. Zack Bayliss had other plans for me.

Eventually, these intentions came to light when I got posted to the US defence research agency's headquarters down the road, for a spot of research and development. This felt like an odd move and I wasn't pleased at first. I didn't consider myself a scientist. But in reality that was exactly what I was. My rigorous, almost obsessive, application of research and experimentation to acquire and hone the skills that I possessed made me more of a scientist than most PhDs.

The R&D team I joined had been working for some years on developing a screening system for detecting 'potential hostile intent', as they termed it. The idea was to develop a non-invasive remote detection system for determining whether someone was about to do something bad. The potential applications of such a system were immense: from spotting terrorists at airport security check-points, to mounting it on armoured patrol vehicles in war zones.

The team had experienced some degree of success to date. Their initial approach had concentrated on developing what was effectively a remote polygraph machine. That is, a machine that could measure physiological changes – pulse, blood-pressure, perspiration – from afar. It did this by bouncing laser beams and microwaves off people, and the mechanics of the system were sound – it achieved the aim of being able to remotely take measurements that approximated those of a polygraph. But the approach suffered from one major limitation: for polygraph readings to be meaningful, a set of accurate control measurements have to be taken for each subject. The challenge of how to do this covertly proved to be a conundrum the researchers could never crack. And a system that flagged up anyone with physiological readings outside the norm was next to useless; being as this would include those nervous of flying at an airport or ill people in a hospital.

This would have been an effective dead end. But the project had some big sponsors and a new project leader was brought in to champion a new direction. This time the approach was to develop software to analyse people's facial expressions, gait and body movements; with the same aim of identifying individuals harbouring malicious intent.

The system was dubbed Hostile Intention Detection Equipment – *Hide*. For those lucky enough not to work in an engineering environment, allow me to explain that the average engineer gets pretty horny over acronyms – like they do about Star Wars T-shirts. Sometimes an acronym happens to spell something tangentially pertinent and they even get excited enough to pee a little.

Oftentimes, they come up with the name first, then crowbar in vaguely relevant words in a random order just to spell it. Before Hide was chosen I had to veto *Stealth Malicious Intention Location Equipment.*

The sponsors of the project also sponsored the researchers at UCSD who ran the tests I'd volunteered for. So when I caused a spike on their charts, Bayliss soon knew about it. By all accounts, *I* was the leading expert in *their* field.

Progress was slow but positive. It took months just to create a system that could filter out micro-expressions, let alone divine any meaning from them. And that was from a full-on face-shot. The fun of dealing with partially-obscured, oblique footage was still to come.

Over time I began to feel very positive about my work. It felt worthwhile. It was all about identifying bad intentions and preventing them from being actioned. That had to be a good thing. I understood the benefit it could have on society as a whole.

But that was all a long way off. In fact, it was still a pipe dream. There could still be hurdles that would not be overcome. In this respect I felt unfulfilled. No one was benefiting right now and that made me uneasy about it. I'm quite impatient, it's true.

So, in my spare time I began to dabble in my own extra-curricular activities, trying to fulfil my self-appointed superhero destiny.

But it wasn't just reading that I practised.
My skills came in two complementary halves.
Reading...
And *writing*.

Fourteen

Learning to Write

Back when I was mastering my people-reading skills, before I came to America, I also began studying the spectrum of techniques that sheltered under the umbrella term of psychotherapy. This umbrella covers a truly massive domain. I'd like to say this is because not everyone responds in the same way to the same therapy - which is indeed true. But the main reason there are so many forms of therapy is that we know less about the fundamental workings of our own mind than we do about the cosmos. When minds are broken, we just don't know how to fix them.

Yet.

However, some things I read did seem to strike a chord with me. In particular I grew very interested in a man named Milton H. Erickson. His lasting influence on the world, direct and otherwise, was so great as to be immeasurable. Many modern therapeutic techniques came in to being through studying this man's work.

His range of techniques were so original and unconventional that the only appropriate way to classify what he practised was as *Ericksonian Therapy*. Although his methods often involved hypnotherapy, his approach was much less direct and authoritative than classical hypnosis. He *allowed* rather than *instructed.* Erickson recognised that resistance to trance resembles resistance to change, and so developed his therapeutic approach with this in mind.

He believed that the unconscious mind was always listening, and that whether or not the patient was in trance, suggestions could be made that would have a profound influence, so long as those suggestions struck some resonance at a subconscious level.

One of his key techniques, which interested me most, was to communicate via metaphor. And many of his metaphors were anecdotal or autobiographical, such as the story of how his own journey began: when he almost died of polio as a boy.

His therapeutic methods seemed to come naturally to him. He had a unique understanding of people and would instinctively know how best to treat someone.

On some occasions he chose to frustrate and aggravate a symptom to gain a response. For example, he might ignore a stubbornly silent family member until they eventually blurt out some telling truth through simple frustration. Conversely he may compliment a symptom and emphasize its positives, such that the subject might learn to accept it or use it to their advantage.

On other occasions he chose to manipulate the physical environment to elicit a response; or seeded ideas by metaphors and stories. Sometimes he even employed psychological shocks and unpleasant ordeals to achieve results.

Crucially, he would tailor his therapy to his subject and their particular needs. It wasn't formulaic. He would *respond* to their reactions; he would set up a feedback loop. This is what so many therapists today do not understand. They learn a particular discipline, they execute their off-pat routine, and they assume it will solve all problems for all people. This is not how it works. Therapy is not about learning a script from a hypnosis book by rote and spouting it at someone who wants to quit smoking. That's analogous to blurting English at people of different nationalities and expecting the same reaction from each.

Therapy is all about finding the *right* language.

But what was the world to do? There was only one Erickson. The best anyone could hope to do was to approximate his skills. In this respect it is a good thing that many forms of therapy spawned from his abilities, even if they cannot match the efficacy of this man's healing words.

So, if Erickson is the Prodigy in the Prodigy-Professor-Scholar model, then the Professor – or one of the Professors – was a man called Richard Bandler. He, along with an associate, studied Erickson's techniques in great detail. They co-authored many books on Erickson's methods, as well as hypnosis, communication and language. Ultimately, they founded the discipline of Neuro-Linguistic Programming. In itself this was an amazing achievement. Unfortunately, many people jumped on the Bandler wagon and NLP gave rise to a cynical corporate money-making machine. This is a shame because its underlying principles are sound and extremely helpful.

Some of the more ethical high-profile practitioners distanced themselves from NLP; whilst others continued to write books with titles like, *Change your life in 10 days: How to become wealthy, successful, good-looking, younger and a Formula One champion with NLP.*

I devoured all the literature I could find on Erickson and all the therapies that followed him. And I got pretty good at understanding how to exploit the mechanisms that I studied.

When I was working for the agency I wanted to put my skills into practise. But my employers and fellow researchers were never really interested in it. They did not appreciate that this half of my abilities was the more powerful half. The more exciting aspect of what I could do.

So I had to go it alone, because I knew that by using my array of techniques I could change people, *help* people. All I had to do was identify the people to help. And to this end I spent a lot of time hanging around in bars on my own. Sad, I know.

If you are not used to it, drinking alone is a peculiar experience. You feel remarkably self-conscious and ill-at-ease. It's odd that it's culturally acceptable to be on your own in a library or a shop or a park; but not in a *bar*. Just after you've purchased your drink is when you notice it. That moment when you turn away from the bar and scan your eyes across the room, inconspicuously trying to find a place to sit. Standing there, with all those people sitting in front on you, you feel like you are on stage, that everyone is watching you. But you soon realise who's on stage – *they* are. They are all busy with each other. It is *you* who is watching *them*. And indeed, that was exactly why I was there.

I was looking for people with some air of distress or unhappiness about them. This was not difficult, because it was everyone. No single person is one hundred percent at peace with the world and that's the way it should be.

There should always be room for improvement, a way forward, otherwise what's the point? And I was the one to do the improving. The world was my surgery and I was open 24-7.

As I was playing out the role of this mysterious saviour character I felt I had to have a 'thing'. Wisely, I decided that my thing would not involve wearing my underpants over my trousers; or in fact any other daring apparel-based experiments.

No, in my case it would be a phrase.

'What do you want?'

Simple, I know, but when asked at the right time, it is also powerful – because it works on so many levels. And when asked, it would be answered at each one of those levels, regardless of the vocalised response.

'What do you want?' I would ask, usually after a long slightly-drunken existential conversation. And they would respond. To give-up smoking; to get a promotion; to be more confident; to woo the girl in the office.

And then ... I would help them.

If I could.

I was in a bar once and there was a bunch of female students getting merry. I noticed that one of the girls didn't fit quite right with the rest, like she was a jigsaw piece from a different puzzle. She looked the part but wasn't hitting the same tempo as the others. Her laughter ended a little too soon; her movements were a little too fast.

After a while the girl headed to the bar and I went over to stand beside her.

'What do you want?' I asked. It was okay to be direct. We were in the same half-decade age-wise and it was a Friday night out on the town. This was the expected mode of contact, at least between people of the opposite sex. It's true, it was a lot easier for me to approach women than men in general, which was a shame in light of my intentions. But give me a break, I can only save half the world at a time.

The girl turned to me with a smile. 'Thanks,' she said, 'but I'm getting a round in.'

She, of course, assumed I was talking about a drink. But some part of her, deep down, would have unconsciously registered the subtle inflection on the 'want'. Some part of her would be answering the question differently.

'No problem,' I said, as we jostled for bar space. 'I'll get them. You a student?'

'Yeah.'

'What's your major?'

'Communications and Media.'

'You gonna be a journalist then?'

She shrugged. An insecure shrug, rather than an indecisive one.

'Why the doubts?' I asked.

She shrugged again before answering. 'Everyone else seems so smart here. None of my family before me ever even went to college, let alone graduated.'

I nodded, more in empathy than agreement, but I nodded all the same. 'Everyone has their limitations, right?'

The girl was a little dazed by my response. This was the point where the stranger hitting on her was supposed to be all encouragement and compliments, espousing just how great she was and how she was going to excel at everything she tried. But, unfortunately, I don't deal in that kind of baseless goodwill prophesizing. I'm not a horoscope.

After a beat, I continued. 'Maybe, it's more important to focus on the task, than the limitation.'

The barman asked what we wanted and we placed our order. The girl ferried drinks back to her companions but left hers on the bar till last. When she came back she took a long sip of her wine, buying time to find a way into a conversation. I helped her out.

'Want to hear a story?' I asked. 'A true one.'

'Sure,' she agreed with a puzzled but curious dip of the eyebrows.

'For hundreds of years there was a well-established myth that running a mile in under four minutes was humanly impossible. People limited themselves based on this belief. But then a man named Roger Bannister decided he wasn't going to be limited by this arbitrary barrier. He stopped thinking about it as four minutes and started thinking about it as two hundred and forty seconds. All he had to do was improve his time by a tenth of a second at a time, until he reached two hundred and forty seconds. And that's exactly what he did. He broke the historic four-minute barrier.

'Remarkably, it then only took *forty-six days* before somebody else did it too, even faster. And now? Now the record for the mile is almost *twenty seconds* inside four minutes. Twenty seconds.

'You see, that's why records are whittled away bit-by-bit. People limit *themselves* by *other people's* achievements.'

The most important thing to know about good therapy, in my opinion – and others would disagree – is not to be authoritative. Not to spout edicts about thinking positive and being confident, because that encourages resistance – like telling an adolescent youth what's good for him. Even those who seek out therapy are sometimes resistant when they receive it. As such, it's important to give the individual the option; to be accommodating and to be *indirect*.

The girl paused before confirming, 'You're right.' She had a mild uncertainty around her brow, as if she was wondering why she had never looked at it this way before. Then concern flooded back in.

'But, I just don't think I'm good enough.'

'When?'

'What?'

I gave a gentle laughing smile. It's important to get smiles right. You can spend a lifetime in front of a mirror just practising this.

'Come with me,' I said. We walked to a quieter part of the bar and found a table to sit at.

'Close your eyes,' I asked, and she did. 'Now imagine your life as a timeline stretching back into the past and out into the future. Can you do that?' She nodded. 'Now point to the past.' She raised a hand and pointed over her shoulder behind her. Some people point left, some point down, some point in really whacky directions, but behind is most common.

'Good,' I continued. 'Now, move backwards slowly along your timeline, until you reach a point where you were not worried about being good enough.' I gave her a moment to do this. 'Are you there?' She nodded. 'Good. Now, tell me, how good are you at journalism now?'

She looked perplexed. 'I'm six. I don't even know what it is.'

'Good. Now move forward, slowly, until you arrive

back at the present.' I gave her a moment. 'Think about how good you are now. Are you better?'

'Of course.'

'Good. Now, finally, move forward a little further, into the future. Tell me, do you see yourself having learnt even more? Having grown better still? Can you see that?'

Her head tilted to one side. 'Yes.'

'Excellent. That's a good trend, don't you think? Now, come back to the present. And open your eyes.'

She blinked a couple of times and then focused on me. I smiled and she reciprocated.

'If there is no need to be limited by the abilities of your six-year-old self then there is no need to be limited by *any* of your past selves. They are just other people, and as Bannister understood, there is no need to be limited by others people's achievements.'

She took a sip of her wine and I took a gulp of my beer.

'I'm not saying anyone can do anything. That's patently not true. But the message is this: don't focus on *limitations*, focus on the *task*. Focus on improving; a little bit at a time.' She nodded pensively. 'Do you think that is something you would want to do?' I gave her the option rather than an instruction.

'Yes.' It was a confident yes. 'I do.'

'Good,' I flashed a broad grin.

There was a pause in the conversation for a moment, as the girl reflected on it. Then she asked a question.

'So, what do *you* do?'

I finished up my drink and stood up. 'I've just done it,' I said, and I offered her a formal handshake. 'Good luck with your course,' I said.

Then I left.

I know this may come across as a little creepy and mysterious, and in a way that's exactly how it's supposed to be. A little mystique adds potency to the message. She will carry this anecdote with her, maybe tell other people about this time she met a weird guy in a bar, and it will only grow stronger. Much more so than if she'd visited her GP for words of wisdom and all the time was wondering if five minutes ago the doctor had had two fingers up somebody's rectum. That takes the edge off.

I don't know if it made a difference in her case, whether she was successful in her goals. I don't even know her name. But I like to think it helped.

And so that was me. That's what I did. Odd, I know.

Things continued this way for a couple of years. I became a transitory figure in many people's lives. Usually just a few hours – but a few hours can make all the difference. It can make people look at the world differently. React to it more productively. It can change them. Just a little. For the better.

But then, all of a sudden, like someone was trying to prove a point, something happened.

I met Gemma.

The girl who didn't need to be changed.

The *One*.

Fifteen

The One

I lived in a second floor apartment for a while when I was working on the Hide system. The second bedroom was employed as an office, the window of which looked out over a municipal park. I used to sit at my desk most evenings, half working, half watching people walking by. After a while you start to recognise people, the regulars. Particularly the dog-walkers. Partly because of their regularity, but mostly because there was more to identify with. They came as a set: human and beast.

One particular young woman came by mid-evening most days with an old tired-looking golden retriever plodding slowly along by her side. She piqued my interest because she was always reading; strolling along slowly, with her nose in a book, whilst her dog ferreted lazily in the grass. I thought this was odd. Dog owners usually interact with their dogs when out walking. She didn't seem to. I wondered if maybe the dog wasn't hers.

The other thing I thought was that she was pretty cute – as if you didn't see *that* coming – at least from the distance I was sitting at. Men have this tendency to bestow angelic beauty upon any woman if she is (a) a long way away; (b) facing the other direction but has nice hair; or (c) on the other end of the phone. The assumption of beauty is a dangerous one, but it gets us through the day – and long conversations with call-centre staff.

I'm ashamed to admit that I momentarily considered taking up jogging and doing laps of the park every evening, such that I might bump into her; but I figured that would be tantamount to stalking.

A few weeks after my obsession had begun, I was picking up my post from the mailboxes over the road and who should turn up to collect hers? Mystery dog-walker.

She had been living in an adjacent apartment block all along. Now, the first narcissistic thought that flashed through my mind was that I was right about the dog she walked not being hers, because they didn't allow pets in these apartments. And off the back of this smug self-congratulation came my opening gambit, which can only be categorised as suicidally inspired.

'So, no dog today then?' I announced.

What the fuck was that? Great job, Aaron. You might just as well have introduced yourself as the voyeuristic pervert from C204 and confided which of her outfits you most enjoyed observing her in! (Dark blue denim jacket, brown skirt and suede boots, in case you were wondering).

I'll save you the transcript of the floundering conversation that followed, suffice to say that she obviously got a kick out of meeting voyeuristic perverts because two hours later we were sharing a meal at the Chili's restaurant down the road. I had already eaten that evening but I wasn't going to mention that when she suggested we go for some food. At least I think that's what she did. She said she'd just come back from a long session at the gym and was starving. I recommended Chili's and that was that.

Anyway, so I had the chance to get to know her slightly more intimately than as a passing pedestrian. And, as we made our way down the street, the first thing that struck me was that she had an infectious spark of fun about her. Lots of people come across as bubbly, but it's often just a façade. Hers was a genuine manifestation of her optimism, which is a very rare quality and one I was beginning to find incredibly attractive.

I remember exactly what we ate for that meal. For starters we shared a *Triple Dipper Combo*. Then Gemma had *Chicken and Portobello Sizzling Fajita*, plus a *Caesar Salad* and *Loaded Mashed Potatoes* on the side; whilst I went for the more modest *Jalapeño Bacon Burger* with *Homestyle Fries*. By the time I was done I felt like I'd ingested a small housing estate, but apparently I just wasn't going to escape without also devouring at least some of a *Chocolate Chip Paradise Pie®*. Fortunately, Gemma did a good job in helping out with the pie – as did the Long Island Ice Teas in a lubricating capacity.

Good job this girl was a gym-fanatic, I figured, because she certainly knew how to eat. She must have read my thoughts or been overly self-conscious about her feast, as she offered an explanation.

'I used to be in the gymnastics team at school,' she declared. 'You wouldn't believe just how insanely hard parents push their kids here. From beauty pageants to Little League baseball; which, by the way, is a national televised event – for fricking kids. So, being a gymnast, where body size is everything, I basically wasn't allowed to eat for the first sixteen years of my life. So I'm making up for it now.' She smiled. Every time she smiled the little scar above her lip became slightly cuter. As did the slightly crooked tooth which dented her lower lip. It's those little imperfections that make a girl so perfect.

During the meal I learned that she was a teacher. And I discovered that the dog she walked was for an elderly friend of the family who lived a couple of blocks away and who was now wheelchair-bound.

After our mammoth eating session – which might just as well have consisted of an actual mammoth – Gemma took her cue to visit the bathroom. This was when it all slotted into place. This was when something fairly obvious finally dawned on me. And it meant that I knew how I could help her; that my question *was* relevant. When she returned, I popped it.

'What do you want?' I asked.

She looked slightly confused. 'In what context?'

'No context. If I qualify the question it will steer your answer. What do you want?'

She paused for a moment then gave a smile that had a hint of realisation to it. 'You ask this of a lot of people don't you?'

Hold on, I thought – *I was supposed to be the mind-reader around here*.

'Maybe,' I replied, caught off-guard.

She took a moment to drop a sugar lump into her coffee and stir it in. 'Why do you ask?'

'Just curious.'

'No, there's more to it than that.' She took a sip of her coffee, playfully stalling.

'Maybe there is,' I conceded, but didn't offer anything else.

'Okay, I'll play your game, if it's that important to you. I shall tell you what I want.'

'Thank you.'

'I want...' she said, finally deigning to give me an answer, and she leaned in closer. 'I want you to stop worrying about *other* people.'

You will not understand just how that answer blew me away. Partly because it was not self-centred, like everyone else's had been. Correction, not everyone else's answer had been self-centred. Some people said they wanted world peace, and such like, but they didn't mean it. I'm not saying everyone doesn't mean it, but they didn't. They just felt that was the kind of answer they should give.

Her answer was not self-centred, but, more importantly, it took me aback for another reason. It meant she understood me. That ... had never happened before.

The walk home was silent to begin with. Not an awkward silence, a companionable one. I was considering the evening's events, which was not wise. Considering and cocktails should not be mixed. In this case it led me to decide what I was going to say next. And what I was going to say next was just about the most dangerous thing I could possibly say. If I ever wanted to see this girl again – which I did – then steering well clear of this subject should have been considered absolutely essential. And yet something made me feel sure I could talk about it. I'd only known her a few hours, but I felt it was safe.

'Gemma?' I queried.

'Yes?'

'How long have you been making yourself sick?' I knew the answer of course. It was just a way of bringing up the subject – so to speak.

For the first time her smile faded. Not to anger or even sadness. Just seriousness.

'Is this what you want to help me with?'

'Do you want me to?'

She laughed. 'No.'

'Why are you laughing?'

'Because of how silly this is, and because of how nobody *realises* how silly it is.'

'What do you mean?'

She stopped so that she could look at me.

'Okay. We just went out and ate a huge amount of unhealthy food.' She indicated the quantity with her arms. 'Like lots of people do all the time. And that's okay, right?'

'Sure.'

'You're not going to send anyone off to the funny farm for this self-harming behaviour?'

'No, of course not.'

'Good. So, if you are allowing people to indulge in this way, then tell me this. At the end of the meal, which is better: to allow frightening quantities of saturated fat, salt, artificial additives – not to mention two-thousand calories – to be absorbed into your body and metabolised; or to flush the whole lot out of your system?'

'But...'

'No buts.' She started walking again. 'It's a no-brainer. And I resent the fact that people consider that anyone who does this has a psychological problem. If someone goes out and gets absolutely wasted on alcohol and ends up throwing-up all that poison into the gutter, they aren't pitied and sent for therapy. Apparently, it's called having a good time. Everyone knows that it's not good for your health, but every now and then it's considered acceptable. So where's the difference?'

I had no answer.

'Like most things, it only becomes a problem when it's obsessive. And I'm not obsessed, not any more.'

'Were you?'

'Yes. When I was a gymnast it was drummed into us that we couldn't weigh an ounce. But fourteen-year-old gymnasts have problems just like any other girl, or boy, and sometimes those problems require ice-cream and cookies and doughnuts to solve them. So we had to deal with it.

'We all did it, some after almost every meal. Your stomach gets used to it after a while. It doesn't even start digesting it. It just kind of packages it up. Then you can get rid of it in seconds. Even in public bathrooms, because you learn how to do it without making a noise.

'Some of my friends got too obsessed. They vomited till their oesophagus ripped and their knuckles bled from supporting themselves on the bathroom floor. Not nice. I was never that bad. And now that I'm done with gymnastics I hardly ever do it.'

We reached the door to her apartment block. We stopped and she turned to me again.

'Don't get me wrong. I'm not condoning it. I don't think people should get involved, just like with alcohol or junk food or gambling, because it can take control. But if you *do* do it, and you do it in moderation, then it doesn't make you a freak or a nutcase.'

This was the first conversation I had had in many

years where I hadn't known where it was going, where I hadn't been in the driving seat. It was … kind of exhilarating. That must sound odd, but it was quite a big deal to me.

'I know I've had an awful lot of cocktails,' I slurred. 'And I know this sounds absolutely ridiculous in my head, but I'm going to say it anyway.'

'Okay.'

'I think you're an incredible person.'

'Good.' She smiled like she'd been expecting it. 'Well that's a lot about my so-called problems. Do you want to know what yours is?'

'Go on.'

'You need to look at things from a different point of view.' That's what I heard her say. 'Do you understand?'

'Yes.'

'No, you don't. Keep saying it to yourself and maybe you will tomorrow.'

She stood up on tip toes to kiss me on the cheek, then she went inside.

Every minute from that point to the next time we met was consumed by thoughts of her.

The next morning I awoke, thoughts from the previous night flooding in like a wave of warmth. And I thought about what she'd said; I repeated it to myself. And then I got it. She hadn't said, 'a different point of view'. She'd said, 'a different point of *you'*.

Of me.

What was the point of me? When I was with other people I always thought it was to read them, to analyse them, to help them. But that doesn't always have to be my purpose. When I was with Gemma I didn't need to help her. She didn't need changing. When I was with her I could have a different purpose; I could be someone else.

Sometimes we all need to be someone else.

That was why she was The One.

Sixteen

Hide

A few months later the Hide project was dealt a blow. Luke Whitman announced that he was leaving the team. He was one of our chief coders and a complete genius when it came to video image processing. Guess who he was going to work for? Hollywood. I was, of course, insanely jealous, but also very excited for him – and growing evermore excited for him with every free pint I was downing at his leaving do.

I figured Monday would be the day to give the team a boost by telling them about my new idea for Hide. I'd been mulling it over for a while and I knew it could take the system to a whole new level.

The limitation with the system to-date centred on the inherent constraint of reading people 'cold'. If you really want to know what someone's thinking you have to see how they respond to stimuli, especially sub-conscious stimuli. I knew this better than anyone. It was my hobby.

To give you an idea of how powerful this approach can be: one study I stumbled across once asked volunteers to fill out questionnaires designed to prime some of them with words associated with the elderly, such as "grey" and "wrinkle". Afterwards, the researchers timed how long it took participants to walk down a hallway, and found that those who had been primed with elderly words walked more slowly than those who hadn't.

And this was just the written word. Imagine the efficacy of the oral equivalent. In fact, you don't need to imagine. You will have experienced it: standing in a room full of people, with dozens of other conversations going on around you. You are only consciously paying attention to the conversation you are having, but there is another part of your brain that is monitoring everything else. And when somebody mentions your name, or a subject you are interested in, then you react.

Most of the target locations for Hide – airports, prisons, hospitals, shopping malls – were ideally suited to feeding sub-conscious cues. They all have public address systems that nobody really pays much attention too. My idea was to feed seemingly nonsense messages over the PA system to elicit reactions from individuals. The messages would consist of fairly non-descript sentences loaded with well-chosen emotive words or sounds.

I need to confess here that this wasn't entirely my idea. A few weeks before I had been watching some old shows of a stage/TV performer who I was a great admirer of. This man started his career as a conjuror but got interested in hypnosis, suggestion and psychology in general, to quite brilliant results in the entertainment field. Anyway, he did this thing on one of his shows where, by looping suggestions through a public address system at a shopping mall, he got about eighty per cent of the visitors to stick their right arm in the air on cue. Pretty neat, I thought. So that's where I stole the idea.

I rolled up to work on Monday set to brief the team

on my notions and plan a way forward with this line of research. When I entered the lab, only a few guys were already in, but there was a mood in the air I didn't much care for.

I sat down opposite a colleague of mine.

'You hear about Luke?'

I shook my head, not liking the tone.

'Car crash. Dead.'

Nothing like breaking it to me gently.

'Jesus, you're kidding? What happened?'

He shrugged to suggest he didn't know the details.

'That's just awful,' I continued. 'Get a job in the movie industry then die in an accident.'

There was a fleeting twitch in my workmate's eyebrows as I landed that last word; a combination of surprise and confusion. Then it was gone.

'What is it?' I quizzed.

He tried to look ignorant for a while, but then realised it wouldn't wash with me.

'You can't just leave a place like this,' he said in a hushed voice. 'Not if you know as much as Luke did.'

I didn't need to ask if he was being serious. There was a fear in his eyes that underscored the belief in what he was implying.

I went home early that day. For the first time I began to question whether I was working for the right side. When I was a kid there were only ever two sides: the goodies and the baddies: cops and robbers; cowboys and Indians. More than anything else, this binary morality was ingrained into me by the Star Wars movies my dad made me watch like they were the modern gospel. But it's not that simple. There are more than two sides. There are *three-hundred million* sides in the US alone:

every man, woman and child working to their own agenda, according to their own complex set of beliefs and motivations.

Understanding this was of critical importance and it bugged me that I hadn't thought this through before. There were only a handful of people who had access to or even knowledge of what we were working on. Who was I to judge that the intentions of these individuals were on the right side of morality? I didn't even know what their intentions were. I'd never met Zack Bayliss in person. Why? Because he was a busy man? Or because he had things to hide? Things to hide, from someone who could read minds...

After Luke's death I started to study things a little more closely; do a little digging. And a few things started to make more sense, like Bayliss never making an appearance, like certain directions we were given. It quite quickly became very apparent ... I was working for the wrong side. Not America, not the Government, not necessarily the agency even. Just whoever was behind this project; whoever knew what it was really all about. Bayliss presumably and maybe a few others.

This put me in something of a dilemma. What we were trying to develop was a powerful tool – weapon even – and I didn't want it used by the wrong people; to the wrong ends. If that was a possibility then it was better that it never existed at all. At the very least it was better that I was not involved with it anymore. But then, I quite liked being alive too.

And then there was Gemma. It was clear now that I was buried deep in some pretty dangerous shit. I didn't want her to get messed up in it.

Apart from the specifics of what I was working on I

had actually been pretty open with Gemma to date. But this time, I couldn't tell her what I had to do. It took months to put everything in place. Then it was time.

That morning I kissed her goodbye a little longer than usual, held her a little tighter.

'Take care,' I said with a smile and walked away, knowing that the time till I next saw her would be at best a long time. At worst ... forever.

Seventeen

Hidden

Six days later a reasonably intact – if slightly charred – canine and premolar were found in a burnt-out van just the other side of the Mexican border. The teeth were identified as those of one Aaron Braunn.

Me.

Apparently, I'd built up some gambling debts and made myself some bad friends; and I'd tried to buy myself out of it with some secret government intelligence software.

The death, of course, was fake. The teeth, alas, were very real. It's not quite as simple as it seems to fake your death by burning someone else's body. You have to make sure none of theirs remain to give the game away. Fortunately, a forensic scientist in Florida had done a little research on the subject, for much more noble causes, I stress.

If you're interested, here's the detail. Providing there is sufficient wicking material, such as clothing, the human body contains enough body fat to burn for about seven hours. The skeleton however takes much longer to burn at these temperatures so there is usually always something left. Dousing in gasoline does not help. That will barely burn for more than a minute before exhausting itself. Without the aid of a crematorium, the only sure fire way – excuse the pun – to completely destroy a body is to put it in the trunk of a car on top of the spare wheel. The rubber of the tyre provides the extra fuel, whilst the body is suspended on the metal rim exposing it to the intense heat. Complete destruction can be achieved after four to five hours.

After completing this process all that remained for me was to throw in a couple of burnt up teeth amongst the rest of the unidentifiable body ash.

The complexity and attention to detail required in this single first step highlights why only someone from inside could entertain the idea of hiding from them. I knew how they operated. I knew what I had to do to avoid their detection.

To this end I had spent the previous six months setting up dozens of fake identities and accompanying bank accounts.

I also did some work at removing my identity within the service. I couldn't actually remove my profile on the system without setting off alarm bells, but I was able to tweak it. And in many ways that was better.

The first thing I modified was the composite face image stored with my profile. Composite face images are created by combining a set of photographs taken from different angles to produce a single 'average' image of one's face. It looks a bit odd to the human eye but when used by image recognition software it produces a much higher hit-rate than using a standard photo. So I switched the image in my profile for an image composed of other people; but I left the main profile image untouched – the one displayed when users look up my details. This was the best strategy because as soon as I disappeared my profile would be springing up on dozens of screens throughout the agency; and if it wasn't my face that appeared people would know the profile had been compromised. It was much more important to replace the composite image so I didn't set off any triggers if I ever passed in front of the wrong cameras at any point in the future.

Something else the agency wouldn't want people to know is that they also collect people's gait profile. The way someone walks is almost as unique as their fingerprints or face, but has one distinct advantage over them both in that it can be used to identify people from a distance. Even cooler still, gait profiles can be used to recognise people from above by the shadow they cast. It won't be long before it is possible to recognise people from satellite surveillance cameras, as soon as the resolution is good enough. Needless to say, I tweaked my gait profile too.

There was one last thing I needed to do before I left; one which would really piss off Zack Bayliss, not to mention a number of others. But this I couldn't do in slow time. This I had to do at the very last minute.

The day I chose to leave was the Friday night before Labor Day weekend. I wanted a long weekend of running before anyone sounded the alarm.

I went into work that day and tried to act normal, which involved attending the traditional Friday team lunch at the canteen. I was operating on autopilot with my mind very much elsewhere – all non-taxing tasks being out-sourced to lower brain functions. This was why only on leaving the canteen checkout did I look down at my tray to find a strangely righteous selection of vegetable soup, cheese-and-onion quiche and a radish salad. None of which I remember buying, but which earned me some perplexed glances from most of my team. They were all very male – and American – and didn't really understand the concept of a meal without at least one previously-sentient constituent. I made a hand waving gesture at the jibes and attempted to keep a low profile.

It's not totally unheard of for me to take the veggie option. Being fully aware that the ruminants are happily belching our world to an early apocalypse, sometimes I feel I should cut back on the meat. Clearly today my subconscious was making some kind of feeble attempt to address my virtue balance.

It was making this attempt because today ... I was going to screw everyone over. Including all the guys I was sharing lunch with, most of whom I counted as friends. Although it would be merely a matter of days before they would gladly be chewing over my own previously-sentient carcass for lunch. As such, I was embarking on a major guilt trip over this final part of my plan. And strangely enough, not eating a cow did not make me feel a whole lot better.

I just needed to hold it together. I needed to keep low, talk to as few people as possible, and ride out the day.

Then, exactly what I didn't need in achieving this aim ... walked right in through the door. Zack Bayliss with some high-profile entourage. Not that Bayliss would even know my face but his presence made me nervous, in the way that the presence of important people does. I'd never seen him in these parts before, with the low-life. He was presumably on a flying visit, showing some bigwigs the facilities.

One of his entourage was his personal assistant – or whatever they call themselves these days. Tanya Scarlett was her name and she bugged the hell out of me. Not that I'd ever spoken to her, so maybe I was judging her too soon. But it was clear to all that she suffered from an acute case of org-chart vertigo. Allow me to explain. The object of an organisation chart is to represent employee seniority on the vertical axes – top to bottom. A quirk of this layout is that the only logical place to put a member of support staff like Ms Scarlett is directly under and slightly to one side of whomever she supports – the big man himself, in this case. This places her vertically above everyone else in the organisation, even her boss's first line of management. Usually this does not pose a problem. But it does in the case of someone like Tanya Scarlett, who is deluded enough to think that her abstract loftiness actually *means* something; and cavorts about the place like some supreme being and sovereign ruler of the land.

There was one other reason why I hated her so much: I found her so annoyingly sexy.

Bitch.

I didn't really understand why this was. And, to be honest, I'd rather just move on and not overanalyse it.

Rumours are of course rife that this PA embarks on a number of out-of-office activities with Bayliss. Whether true or not, I'm sure the primary source of these rumours are her own lips, and indeed hips, as she prances about on her power-heels with her unmistakeable *I'm-shagging-the-boss* swagger.

Harlot.

The rest of the group were all male, smart-suited and hobnobby. I did not know who they were but I would be willing to wager that their collective power was significantly greater than that of the president himself. For this reason, I did my best to ignore them.

I brought a spoonful of soup to my lips, remembering with disappointment that it wasn't clam chowder. I'm not sure of the exact environmental impact of clams but clearly my subconscious thinks they should be avoided along with the ruminants, from a virtuous planet-saving perspective.

Then something really unexpected happened. As the Bayliss rabble passed by our table, in a haze of sycophancy, little Miss Sassy Pants herself looked right at me. And do you know what she did?

She said, 'Hi'.

Hussy.

I was rather caught off guard. All I managed was a stunned smile in return, before missing my mouth with a spoonful of clam-less broth. The reason I was startled was that I wouldn't have expected her to have any idea who I was. Did she know who I was? Or was she just doing the friendly 'Hi' thing? I hadn't noticed her say 'Hi' to anyone else. Jeez, that's all I bloody well needed. On the very day that I needed nothing but to melt into the walls, I was suddenly 'known' by the upper-echelons. I was suddenly being 'Hi'-ed at by a woman who flirts around in the corridors of power – and indeed *fondles* around in the *trousers* of power.

Today, of all days, I was not handling so well. My immaturity was showing through. I was not quite a grown-up in a very grown-up world.

After work I made myself scarce until midnight, and then returned. On my way in I nodded politely to the security guard in reception.

'I'd forget my head if it wasn't screwed on,' I said with a cheery smile, by way of explanation of my presence. The guard glanced up from his security monitor-slash-TV just long enough to return the smile, and I made my way up to the lab.

The lab was dark. I stepped in and as I made my way to the far side the fluorescent lighting flickered into life sporadically down the room.

At my desk I booted up my machine to set about my deleterious handiwork. I remotely logged into the repository server with the deviously-acquired admin password. Passwords are still the chink in any security system's armour. Correction, password *owners* are – they're easier to crack.

And so it was time for my final task.

My job here was simple. All I needed to do was delete the source code for Hide. To extinguish it from the hands of power.

This had taken quite some preparation, because all the local file servers were backed-up in a number of off-site locations. That's just standard protocol. As such, it took weeks of social engineering to get into a position where I could modify the backup policy, and turn off the backup for our systems. Luckily, the thing about backups is that nobody notices their absence until they are needed. Once the backups were removed I figured the servers would be written to enough times to make any residue of the data unrecoverable.

That done, all I had to do was purge the local repository. But that was one task that would be noticed immediately. So this had to be the last thing I did before turning out the lights – on the lab and on Aaron Braunn.

So, there I was, habitually twiddling a ballpoint pen around my thumb; all set to issue the command to erase over a year's worth of hard work. My hard work. My friends' hard work. And I discovered something I really should have anticipated. I discovered that twiddling a ballpoint pen around my thumb was about the only thing I was ever going to achieve. Because I could not bring myself to do it. It seemed so ... irreversible. It would be like killing my baby.

I sat there for a while longer, grappling with my conscience, until I finally conceded that it was never going to happen. Not like this.

So I had no choice. If I was ever going to get out of here, having achieved my aim, I had to take a copy of the entire thing first. But considering that the sole intention of this whole charade was to prevent the software falling into the wrong hands, it would be pretty dumb to just start walking around with it in my pocket.

So I began the process of encrypting the copy with a key so large that even NSA weren't going to crack it without a global distributed computing effort or a string of quantum computers.

However, this presented me with a problem. I did some quick maths regarding encryption algorithms, and calculated that the process of performing serious number-crunching on a serious quantity of data would take a serious amount of time – squared. And such amounts of time did not feature in my original plan. So I needed a new plan. It didn't take long to arrive at one because the new plan was very similar to the old one – with about four hours of hanging around in the middle.

Remarkably, I eventually grew bored of twiddling my ballpoint and I found myself nervously pacing up and down the corridor instead as I waited for the numbers to be crunched. I tried drinking the coffee-approximation vended by the machine in the lobby, but it was only the colour the machine ever got close to approximating with any real success.

There were a few sofa-bench type affairs clustered around a coffee table near the machine. I perched myself on one of them to begin my second cup of coffee-coloured liquid. By this point I figured I had a couple more hours to wait. And so I waited.

And waiting made me worry. I needed to be gone by now. What I was doing was seriously bad news – for me that is. I believed I was doing the 'right thing', but there were people who wouldn't see it that way. And those people were pretty powerful. This was some real deep shit I was getting myself into one foot at a time – and I could almost begin to smell it. As soon as I could, I needed to ditch these cruddy shoes and get as far away as possible.

As I sat there, amidst the drab perfunctory surroundings, with nothing but my paranoia for company, I started to feel that the walls were judging me. They stood around me like schoolyard snitches threatening to go tell on me. And, paradoxically, as the silence solidified around me, the childish taunts began to crescendo toward a deafening cacophony inside my mind.

I was, by all accounts, losing it.

At that moment an eerie and hauntingly realistic flash of déjà vu washed over me and brought with it a deep bout of nausea. It snapped me out of my downward spiralling reverie but if it were a portent of any future event then I did not anticipate its arrival with glee.

I needed to be gone. Now.

Then ... the deafening silence was broken, by something much worse.

Footsteps.

My stomach flipped. The steps were coming from behind me, from a corridor the other side of a door. I couldn't move. Whoever it was would be able to see me through the glass in the door. If I scuttled back to the lab it would imply wrong-doing. So I had to stay put.

The footsteps were slower than normal walking pace: slow ... careful ... steps – as if intentionally building suspense. They were hard-soled shoes making a crisp clop-clopping that echoed toward me. All I could think of were those power-heels of that blasted PA Tanya Scarlett. She knew! That was all my mind could think. She was here to get me. That was it. It was all over. It wasn't fair. I was only twenty-four. I was way too young to die. I hadn't even been to Disneyland yet.

The footsteps stopped. There was a beep as a security pass was waved. And then the door opened.

This, I knew, was the point I had to begin standing. It would appear just as odd if I did not react at all to another individual at this late hour.

'*Sir*?' It was a male voice. I finished standing and turned to face its owner. Then it delivered something that wasn't in any of my pre-conceived scenarios: 'Would you like some *real* coffee?'

It was the security guard from downstairs, holding out a large steaming mug of black coffee.

'It's Colombian,' he said proudly. 'Freshly ground.' He leaned in. 'I've got a coffee-bean grinder under my desk.' He delivered a smile and a conspiratorial wink, as if keeping a contraband coffee-bean grinder at his post was the greatest crime against his nation.

I realised my jaw had been hanging open a moment too long and pulled it shut.

'Thanks,' I said as I approached to take the mug.

'I was watching you on the monitor,' the guard continued, 'drinking that vending machine muck. Thought you could use some of the good stuff.'

Damn it. I hadn't even noticed the camera in the vestibule. My paranoia slipped into overdrive. My mind whizzed. Surely, there was nothing I'd done on camera that looked suspicious? Had I been consuming a beverage in an incriminating fashion? I reeled myself in. Clearly not in the eyes of the security guard, and that was all that mattered. I just had to make it through tonight.

'Very kind,' I said as I took a sip from the offered mug and suddenly felt like the worst human being alive. This stranger had held out a hand of friendship. He had initiated an unsolicited act of kindness. And I was betraying him. In the next room, on his patch, on his watch, I was conducting *real* crimes against *his* nation, against *him*. And at the same time I had the audacity to stand here and drink his fucking coffee. I might just as well be pissing in his face.

Regardless. Now was not the time to crumble. This was about survival.

'Couldn't sleep,' I said. 'Have this problem I've been trying to crack. Keeping me awake. Figured I may as well be awake here.'

The guard nodded. 'Well done for your dedication.'

'Craziness more like.' I attempted a laugh. 'Anyway,' I inclined my head toward the lab, 'best get back to it.'

'Of course. Good luck with that problem, sir.'

'Thank you.' I headed off. 'And thanks again for the coffee,' I called as I took another sip.

Shit. Now I'd gone and walked off with his Kennedy Space Center mug. He probably intended me to stand there with him, exchange some company for his coffee. What sort of unrelenting scumbag was I exactly? That was it; I was going straight to hell, without passing Go. Lucifer wasn't even going to wait for my ever-nearing death. He was just going to suck me through the floor right now. Briefly, I entertained the idea that this was a fairly attractive proposition.

At almost four in the morning, the encrypted copy of Hide was complete and stored neatly in my portable storage device – jacket pocket. I issued the command to erase the Hide software code. Then I installed a little app to write zeros then ones repeatedly across all the clusters of the hard-disk a few hundred times.

Then, I went.

On my way past the front desk I dropped off the security guard's mug. 'Great coffee,' I said. 'I won't tell anyone about the grinder,' I added. *It's the least of your worries*, I thought.

He smiled and winked again. 'Good night, sir.'

I prayed he wouldn't get into any trouble.

Eighteen

Paused for Thought

I was pretty sure no one at the agency knew about Gemma, but I didn't want to chance it. That's why I had to go completely off the radar for a while. That's why I couldn't tell her. She needed deniability in case anyone came calling.

The next six months were as close to unbearable as my inexperienced soul could imagine at the time. Although it was to prove a useful taster for the rest of my life. I desperately wanted to speak to Gemma – for all she knew I was dead. For all *I* knew *she* was dead. But picking up the phone was way too risky. NSA were all over the phone lines these days.

I tried my hand at being a tourist for a couple of months, embarking on a low-key tour of New England. I'd never been up there and was kind of curious as to just how Englandy it really was. Conclusion: more cars, less teapots – much like the rest of the US.

After that I settled in New York, for no particular reason other than there is a song that suggests you should do it at least once in your life. I don't advise basing life strategy on popular music – but then it's probably as good a method as any.

The days began to feel almost viscous as they passed

by ever slower. I waded through them in a continual fog of non-existence, trying to find myself – a new self. There was nothing left of my old life, not even my name. I needed to shop for a replacement, and New York was supposed to be good for shopping, but something was holding me back. Something inside was not allowing me to make any decisions. After a while I realised why that was. I didn't want to make any decisions about where my life might go until Gemma was here to make them with me. That was the least I could do. That was how I was to show commitment to her; if she could ever stand the sight of me long enough for me explain.

I planned to wait six months from my disappearance before getting back in touch. Until then it was like someone had pressed pause on my life, and all I could do was wait until the remote-control wielder got back from the bathroom to continue with the show.

Finally, the day arrived. I'd had plenty of time to think about how I would do it. I couldn't call or email; didn't want to leave my trace of electrons. And I couldn't pay a visit in person either because I didn't know who was snooping around my flat, which was right next to hers.

Lucky, I recalled those antiquated papery things we used to stick stamps on. It's somewhat ironic that in this age of advanced cryptography, the most secure way of sending a message to someone is by post. Even if it were intercepted it couldn't be traced back to anywhere more specific than a city district, with no record of who posted it.

I knew this was going to prove a tough letter to pen. I wasn't sure how best to phrase it. 'Sorry, forgot to say, I'm *not* dead!' But then I got worried about being too specific in case the agency did know about Gemma and were intercepting her mail. So I had to be cleverer than that.

I mocked up a letter from a fictitious *American Eating Disorders Association* informing her where and when the next social event was being held. I was the only person in her world that knew about that part of her life – at least, I hoped I still was – so I trusted she would understand the message. I knew she would be pretty pissed at me referring to her as having a 'disorder', but I figured this would be quite a long way down the list of things she hated me for right now so as not to count.

I stood at a blue mailbox on the corner of a street. I've always had trouble posting letters – literally, I mean – and hitting Send on an email. Not very often do you hand over control of something so instantly and irreversibly. One way or another my life was going to change on the words in that letter, and I was finding letting it go hard to do. After what seemed like about an hour some old man tottered up beside me with a bundle of mail. I steeled myself. If this old fella could post a whole stack of letters then I should be able to handle one. I let it drop and it was gone.

Two weeks later I waited expectantly in a diner in the middle of nowhere. And only at this point did I realise how ironic my choice of venue was for this supposed social gathering of the *Eating Disorders Association*. I might have smiled, if I'd remembered how.

Pushed aside was a plate sporting two half-eaten waffles. In my hands I was cradling a bottomless mug of coffee which was beginning to test the bottomless patience of the waitress – who, incidentally, most certainly wasn't bottomless. She glided over again to top me up, continually chewing on gum like a grazing camel.

My eyes flicked to the door every time it opened, but each time they landed on no one but a stranger. I'd been there for almost an hour and now something was growing acutely urgent – my need to pee. I didn't want to leave my post but my bladder had other ideas.

I headed over to Chewy behind the counter to explain that I was waiting for someone and to ask if she could keep an eye out for me whilst I visited the bathroom.

Then, the door opened, and this time my eyes fell on known territory. Only it was different. She was different. Her hair was shorter. She seemed thinner, even though I hadn't realised there was anywhere she could have been thinner before. The clothes she wore didn't seem like hers – I didn't recognise any of them.

Suddenly, I experienced a pang of fear as I realised what these changes represented. They were the changes of a woman that had moved on. But what was I expecting? Six months was a long time. The question was, could she ever move back?

Neither of us stirred. Neither of us spoke. The tension was such that even Chewy's lower jaw stopped rotating.

I turned my body to face Gemma but took no step forward, so as to offer an open posture without rushing her. This was her moment. She was boss. It was important this was understood.

Eventually, Gemma walked toward me with purposeful steady strides. She stopped before me, then she slapped me across the face. Hard. Fair, I thought. I didn't move. She slapped me again.

'I need to explain,' I said, rather obviously.

'Yes, you fucking do.'

She started to pound on my chest with clenched fists. I let her for a moment before grabbing her wrists. She struggled against me as months of anger and frustration burst out. I pulled her in, wrapped an arm around her and held her firmly. She resisted for a moment, writhing in my arms, but then she gave in and began to sob.

'Never leave me again,' she whispered into my chest through tears.

'I won't,' I said, genuinely not knowing how hollow that promise was.

Nineteen

Nascent Truth

Gemma joined me in New York. She worked as a placement teacher, and I freelanced out my skills. To begin with I could not be too overt as to what I was offering, and I touted myself as a Business Negotiator. I knew I could come in handy in the boardroom as an advisor, with my unique skills at communication. To get the ball rolling I had to offer my services on a trial basis, gratis – or at least do a little demonstration of my abilities.

After a few legit contracts I started to make some slightly greyer contacts. This suited me as I wanted to keep off the radar. Fortunately, no one who hired me was ever likely to shout about it. Secret weapons are best kept secret.

The establishment of my new life was complete and I was, dare I say it, *content*. I don't have the kind of temperament that allowed me to be actually *happy*, but I had finally reached a place where I wanted to stay.

For a while, at least.

Time passed and there was never a knock at the door. Even if the agency didn't buy my dying stunt they obviously couldn't find me, and that was good to know.

One year after fleeing, Gemma fell pregnant with our child. To describe the emotion I felt at this news I won't resort to such clichés as, 'the happiest man alive', because I'm not so dumb to believe they mean anything. But I finally understood why people feel the need to spout such twaddle. This was quite a significant development for me. It's true to say that I reached a new extreme on my emotion scale.

Then...

Twenty-nine weeks later...

I plummeted to the other extreme.

It began with a pain in Gemma's stomach and a tenderness about her abdomen. Then later that day she called to me from the bathroom saying she was losing a lot of blood, and that it wouldn't stop. I was overwhelmed by a sickening fear that I can't even begin to describe. But I was lucid enough to get her into the car.

By the time we reached the hospital Gemma was in extreme shock and they took her from me immediately; left me standing all alone in a clinically white corridor as they whisked her away from me.

There can be no greater sense of impotence felt by a man than when he finds himself pacing uselessly up and down a hospital corridor as his family fight for their lives without him. This was possibly the only time in my life when I wished to believe in a god. Any god would do. So that I could fall to the ground and pray till my knees were raw.

So that I could do my bit.

But I didn't believe in a god. And no god decided to visit itself upon me in my moment of need.

So I just paced...

I was not present for any of what followed but I pieced it together later. Doctors sometimes aren't keen to talk in medical terms because they think you won't understand. But I needed to understand. Every last detail.

Gemma had suffered a major placental abruption: the placental lining had separated from her uterus. She had lost a lot of blood so they gave her a blood transfusion immediately.

The complication led to something called disseminated intravascular coagulation, which means that blood clots were forming inside blood vessels throughout her body. It prevents normal blood coagulation and in Gemma's case led to her starting to bleed from her skin, mouth, nose and pretty much every other orifice in her body.

Due to the nature of this condition the decision was made not to attempt to deliver the baby by caesarean section and so a natural birth was induced.

The baby was born successfully.

But she survived no longer than a few minutes.

The only saving grace was that Gemma was no longer conscious to witness this. Her organs began to fail one-by-one and she was rushed into intensive care.

And all this time ... I just paced.

Now I will allow myself to use a cliché because it *does* have meaning. The next eight days were the longest days of my life. I probably got hours of sleep that barely ventured into double figures over this period. I spent most of it on an uncomfortable plastic chair drinking weak vending-machine coffee.

Eventually, Gemma pulled through and was able to

leave intensive care. Then I had the task of telling her that our daughter had died.

And so began the task of rebuilding our lives. Although it turned out that we were not such great builders. Our relationship never really recovered. And if I'm honest, it was mostly my fault. The final nail was only a little thing.

It was late, nearly midnight. I was rummaging for morsels of entertainment amongst the perpetual trash of late night TV. Meeting with no success I made my way through to the kitchen and poured myself a gin and tonic. I poured a second in optimistic anticipation of Gemma's return. No ice, it hurt her teeth. It hurt mine too sometimes but in my opinion a G'n'T wasn't complete anywhere but on the rocks. I smiled as I recalled the number of occasions Gemma and I had had that conversation.

I carried both drinks back through to the living room that flickered under the light of *The World's Scariest Chip Pan Disasters*. As if on cue I heard a key at the door to the apartment and headed down the corridor to greet Gemma with a kiss and a gin. She seemed to welcome the latter more and she smiled at me with a widening of her eyes that indicated just a hint of distance that hadn't been there before.

We'd been together two years and she hadn't hidden anything from me. Nothing big, nothing bad – nothing I couldn't live with. I get used to knowing people's little secrets.

I'd always felt that her name was apt. She was to me a gem amongst a sea of dishonest people. A rare find – someone I could be with. But that night was going to be different. Her shine was going to tarnish. She would no longer be my flawless Gem.

'Good day?' I asked.

'Yes, thanks. Busy, you know.'

I knew. We exchanged small talk for a few minutes and I knew. She didn't need to tell me. I figured it out. Well, I figured out there was something I needed to know about where she'd been, who she'd been with. She filled in the details for me when she knew she had no option.

She'd been with her ex-boyfriend, Sted – what sort of a name is that? I met him just the once, and that was about three times too many. He was a bit of a lout in my opinion but then my judgement was clouded just a little. There is no person more abhorred in this world than a lover's ex. They are your nemesis. The one person you have to compete with at every level. You can take being slaughtered at squash by your best mate or surpassed in the kitchen by your mother or beaten to the bonus by your colleague, because secretly you know how much better you are than them at everything else. But with your lover's ex, there is no option; you have to succeed them in every sense. And you know that it'll only get harder. Because time has this annoying habit of toning down, even erasing, the bad memories from past relationships, leaving the rosy parts to shine through like diamond in kimberlite. So, you're fighting a forever-strengthening opponent as you are only weakened through an attrition of daily life that just makes you a less nice person to be with. And one day you realise – and you don't have to be me – that you don't match up. In some tiny respect in their eyes you're just not quite as good. And as soon as you realise that, the bond is weakened, sometimes beyond repair.

That night I realised.

It was his idea to meet, not hers, and nothing happened. In fact she told him where to go, and it wasn't anywhere pleasant, like Santa Barbara. He hadn't treated her well and she was sensible enough to know that she wouldn't be better off with him. But I didn't want to be someone that she was 'better off being with'. I sensed her feelings for him, her passion. Passion that only seems to arise for people that treat you like shit. I have experience of this. It's odd; I can't explain it.

There's always been this distance between me and others. My all-too-intimate knowledge tainting my view of their personas, sullying what might otherwise be such a pleasant sight – before even the first handshake is unclenched. The human mind is a beautiful and amazing thing. In much the same way that childbirth is. It's all about choosing the bits you see. The product. The rosy-cheeked mother, the miraculous bundle of life, the proud father. With the mind it's the same. Avoid the seedy, distasteful parts and what you see is quite respectable. A person, with flaws, sure, but generally wholesome. But it's such a narrow view, like reading the authorised biography of a two-bit sports personality, one of many twee books lined up in a yuletide bookshop display, spouting amusing anecdotes of an inoffensive life. Trust me, it's not the whole story, it never is.

I see the books too but I get to see all the pages that never reach print, the ones you'll never read. That's why I prefer to leave the books on the coffee table and go about my own business instead. That's why I turn away, especially from those closest to me, the people I love, the people I want to like.

All my life I've been standing in the middle of this

frozen lake, even those closest to me reaching out from a faraway shore. At least since meeting Gemma there had been one person standing with me. Somehow she had instinctively known the path to take to find her way to my place on the ice. I had allowed her to edge tentatively towards me, and then one day I turned around and she was standing right there beside me, hand in mine and prepared to face the world with me together.

That was how I'd hoped it could stay, but deep down I was far too well acquainted with my foibles to believe that it would, and on that night of Gemma's clandestine meeting, I was proved right. Things changed. Every moment that passed thereafter I found myself pushing her away. Sliding her across that ice. Looking on helplessly until she was a mere silhouette against the backdrop of my life; standing there, shivering on the bank with everyone else I had ever loved. Between us stretched an expanse of thin ice that every morsel of communication had to journey across. In the end the journey grew too tough.

I knew what I had to do. I gathered the few things of mine that I didn't want to leave behind and went. I wanted to explain, but I didn't – I couldn't.

The alley was narrow, the buildings either side towered above. Steam snaked out of grates in the road. It was quiet as it always was in the city after dark. Gemma had followed me down to the street. I didn't know if she just wanted to make it harder for me as I left. As we stood in the night air we held each other tightly. I felt her fingers dig into my flesh and smelt the familiar aroma of her hair as her head nestled under my chin. I loosened my grip but her grasp only tightened. I knew she would never end this embrace. I pushed her away gently. Her eyes were filled with dew.

'I'm sorry,' I said and I took a pace backwards. 'I'm so sorry.'

Her eyes screamed after me and I felt my heart tighten, but I had no choice. I turned and I walked away and with every step I felt those eyes burning into my back. I swallowed hard, breathed deep and kept walking without looking back, every step heavier than the one before.

I made it around the corner before the tears began to flow.

I never did look back. I've been walking ever since.

PART THREE

Questions

Twenty
Silence

From that moment to this there have been no events in my life that I feel worthy of narration. The same cannot be said of Gemma. Her years were far from uneventful – though not in a good way.

Some time after I left, there was another man, of course. I don't know the details. I wouldn't want to. But I know that it didn't last. And I know that Gemma had a daughter by him.

I didn't find out this detail until a year ago. Or to put it another way: I didn't find out this detail until it was too late. Until Gemma had lost her second child. After six years this time, rather than six minutes. Not that that matters. Not that it makes a difference. Having only lived through one of these losses I can't begin to speculate which is worse. But I know this: neither six minutes nor six years constitute a life. Only a tragedy.

I know I bear no direct responsibility for these events. But at the same time my decision to leave was the butterfly flapping its wings. If I hadn't left, things would have played out differently. At the very least, I would have still been there for her.

For these reasons, and many others, which can remain unspoken, my thoughts tend to spend a lot of time wallowing in the past these days. Understandably, I feel.

But for once, right now, my thoughts were not sojourning in history. They were standing right here beside me at the bar in BlueJay.

I was supposed to be here to meet Burch's contact, but I had been rendered somewhat distracted. A few moments ago a woman entered my sphere of awareness in much the way that a brick might enter a sphere of custard – with great consequence.

I had been observing a couple of guys nearby – one of whom I recognised as a local baseball player – when a manager-type-person brought over and introduced a woman to them. And since that moment my thoughts were no longer my own to command. It wasn't her striking Latin features or her attractive wine-coloured frock. It was something else entirely.

And maybe now I can explain.

When it comes to leaking one's thoughts through actions and expressions, some people are 'noisier' than others. Some are faint and have to be scrutinised for some time before anything concrete can be gleaned, whilst others are so loud that it takes no effort at all. And between these extremes there is a whole continuum of people, along which anyone can be placed. At least, so I thought. Until now. Until seeing this woman. Because ... she didn't fall on this scale.

She was ... silent.

Totally silent.

I couldn't explain how that could be. There is a hard-wired physiological connection between one's unconscious thoughts and their body – particularly the face. And whatever overt picture is intentionally painted

– false or otherwise – the truth is always there, in the detail.

But with her, there was no detail.

And what did this mean? It meant that where everyone around her was transparent to me, she was ... opaque. And as much as it piqued my curiosity, it also freaked me out, because I'd never met anyone like this before. Ever.

It's hard to convey the intensity and the bizarreness of the discovery. To me it just didn't fit into any current frame of understanding. She may just as well have been levitating.

Of course, being faced with such a novel scenario I did exactly what any normal, decent person would do. I stared at her blatantly for much longer than was polite. After a time I grew aware of my social transgression and embarked on a noble campaign to point my eyes elsewhere.

The baseballer's original companion had left since he would have been the third who made it a crowd. I watched the sportsman for a few moments as he made his best plays. He was the yang to her yin. Where she was an enigma he was an open book. Anyone in the bar could have had him all figured out in a matter of minutes. In short: he was a cock.

It was clear he fancied the mystery woman, but he fancied getting her upstairs rather more than he fancied planning a family or even a romantic meal. Suddenly my instincts were to protect this woman rather than move on. But that was madness. I didn't even know her. In fact, she was the first person in my life who I knew nothing about. For all I knew she could be more depraved than any of the recalcitrant degenerates I'd had the misfortune to deal with over the last decade.

Besides, she was in the company of a good-looking, wealthy and successful sports star. She wouldn't give the prospect of talking to a lonely fool like me a second consideration.

I hovered in some kind of out-of-kilter stupor for a while. Then, as if to remind me of what I was really here to do, there was a buzz-buzzing in my pocket. A short buzz. A new text message. It was Burch's phone. I ignored it.

I had to step back for a moment. My mind was in fragments in a way I was entirely unused to. And I had the unnerving sensation that this was another of those butterfly effect moments. That my life could go either way based on how I decided to play this one out. It seemed I was standing at a juncture. Not a crossroads, just a single point on a very long road. And I could go one way or the other. Forward or back.

Not that I felt this mystery woman would figure significantly in my future, but she represented something entirely new to my plane of existence. From her I could learn something – about myself and other people. Something I didn't already know. Maybe something significant. And that felt like a positive step forward.

But that was not my intended mission here. I was here to find out the truth about what had happened to Gemma and Pearle. To discover why a man was framed for the murder of a girl who supposedly died of natural causes. In short, I was here to further dwell in the past; to feebly attempt to exorcise a demon that may never wish to be slain.

So what was it to be? Future or past? Forward or back?

I did not hesitate in doing what I always do in such times of indecision. I procrastinated vigorously until there was no longer a decision to be made.

The couple stood to leave – all laughs and flattery. And when they did ... I bit down and watched them go.

I regrouped for a moment, took some deep breaths and recalibrated my mind. Fantasies had to be put to one side. I had to get back into the real world, back into the now.

When normality finally returned I fished Burch's phone from my pocket and read the message. All it said was, 'Table 41'. Clever, I thought. Not even a regular punter could actually locate a specific table without stumbling from one to the next peering at the brass plaque on each. Or alternatively asking a member of staff, from which would ensue much turning and pointing. Either way, it gave him a chance to witness my approach, to clock me before I clocked him.

The man Burch was here to meet clearly wanted to see him coming. I, on the other hand, didn't want him to see me coming, because I was not Burch, and I wasn't clear whether or not the two had previously been acquainted.

So, I had to get clever too. I motioned to a nearby member of the bar staff. When she approached, I leaned in.

'Don't look,' I said in a mock-hushed voice, 'but it's my friend's birthday, over on table forty-one. Would you be so kind as to deliver a special bottle of champagne to his table.' I gave her a theatrical wink and handed over much more cash than was necessary. It always felt like you should stuff it down their tops in this place.

'Certainly sir,' she said obligingly, as if I had, and flashed me a well-glossed smile.

BlueJay is the kind of establishment that looks after its wealthy clients. It's the kind of place that considers itself as actually having clients – as opposed to just customers or piss-heads like most drinking houses.

Four minutes later, there was a small commotion over at the back of the room as two waitresses burst into a suitably high-profile and embarrassing rendition of Happy Birthday, with a cork-popping finale and a round of applause from nearby drinkers. There were three guys at the table who all looked a little confused but played along with it rather than create an even bigger scene.

I took my cue to approach the table; and did so with the mock wobble of a beer-laden man, before plonking myself down at their table.

'I didn't know it was your birthday,' I said in over-familiar tones. A carefully chosen opener that could just as well come from a long-time acquaintance as a random, slightly-tipsy stranger from a neighbouring table.

The three men looked at me with a hint of suspicion, still slightly in shock from the whole serenade thing.

'Who are you?' said the largest of the three gentlemen, sitting in the middle.

'Who do you think I am?' I said. A nicely ambiguous response, but delivered in such a way as to make his question sound dumb.

After a moment the large guy said cautiously, 'Bigby?'

I faltered momentarily – on the inside only of course. I should have anticipated that these guys would not be using their real monikers in business dealings. I couldn't be sure but I had to work on the assumption that Bigby and Burch were one and the same.

I put my hand out. The big guy took it.

'Chinny,' he said by way of introduction, then nodded to each of his comrades. 'Lips and Nino.'

'Gents,' I nodded.

Chinny was dubbed so either because he had none or many of the said body part, depending on your definition. He was large and balding, and wore a shiny grey suit and a shirt that looked uncomfortably tight around the collar. Between his fingers he rolled a fat smouldering cigar.

Lips was a stocky guy with a skull that looked built to withstand most assaults from fists, bats and small incendiary devices. I didn't wish to speculate as to the origins of his handle. I also didn't want to ever find myself on his bad side, but I feared a full circumnavigation would turn up sides of no other kind.

Nino was less chunky, more weasely and greasy-haired and who looked the type to be terminally twitchy.

The hierarchy was clear to all. Chinny was the boss, Lips was the muscle and Nino was the smarts.

I also knew who I was now. I was Bigby for the next few minutes. So I could drop the inebriated stranger act and slip casually toward sobriety over the course of the conversation.

There was still a whisper of suspicion about the boss's eyes so I felt I had to re-affirm my personage with the only fact I knew about this situation from our previous text conversation.

'So, what's so special about BlueJay?' I asked, enquiring as to why this had to be the meeting place.

'Nothing,' Chinny replied flatly, not wishing to

elaborate. It wasn't that he didn't want to tell me, I sensed, but that he didn't actually know. As if he'd been instructed to meet here. That was interesting. From my supposed throw-away question I'd gleaned something potentially useful. I stored it away for future reference, just in case it became important.

'So how come you been banged up?' Chinny asked to deflect the attention back to me. 'You been a naughty boy?' He gave a wicked smile.

'I wish I had. But nope, some bastard's set me up,' I said. 'You boys wouldn't know anything about that would you?' I left a pause just long enough before I started to laugh. Long enough to see the marks of surprise about their eyes that confirmed they had nothing to do with it. I sighed inside. It appeared my current route may be heading for a dead end. And I was heading there pretty fast so I hoped it wasn't bricked up.

But the journey was not certain to be a wasted one. Not just yet. For I had a dual purpose in being in this place. There was one more thing I wanted to know from these men. Although, I guess you wouldn't know what.

Maybe it's time you did.

The thing is, I lied earlier. Well, I misled you anyway. When I said that nothing had happened to me in the last ten years worth talking about. In fact, a lot happened in those years. It's just that I'm not so proud of much of it.

It started when I left Gemma. After that moment I kind of turned a corner – both literally and psychologically speaking. Originally, way back in college, I began learning my skills with the aim of helping people. To seek out people suffering from internal troubles; and to resolve their issues – if I could.

That may sound a bit do-goodery; a bit up-my-own-arsey. But I'm not claiming my motivations were anything but selfish. I don't believe humans are actually capable of true altruism. It is an impossibility of nature. All human actions are instigated to satisfy some biological imperative, some internal need. Need of self, not need of others. We are driven by fundamental visceral mechanisms: pain, hunger, pleasure. So if I want to help someone else, it's because I have a desire to, because it makes me feel better.

This is true of all so-called 'good' people. But before you saddle up your high-horse and come galloping in, just let me say this: it makes no intrinsic difference. If someone wants to help old ladies across the road because it makes them feel good, that's still a damn sight better than wanting to, say, punch someone in the face because it makes them feel good.

Ultimately, people are neither good nor bad, just a huge bundle of conflicting desires. In turn, their actions are neither good nor bad, just a reaction to an even huger array of external stimuli.

The point is that I don't consider myself holier-than-thou. I understand that for whatever reason, it was extremely important to me to make a positive impression on the world and the people in it. So that was the purpose of my scholarly early-adult years.

After Gemma, though – after losing a child and walking out on a lover – I became prone to much darker thoughts than I had ever experienced before. And these thoughts led me to wonder if perhaps I could improve the world in another way – a darker way. An indirect, but farther-reaching way.

I wondered if, rather than seeking out sad people and

making them happy, maybe I could seek out bad people and make them ... dead. To cut the cancers from society.

And so began a new chapter in my life. One that I could write a book about in itself. It would start with a trip to Colombia, where I would learn far more about the human condition than I ever believed there was to know. I had some pretty eye-opening experiences in that country. But they have no bearing on the here and now, and suffice to say that I never did go as far as killing anyone. It appears I do not have the confidence of mind for executing that immutable action – as proven again when I dumped Burch in the gutter the other day. So it seems I don't quite have the mettle to be the next masked crusader – which is just as well as I don't quite have the legs for tights either.

However, it's fair to say that I did do some things that my mum wouldn't be proud of; some things that may be considered as wrong in a two-wrongs-don't-make-a-right kind of way. But that doesn't mean they were not justified. Sometimes a second wrong is the quickest way to redress the cosmic balance. Sometimes, not always.

With many bad people doing bad things it's simply a case of informing the appropriate authorities: police, traffic warden, park ranger, whoever. But this approach is not always going to produce the desired effect. Sometimes, it's down to me and my wrongs.

On occasion it's enough just to perform a little intimidation; because with many wrong-doers – the small-time, fringe variety – it is enough for them to know they are being watched to stop them doing whatever it is they are considering.

But when it comes to bigger things, I have to play much cleverer games. This is my party trick. This is what I do best; what has the greatest results. Essentially, it entails turning the bad guys against themselves. I wind them up like little clockwork toys and point them at each other; and then I walk away knowing that whatever comes next is their own doing – mostly.

Anyway, because of these little games I like to play, my purpose at BlueJay was twofold. Firstly, of course, I wanted to find out who had set up Burch and why; and I'd already drawn a blank on that front. But secondly, I knew that if I met some of Burch's associates, I might find some bad people worth messing with. It all depended on their particular brand of badness. I already knew that whatever game they were into was illegal. But that was not enough, because legality and morality are not entirely well aligned. Partly because the latter is subjective and culturally dependent, but mostly because the former is based on nonsensical ideologies.

Some cases in point. In California, it is illegal to play bingo, yet legal to sell carcinogenic substances for inhalation. It is illegal for a twenty-year-old to buy a pint of weak beer, yet legal for a hormonal sixteen-year-old to drive a 3.5 litre killing machine down a five-lane freeway. Go figure.

So, yeah, I work to my own code. That sounds far more renegade than it's supposed to. It just means I don't waste my time on benefit fraudsters and double-yellow parkers.

I continued my conversation with Chinny and his colleagues, to establish the details I sought. This is not as hard as it seems with a little practise, especially if you have a funny accent – as I do to them. If you put a foot wrong they just assume they misunderstood you, on the most part. That gives you a few chances. And a few chances are all I need.

I did discover what they were into. And it was a huge disappointment.

The rug trade.

Fake branded fashion apparel.

To give them their dues, they were into it in a big way. We are talking container loads of the stuff, shipped in from Asia. All destined to be distributed to the gangs of New Meadows, to be filtered down to their guys on the streets. This was all very interesting and, yes, illegal, but to be frank, I couldn't give a shit about the rug trade. For my money, it wasn't doing anyone any serious harm.

So my job here was pretty much over. Time to make my leave. I shook hands on a deal they thought was too good to be true, and walked away.

That evening I took another soak in the tub – to loosen my thinking muscles. I re-ran the evening's events through my soggy mind. The fact that the men I met were into the rug trade, a pastime not worthy of my further attention, was not such a major disappointment. I could live without that kind of work for a few days.

Of greater annoyance was that these associates of Burch genuinely had no idea about why he had been set up. They didn't even seem to have much of an idea as to why they were meeting in BlueJay either. A legitimate fashion outlet did seem like an odd choice of venue for forging deals in illicit goods, rather like plotting a money laundering scam in the lobby of the Federal Reserve. I got the solid impression they were acting on orders from higher up the food chain. And Burch himself didn't have a clue as to why he'd been set up either.

Clearly, they were all pawns in some larger game of

chess. I had no idea as to the stakes of the game, or who the players were. I briefly entertained the idea that I was a pawn too, but that didn't seem plausible. I can see through anyone's attempts to play me – Aaron Braunn to King Four would not go unnoticed.

So, it was all a bit of a mystery. But then something unexpected happened. In the context of my own brain that is. I suddenly began to wonder whether I actually wanted to unravel this particular mystery.

Why?

Because another mystery entirely had begun to play in my thoughts instead: the woman at the bar – who was now running amok like a small child in a toyshop. I wondered if I'd chosen the wrong direction earlier, when I turned toward the past.

Maybe I did need to look to the future now.

Maybe I needed to find that girl.

To find myself again.

Twenty-One

Reality Check

Conner was making a habit of waking to new pains; on this occasion a stiff neck and a dead arm, courtesy of his restless night on a Holiday Inn sofa. He filed his new ailments along with his existing ones and pulled himself into a sitting position.

Mila was still asleep. Sleeping like a heavily sedated baby, in a comfy king-size cot. Conner decided that if she was just going to rub it in his face like that then he'd leave her to it. He pulled on some clothes and headed out in search of breakfast. Considering everything that had taken place, breakfast was pretty much the only short-to-medium term event he could reliably plan for. Beyond breakfast everything was all kind of murky; greyer than the Holiday Inn scrambled eggs that he opted to avoid.

Conner picked up coffee and pastries from a store down the street and returned to the hotel room to find an unoccupied bed, and an occupied bathroom – as far as the noise of a rushing shower was an indication of occupancy. A recently acquired streak of paranoia coupled with too much movie-watching prohibited him from jumping to any obvious conclusions, such as the aforementioned shower rushing over a naked Mila – as much as the thought appealed. He stood motionless, ears pinned back, and after a moment there was the sound of movement from within the room. There was somebody in the shower, which was a positive start. He took a step toward the door.

'Mila, I'm back,' he called.

A brief pause, then, 'Okay, almost done,' came the response, in a reassuringly familiar voice, much to Conner's relief.

Conner took a seat and flicked on the TV for company. The beautiful faces of über celebrity couple, Danny Rubeck and Sadie Winters, flashed up at him. Their image had started appearing all over town recently, the stars of some mysterious ad campaign that didn't reveal what was being promoted – presumably to create some kind of anticipatory buzz. Conner tried desperately to care less but failed, and began channel-hopping in a futile search for something less a waste of his time.

A few moments later – okay, quite a few moments later – Mila appeared from the bathroom, fully dressed in last night's clothes and drying her hair with a towel. She perched on the end of the bed and Conner handed her a coffee.

'Thanks,' she said as she took it.

Conner turned off the TV and they both stared at the white walls for a while, not speaking. Conner was particularly aware of the untenable situation they found themselves in, which made it hard to know where to start talking.

Mila knew where to start. She'd known for a while, deep down. And as it wasn't directly associated with their recent attackers it was a topic she favoured focusing on. She took a deep breath and let it out as a sigh, and just let the words tumble out with it.

'I don't believe any more, Conner,' she declared as if confessing a sin; as if it was God she was referring to. But she knew this was way more important to Conner than any mere deity.

'You don't believe in what any more?'

'In our cause.'

Conner knew what she was talking about. The cause of trying to bring the rug dealers to justice. The cause to which they had both sacrificed countless days and nights.

'And it's not just because of all this,' Mila continued, gesturing to their surroundings, highlighting their current predicament: holed up in a hotel room, on the run from persons unknown, the victims of recent beatings and kidnappings. She shuffled along the bed toward where Conner was sitting opposite, such that their knees were almost touching. 'I just don't understand who we are trying to protect,' she said, looking at him now. 'The goods these guys are selling on the street are just as good as the genuine article, but at a fraction of the price. Isn't that called competition? Isn't that *good*?'

Conner responded for the first time, in agitated tones. 'It's not about the quality of the *material*; it's about the intellectual property in the design. It's about the *designers* being stolen from.'

'The designers? Do I have to care about them too?' Mila shook her head as if to say that it wasn't enough. 'If they were struggling to feed their children then maybe I *could* care. But if counterfeit sales means a designer gets only *two* hundred thousand a year instead of three; or the CEO gets *four* million instead of five;

and they have to – I don't know – sell one of their condos or something; then it's hard for me to feel their pain. It's hard to worry about them. It really is. You know?'

Conner grew more agitated. This was his life's work. This was his belief system.

'But that's too narrow a view – that's the effect when there are laws in place and people like us trying to uphold them. If there were *no* rules, *no* enforcement, then it would be a free-for-all, and the outcome would be much worse. The legitimate companies that invest in developing new products wouldn't exist at all if the law wasn't there to protect them. The world would be a poorer place because of it.'

'No.' Mila was confident in her disagreement. She stood up and took a couple of paces before turning back. 'That may be true of technology; artefacts of real invention and ingenuity that take years to develop. But when it comes to *fashion*, it's the other way around. If the companies didn't screw the consumer with ridiculous prices then there wouldn't be a viable counterfeit trade in the first place.'

Mila moved to the window and drew open the curtains. She looked out in silence for a moment before she spoke again.

'Look around you, Conner. This whole *town* is fake. It *runs* on fake. If that Irish bar you like so much wasn't here in New Meadows, feeding off the *intellectual property* of hundreds of years of Irish heritage, maybe you'd actually want to *go* to Ireland to experience it. But you don't need to because you have a cheap knock-off copy *here*.' She turned to look at him. 'Why's that not illegal?'

'That's not the same and you know it.'

'It's only not the same because there isn't a billion dollar Ireland Inc lobbying the government and bribing the officials to *make* it the same. Corporate law is written by the corporations. It's not about what's right and wrong.'

Conner approached the window, but he didn't look out. He looked at Mila.

'But people are getting *killed*. They're getting murdered, because of this trade. Don't you care about that?'

'Yeah, and cops are getting beaten up.' Mila sighed. 'Listen. I know people are getting killed, and that's bad. But are we helping? Really?' She turned to face Conner. 'The fact that this activity is deemed illegal is what has driven it underground; driven it into the hands of the kind of people who are wont to kill each other. The very fact that *we* are out there –' she pointed out of the window '– trying to bust their asses, is what makes it such a hostile environment in the first place. On every street in the land Starbucks and Costa compete on the same turf, right next door to each other, and hardly anyone ever gets shot because of it. To the best of my knowledge, no one's ever had a *cap busted into their ass* over the sale of a venti mochaccino and blueberry muffin. Because it's not illegal. Yeah?'

Conner didn't know how to respond. He placed both hands on the window sill and stared down at the street below. Mila took a step toward him and placed her hand gently on his. Then she spoke with a softer voice, one with no tones of confrontation.

'It just seems like we are letting City Hall write our own morals for us. And then we're risking our lives to protect them. That doesn't make any kind of sense to me. Not any more.' She took his hand as he stood staring out of the window. 'Look, don't get me wrong. I *do* see the bigger picture. I'm not saying the law is wrong. I'm not saying that what we're trying to do is not the right thing. I'm just saying that I can't care enough about it any more. Not when the only victims are the criminals themselves and the overpaid industry execs. And now *us*. You understand that don't you?'

Conner didn't respond; didn't turn to face Mila. In part because he was scared that he *would* understand, and because he didn't know what that would mean for his life. He didn't have anything else to believe in.

'You know as well as I do what Bigby has been questioned over before,' Mila continued. 'His unsavoury behaviour towards young girls. Maybe he didn't commit the murder he's in jail for now. But if letting the Feds stitch him up for something he hasn't done keeps him locked up for a while then maybe that's more important than bringing down a chunk of the rug trade, cos who knows how long that will take or what good it will do anyone.'

She let go of his hand and moved away from the window. 'I guess this is the point where I'm supposed to grab my bags and leave. But I don't have any bags ... or anywhere to leave for.'

Conner turned and leaned back. 'So what now?'

'*Now* now?' she questioned.

'Good place to start.'

'Okay. Now, you escort me back to my apartment so I can get some clean underwear. Assuming you think that's wise?'

Conner burst into a smile. 'Oh, from a strict hygiene

standpoint, I think that's very wise.' He winked.

Mila laughed coyly. 'You know what I mean.'

'I do.' His smile made way for contemplation. 'And then?'

'Then I'm going to take some time out. Go stay with my mom for a bit. I like the idea of being in a whole other state for a while. In both senses.'

Conner inhaled deeply and let out a long sigh as his face dropped. Then he kicked the back of the sofa making Mila jump.

'Shit!' he exclaimed.

'What?'

'That really hurt.'

'An outcome that could've been predicted, I fear.'

'I know. I didn't think it was going to be that hard.'

Mila tilted her head to one side with a sympathetic half-smile.

Conner began to nod slowly. 'I think you're right. I think it's a good idea for you to get away from this for a while. As much as I hate to admit it.'

'What about you?'

'I...' he paused for a moment. 'I'm not sure just yet. Try to figure out how to operate without my left arm first.'

Mila took a moment to realise he was referring to her. She smiled at him sweetly to acknowledge the compliment.

'Sorry,' she said genuinely.

Conner stayed with Mila as she packed up some belongings at her apartment. Then he drove her to the airport and hugged her goodbye. As simple as that, a significant part of his life was gone. Again.

That afternoon he walked into town. Some automated part of his mind had registered today as a Bad Day and sent his body off to find Something Good to make it all better. If nothing else that meant he had a clear-cut no-messing plan right up till the end of the day – tomorrow morning in fact – and he was presently very pleased about this level of short-term clarity. He wasn't going to give Today any more chances to mess him about. Unfortunately, Today had different plans and delivered him a text message to let him know about it.

He flipped his phone open to find a message from an informant of his. The gist of the content posed the following riddle. If Bigby is in jail ... how come he was able to make a deal in BlueJay last night?

'Shit!' exclaimed Conner as he turned around and headed back into the unknown.

Twenty-Two

First Encounters

For the second night in a row I found myself rubbing my averagely turned-out shoulders with the very well-groomed examples to be found on the clientele of BlueJay – bar, restaurant and fashion emporium. I was here for quite a different reason this time. It was still all about a girl – what can I say? I'm a man – but this time, a different girl. Mercifully, she had largely occupied my waking thoughts over the last day and had done a good job of making sure I didn't have any sleeping thoughts too – not in any dodgy way I assure you. She was just an anomaly in my world that I needed to know more about.

I located the barmaid I'd seen talking to the mystery woman the previous evening. I approached the bar and she smiled at me through striking – verging on scary – make-up.

'What can I get you?' she asked.

'Dos Equis, please.' I found myself in the mood for a Latin beer this evening. And I was swiftly presented with one, thanks to that efficient American bar service I'd become so used to paying a buck for every time I ordered a beer.

'Thanks,' I said, and was sure to ask her another question before she got any of my money. 'What's your favourite tipple?'

After a brief pause whilst she processed the information she responded. 'I'm a typical white wine girl myself.'

It was of course just a control question because I intended to mine her for more useful information. A control is important. You may have heard of eye accessing cues, a theory posited by the NLPers, such as: glancing up and to the right is an indication of recalling a memory. There is some basis to these rules but they are too generalized to be of any use. The only rule you can be sure of is that if someone is trying to deceive you then they will behave slightly differently, in some small way. So knowing how the barmaid expressed herself when she responded to an innocent innocuous question about her favourite drink was all important.

I began fumbling dollars out of my wallet as I casually offered another question. 'You don't happen to know the girl who was in here yesterday with that baseball player, do you? They were sitting right over there.' I nodded across the bar.

She pouted her lips and shook her head as if she was trying to recall. 'No,' she said, 'I don't think I do.'

She was lying.

I put some cash for the beer on the bar-top. 'Oh, shame. I'd really like to speak to her.'

'I'm sure you would,' she said with a wink and smile. But it was not difficult to spot that her smile was as fake as her tan. Anyone can spontaneously display a beautiful beamer on their face at will. But to the educated, its construction will give the owner away. Specifically, a fake smile will only flex the muscles at the corners of the mouth. Whereas, an involuntary smile, generated in response to a genuine emotion, will also tighten the muscles that encircle the eye. It is almost impossible to tighten these muscles on demand, and it is equally difficult to stop them from tightening when you smile at something genuinely pleasurable. It's called a Duchenne smile and the bartender's was not an example of one.

'I wish I could be more help,' she added as she started to wipe down the bar with a damp cloth.

'Oh, that's a pity,' I continued with a touch of despondency. 'I was kind of hoping to put some business her way.'

'Business?' There was the tiniest of falters in her nonchalance. 'How can you put business her way if you don't know what her business is?' She didn't look at me as she continued to slide a cloth across the bar, trying to pretend she was just playing along at small-talk, but her tone had lost its usual built-in note of over-politeness. She was interested in my interest.

'Oh I'm in the fashion industry. She had a certain ... you know ... something.'

'Oh yeah, I know,' she agreed with little sugar-coating over her contempt. She was suspicious of me. Rightly so. Personally, I wouldn't trust me as far as I could vomit a barstool. But this was a good sign. Her air of protectiveness clearly meant she did know the girl I was asking after.

Time to play meek. They will inherit the earth after all. And are more likely to be trusted. 'My apologies,' I said submissively with a slight bowing of the head and my eyes falling to the bar. 'It was rather forward of me to ask.' I slid off the stool on which I'd been perched and turned to move away. Just as I did the barmaid spoke up.

‘She’ll be in at nine,’ she said.

I looked back and smiled. ‘Thanks,’ I said and I raised my bottle to her.

Whilst I was waiting I met a guy at one of the other bars in the place, the big long one down the side, rather than the circular one in the middle. He needed my help. Usual stuff: relationship, job, indecision. I told him something I tell a lot of people. Life is like buying a pair of shoes. I’ll leave that one with you.

A little after nine the still-unnamed enigma girl caught my eye taking a seat over the other side of the room. She was alone, but probably waiting for someone – maybe the baseball guy, maybe someone else. I couldn’t quite figure out what she did for a living. I was pretty sure she worked at BlueJay; got the impression that this was her ‘patch’, whatever that meant. I hoped it didn’t mean one thing that it could. My best guess was she was some kind of high-class escort, but also linked to fashion, considering the venue. For once in my life I would have to find out the hard way, if I dared. I had been anticipating the challenge with excitement, but now that the chance to speak to her had finally come I was scared. Scared at the prospect of speaking to a person who would respond only in words. I’d always been spoilt by having the upper hand in conversations. Now, being equal would be my weakness. An archer without his bow. My heart was thumping so hard I could feel it in my temples. But it was an opportunity that I couldn’t allow myself to waste again. I stepped up and walked over to her.

As I approached she saw me coming and turned to me.

‘Look,’ she said before I had chance to speak, ‘I don’t

know what you want from me but I'm not interested.' She'd obviously been warned about me by her friend behind the bar. I admit it didn't look good. It looked like I was some kind of obsessive stalker. But then, filling the main criteria of stalking and being obsessed, I did seem to fit the bill rather neatly. Armed with this sudden revelation about myself I was caught a little off guard and wasn't sure what to say.

Moreover, I didn't know what to say because I didn't know what *she* had said. I know better than anyone that people don't always mean what they say. Sometimes they even mean the exact opposite. So often words are just served as a distraction from the truth, like a cooling breeze over skin burning in the midday sun. How do people cope when they don't know which is the case? She was either just being cautious or she genuinely wanted nothing to do with me. I didn't know which, but common good manners suggested that I assume the latter.

'Sure,' was all I said and I turned away. Something about that moment as I turned away caused my mind to snap to a different time and place. I was overcome by sinking dread as my mind was seduced by a vivid image from the past. A night-time alleyway, tall buildings towering above on either side, smoke snaking from grates in the road. And a girl. Tearful. Arms clamped around me.

I hadn't always been alone.

I'd made myself alone.

Ten years ago when I walked out on Gemma.

It took me a long time to realise how stupid that had been. After a lot of soul searching I'd come to some conclusions about myself. I was different from everyone else, it was true, but the rules didn't change just for me. Sometimes people think things you don't want them to think, feel things that you're not comfortable with. But that's just tough because that's the way it is. It may be worse for me than anyone else but that doesn't make it any different. I realised I had to learn to live with these things else forever live alone. And I'd decided that it was Gemma I wanted to learn with. Of course, by the time I'd figured all this out, it was too late.

Jackson Burch had no involvement with the incident a year ago; the virus that infected Pearle and Gemma. Most likely, no one had. Most likely, there was no foul play at all, as originally declared. But ultimately it made no difference, because only one person was responsible for expunging them from *my* world, and I have to avoid the awkward stare of that person every morning of my life when I stand in front of the mirror. I walked away from them and now it's too late to walk back.

My mind snapped back to the present. A light-headedness washed over me and I had to reach out to the back of a chair to steady myself. As I paused I swirled the remains of my beer around the sides of the bottle and collected my thoughts.

It was all very clear.

It was time to stop walking away.

'I thought I said –' the mystery woman began on my second approach.

'I know, I know,' I cut her off as politely as I could. I may not be able to read her, but I still had my other abilities. I still knew how to pull off non-threatening and innocent, or any persona, better than anyone. And I had to assume she was not also impervious to my charms, so to speak.

'Okay, I am not involved in fashion in any way. I don't know who you are or what you do. I don't even know your name. But I need to speak to you and the reason I need to speak to you is very difficult to explain.' I spoke with urgency because I knew her patience-clock was ticking. Plus the use of succinct phrases engenders a belief that you're actually going to get to a point.

'Try me.'

I hesitated momentarily, not quite knowing how to continue most efficiently. 'It has to do with the adage "Since we cannot know all there is to be known about anything, we ought to know a little about everything". And I know *nothing* about you.'

She snorted a sardonic laugh. Damn it. That was not good. I was floundering. This would be so much easier if she were a murderer. Maybe she was.

'So, are you saying you know something about everyone else in here, except me?' she said confrontationally.

'Well, yes.' That was better. Few words. Straight to the point.

A raise of an eyebrow indicated that this was not the answer she had expected.

'Okay, what about him?' She nodded to a man standing nearby, swigging from a stemmed glass and talking energetically to a woman in a red cocktail dress.

I looked at him for a short moment.

'He works in the city as an actuary but says he's a banker because no one knows what an actuary is, and he chats up women – not very successfully – by lying about the size of his bonus last year.'

I admit, most of that was guesswork, but I promise, it

would be pretty close to the truth.

My female challenger looked slightly incredulous.

'And her, pulling the beer?' She nodded toward the bar.

I smiled.

'She's your friend. She met you in here where you both work. She hates working here because she wants to be a designer. She told you that some guy was asking after you that was a bit odd but had a nice ass.'

She smiled coyly – genuinely I presumed – then looked at me with a questioning brow.

'Okay, how about these two?' She motioned to the couple on the next table.

I didn't need to study them. They'd been in my line of observation for long enough for me to already know what I needed to. But this time I decided to give more away ... about me that is.

'From their clothes we can tell this occasion is of a romantic nature, yeah? A date. But there is a stiffness in their posture, a nervousness in their movements, which suggests they are not well acquainted. So, this is maybe a first or second date.

'The guy is quite a snappy dresser and seems confident enough; the type who would know his way around the drinking establishments of town. Yet, when he went to the bathroom a few moments ago his companion pointed him in the right direction. It seems unlikely that this guy hasn't been to BlueJay before if he lives here. So I figure he's from out of town. I'd say they met on an internet dating site. You'll probably find that he has trouble meeting girls because he works in a male-dominated industry – maybe IT.' I took a casual glance at the couple. 'There's one more thing. He has this weird fidgety thing with his right hand. I think he's a smoker but he lied on his profile. Although with good intentions because he wants to give up.'

At that point I took a cigarette of my own out.

'Hold on,' I said and I approached the couple. 'Hey, have you got a light?' I asked, directed to the man.

'Err, no, I don't smoke.'

'No worries,' I said and returned to my new acquaintance.

'What did that prove?' She asked.

'Well, there was a pause in his response which is not surprising because I caught him on the hop. But also, when I asked the question his left hand involuntarily moved to his jeans pocket, where he usually keeps his lighter.'

There was a moment of silence before the enigma woman spoke again.

'Okay, so you know things about people. What does that have to do with me?'

She was sitting at a high-table and I was still standing across from her. Sitting would be the wrong move; considered as a sign of arrogance.

'You may not know this, but you seem to be quite special. I can discern a few things about you from your clothes, skin-tone, etc. But that's it. You demonstrate none of the involuntary behaviours I am used to analysing: gestures, facial expressions, voice patterns.'

She looked totally confused at this point, so I continued quickly.

'Okay, I know this sounds like I'm totally crazy, or the most elaborate chat-up routine ever, but ... but I really need you to let me buy you a drink.' Pause. 'Ten minutes of your time is all I ask. Then I'll be gone. I promise.'

She considered this for a moment.

'Gin and tonic.'

'Ice?'

'Of course!' she said as if I'd asked a silly question.

Whilst I was fetching the drinks I had time to contemplate the best way forward, considering potential time constraints ... and drink-being-thrown-in-face constraints.

'Right,' I began on my return, this time allowing myself to take a seat opposite her. 'I don't want to waste too much of your time so I'm just going to jump right in with a little experiment.'

'Okay,' she said apprehensively.

'Nothing complicated. I'm just going to ask you five questions and I want you to lie on one of the answers, but don't tell me which. Okay?'

'Okay.'

I asked her five questions. All with simple, objective answers, but which would involve recall such that she'd have to pause and think. I asked her the colour of the door of her last house, the model of her first car, what she had for lunch yesterday, the name of the first person she kissed and her last holiday destination.

She answered each one without a flicker of discernable difference: eye movement; flushing of cheeks; pacing of words; tone of voice. Nothing.

'You definitely lied on one of them?' I enquired.

'Yes, first person I kissed was called Steve not Ben.'

Well, that clinched it. If the original answer hadn't been a lie then her last statement was, and there was still no change in delivery.

'Don't take this the wrong way,' I said. 'But you are

the best liar I have ever met.'

'Gee thanks.'

'No problem,' I said. Then I thanked her for her time with a smile and stood to leave. I didn't want to leave, but that was the deal and sticking to it was the only way to build trust. But before I walked away she put out a hand.

'I'm Karla, by the way.'

'Oh.' I took her hand and said something unexpected. Something I hadn't said in a long time.

'I'm Aaron.'

Twenty-Three

Different Views

Conner wasn't entirely sure why he was heading to BlueJay right now; what his key motivation was. Considering, that is, that he had been threatened – by various parties to varying standards of persuasiveness – to stop pursuing the Bigby case.

Maybe he hadn't consciously thought it through at any point and it was just an impulsive reaction to receiving the tip-off.

Maybe he was personally intrigued as to how Bigby managed to pull off being in two places at once: holed up in a prison cell and yet also in a bar doing a deal.

Or maybe ... maybe he just wanted a beer.

Whatever the reason, that's the way his feet were taking him.

He'd met up with his informant in one of their usual shady places. His name was Jaz. He teetered on a very low rung of the Scrips hierarchy, but his brother was a much bigger player. Conner had arrested him a couple of years before and the trader was more than happy to cut a deal to get off the hook. That's how most grasses start their relationship with the cops. Through his sibling, Jaz could glean information that would otherwise be way above his pay grade, and he was always willing to share it – for the right price.

On this occasion what he knew was this. Some new suppliers had turned up on the rug dealing scene of New Meadows, saying they had several containers full of gear arriving at the docks in California. They had made a provisional deal with Scrips, and had arranged a meeting with Bigby to discuss shipping their 'wears' to New Meadows. Bigby was kind of the FedEx of the underworld. He knew how to get things from A to Z, avoiding all the right letters in between so as not to come to the attention of any authorities. According to the sellers, this meeting had taken place the previous evening. But the Scrips buyers knew that Bigby was incarcerated and, indeed, incommunicado.

For Conner, this was not particularly useful information but it was at least intriguing. And if he had been officially on the case he would have requested the previous evening's surveillance recordings from BlueJay. Simple as. But he was *not* officially on the case, and moreover there was the whole aforementioned being-threatened business to consider. As such, low-profile was the order of the moment.

The best low-profile plan he could think of was to head to BlueJay and discreetly flash a picture of Bigby at a few members of staff. As to be expected, the plan didn't get him very far. The picture of Bigby met with only blank expressions. After a while he was starting to grow concerned that he was pushing his luck, and was happy to arrive at the conclusion that his motivation in being here had been beer all along. That was a goal he was confident in achieving.

Conner sat himself down at the bar and was shortly furnished with his cold beverage of choice. He glanced up at the screen above the bar, which was showing a baseball game. He watched it for a while without really watching it, and shortly it slipped into a commercial interlude. He was greeted by those two beaming faces again; the celebrity couple of the decade, Danny Rubeck and Sadie Winters. The advert was as mysteriously uninformative as all the rest, only hinting at some event, some four-weeks hence. The evasive nature was supposedly a tactic to heighten tension. Conner had less than no interest in whatever it was the stars were peddling, and so was particularly annoyed that he was totally sucked in by the ploy; that he found himself wondering on the subject – just for a moment. He strived to shake the thought from his mind, figuring it would have no bearing on his life.

He figured wrong.

A man sat down in the seat next to him, shaking his head disparagingly at the diamond-studded actress and tutted audibly.

Conner turned. 'Not a fan?' he enquired sociably.

'I wouldn't say that,' the man replied. 'I actually quite like her as an actress. It's just that she represents a lot of what's wrong with the world today.'

'And what's that?'

'Extreme inequality. Consumer exploitation. She earned eighty million dollars for her latest movie. She may be supremely talented, but is she worth that? Is she eight thousand times more talented than an unknown actor?'

'I guess not. So?'

'So, it's odd. If she were a city banker earning that much she'd be reviled. Instead she is adored.'

'She's overpaid. I'll give you that.'

'She's a symptom of a broken market, that's what she is. Do you know how much they spent on her latest sci-fi blockbuster?'

Conner shook his head.

'Five hundred million dollars. Let me put that another way.' The man spoke each word in turn for emphasis. 'Half ... a *billion* ... dollars. In a world with as many problems as this one, how can it make sense to spend half a billion dollars on the production of two hours of cinematic entertainment? There is way too much profit being made in the movie business. And profit is *bad*.'

'Profit is *bad*?'

'Of course.'

'Why?'

'By definition it means that a firm has overcharged its customers. Consumers are being screwed. There shouldn't be *any* profit in a perfect economy. It means something is going wrong in the market. There is some sort of barrier to competition, which ultimately means the guy on the street is losing out. Just the same in the music industry. And the big sports. Too much money is made by too few people.'

Conner didn't usually question the ways of the world like this. He didn't generally set out to scrutinize things that seemed in no need of analysis. Now he was realising that far more of the world's accepted facts were open to be challenged.

'So, what's the answer?' he enquired.

The man thought about this for a moment over a sip of beer, before delivering his response.

'Piracy,' he said. 'Partly, at least.'

'Piracy? You think that's a good thing?'

'Well, I can't condone people doing it on a mass

scale, people making money out of it. But as far as copying the occasional movie or music track is concerned, and passing it around for free, I can't argue against it.'

Conner frowned at the suggestion. The thought was not sitting nicely with his sensibilities.

'Why do you say that?' he asked.

'Because it's helping. It puts a squeeze on the industry profits, which fortunately affects the big firms most. Those with the ridiculous marketing budgets and endless payrolls. Piracy happens to re-distribute spending from the big players to the small.'

'How come?'

'Because almost everyone has a conscience that kicks in somewhere, and people are far less inclined to screw over the small-time players than the mega-rich superstars. Someone will pay to go to see a local band, might even buy a copy of their album whilst they're there. Then they'll go home and illegally download a Madonna track and not give a damn about it. That's the way it goes. It's a weird state of affairs but piracy is doing good right now.'

Conner gazed wistfully back at the TV screen. 'It's kind of crazy that something that's supposedly bad, illegal even, can have such a positive effect on society.'

'Things are never black and white,' the man confirmed.

Conner nodded slowly. 'I'm starting to realise that.'

The two guys talked for a while longer before Conner finally left and returned to the path he had set out on earlier that day. Shortly he found Crystal Seth loitering lucratively out the back of one of his favourite dives.

'Hey man,' said the dealer. 'What can I score you?'

Only at this point did Conner question what he was seeking. He thought for a moment about the various wares offered by this man and what effect they would have on him, then replied.

'Actually, nothing.' He walked away and headed home. He couldn't quite explain it. There was no doubt he'd had a run of Bad Days, yet something was different.

As he walked, he started to consider the conversation he had had in BlueJay and in particular how it related to his own line of investigation. Was there any difference between pirated media and counterfeit clothes? The big name clothing manufacturers – the Branding Machines – were just as profitable as the major movie studios and music producers, so maybe the same arguments applied: that the extent of their profit margins was a metric for their exploitation of the public. So maybe they only had themselves to blame for creating an environment where counterfeiters could flourish. Did that make rug trading okay? Probably not. But did it make it bad – a bad thing for society? Or was it the ultimate form of competition? That was a question Conner found harder to answer.

The counterfeit clothes industry did seem to draw many parallels with the drug trade that it had replaced, and the drug trade surely *was* bad. Or was it only really the tabloids that aligned these two industries? It was true that the dealers themselves were just as unsavoury. Many of them were the actual same people. But the product was quite different. The product of the rug trade was not addictive and deadly. It was, well, t-shirts.

As if the arguments were not complicated enough, there were now an increasing number of mind-altering drugs that were legal, albeit 'natural' and supposedly less harmful.

To Conner, nothing seemed to be clear anymore. Particularly his own thought process. Where there were once neatly delineated boundaries, there was now just an amorphous blur.

In many ways the conversation this evening echoed that of his last one with Mila. Together they compounded the realisation that he just didn't know what he believed in anymore. What was right and what was wrong. What was black and what was white. And maybe that wasn't a problem. Maybe he could live with that uncertainty. But there was one thing he *did* need to know.

He needed to know what he wanted.

What *did* he want?

● ● ● ● ●

That weekend Conner found himself doing something he would not normally seek to do. He was looking out at the ocean. He was here at this specific spot for a reason. He needed to be here to learn something about himself.

When he and Lisa had got married they had no grand designs to travel anywhere exotic for their honeymoon. Instead they hired a car and did the whole West Coast thing. They stopped off at the major cities, of course, but for most of the driving they stuck to the coastal route, picking out motels they liked the look of to stay in each night.

Conner and Lisa both grew up in the land-locked state of Nevada, and went to college in New Meadows where they met. This inland upbringing affected them in quite different ways. For Conner, it released him from an ancestral throwback; freed him of the constant need to be near water, which he was aware afflicted so many. He knew that for most people a vacation was simply not a vacation if a lake or river or ocean was not involved. Conner saw this as a needlessly restrictive response to a time when local expanses of water were vital to survival.

For Lisa though, her early years of growing up far from the smell of salt air had given the ocean a mystical allure. She was drawn to it.

They spent two weeks travelling down the coast, which was the longest period of time, before or since, that Conner had ever had off work. Near the end of their trip they shared one of those magical, timeless moments; the kind that will always stand out as a time when things were just … well … right. Simple as that. Such a moment can never be planned. The mere act of forethought denies the chance of such an experience.

Serendipity is king.

Sometimes the planets just align.

The morning when the planets were aligning for Conner and Lisa had begun with them sneaking a few items out of the breakfast buffet at the motel they had stayed at the night before. The hoard consisted of a few rolls, ham, cheese, and some pieces of fruit; with which they made up sandwiches for lunch. It's not that they were cheap, or particularly poverty-stricken. It was just that, like many, they both got a surge of satisfaction from making the most of a situation – of not letting things go to waste.

A few hours later they pulled into an innocuous viewing-point, one of the many thousand dotted along the coastal route. It was just a small one and there were no other cars around. There was an information board detailing the local wildlife and a map of a footpath that trailed along the cliff. They set off along the path which wound its way through the coarse bushes along the cliff top. After a short while they came across a rickety wooden bench, which they decided to camp at to feast on their illicit luncheon.

Either side of them stretched the majestic white face of the cliff. The sun was warm on their bare arms and faces. There were no people, no traffic, no pressing time constraints. And in front of them there was a one-hundred-eighty degree view of the ocean.

And that was the moment. Nothing complicated. Just a place. A time. A person. That's all it takes.

And sandwiches sometimes.

It is moments like this that make two people become a couple. Some people believe that there is only one person in the world for each of us. This is a fallacy. There are, in fact, none. Zero. Not to begin with, that is. Because your *one* does not exist until *after* you have met them. Until after you have shared moments like this. That is why they are so important.

And if you lose your one, then you have to start over. From scratch. From zero.

Conner and Lisa returned to this spot in the years that followed, before the birth of their son. Lisa always insisted that the outlook from this place was her favourite view in the whole world.

Conner didn't agree with her, not about the view. His feeling was that the ocean was always the same. Always flat. *His* favourite view was from a lookout atop the hills that flanked New Meadows. From there he could see the whole town. And it was never the same; it evolved. Buildings would be flattened. New ones would spring up, one floor at a time, seemingly at the will of the spindly looking cranes that perched on top. Lights would buzz up and down the highways, and ping on and off at windows. There was always something different to see. Always something going on. That was why Conner preferred that view.

But now he sat once again at their spot near the ocean, as serene and beautiful as ever – as even he would admit – and sure enough it was exactly the same. He dug deep to see if his feelings had changed. But no, for him the New Meadows cityscape was still the more awesome of the panoramas.

Their difference of opinion over the matter of scenic beauty did not trouble Conner when they had sat there all those years before. Why should it have done? It was only a small thing. But it is hard to tell which little differences will open up into massive fissures, far too vast to cross. Conner wondered briefly whether this difference was the beginnings of the fracture that drove them apart. His horizons had always been close by. He had no great desires to move from the region in which he'd spent his life; no wish to escape his career. Maybe Lisa's love of this vista, out over the ocean, to a horizon as distant as one could be – maybe that was indicative of a deep-seated desire that was at odds with his own. Maybe he could have seen that way back then.

Conner considered this possibility for a moment and he eventually came to a conclusion that it was all hokum. It was the kind of sentimental, poetic nonsense that you'd find in a romantic novel. The truth is that to every personality there are a million different facets, and no two people's are angled exactly the same way – that's just a statistical impossibility. There is no pattern, no rhyme or reason, no magic formula. Some couples just work, some don't; and some have to *make* it work. All outcomes are possible. And having differing opinions over scenic spots or sports teams or sandwich fillings, does not manifest as a fundamental stumbling block; does not *mean* anything at some higher level. It's just part of the minutia that makes a relationship interesting.

But there was one fundamental point Conner could draw from his trip to the coast. As he sat there, the significance slowly dawned on him. The salient truth was this. In his time of troubles, when everything had got too much for him, when he needed to seek answers ... *this* place was where he chose to run to.

This place ... so intrinsically connected to Lisa.

There was no tenuous link to be drawn from this fact. It was all very clear.

She was what he sought.

She was what he wanted.

Twenty-Four

Opening Up

The evening after first meeting Karla, we met up again and went for a meal. After that, we saw quite a lot of each other.

She was different from Gemma. Gemma was comfortable, easy to be with, funny. If I were to make a TV analogy then being with her was like watching a good comedy. Karla, on the other hand, was more like a documentary. She was intense, fascinating; harder work sometimes, but entertaining, definitely. That's not to say that Gemma wasn't interesting or Karla wasn't funny, but there are degrees of everything. You know where I'm coming from.

On our second night out we got to the subject of what she did for a living. And it turned out to be something I didn't even know existed as a career – which was kind of the point.

First, let me give you some background. About the curious anomaly of fashion.

Some people say that they are not affected by fashion. They say they just wear what they 'look good in'. But here's the rub: what they think they look good in changes with time. Even for those who are not fashion 'victims'.

Some clearly take their appearance to the dangerous extremes of fashion and dress up like clowns, presumably for the entertainment of the rest of us. But aside from these, us Average Joes and Janes are also affected, just more subtly. The width of our lapels, the size of our hair, the flare of our legs, the cut of our jib. The fact is that we can look back at old pictures of ourselves and be appalled by what we see, by what we once truly believed was totally *groovy*.

This *would* be unremarkable. After all, everyone's tastes change with age, be it food, music or holiday destinations. But with *aesthetic* taste something spooky is afoot: everyone's palate changes together – in sync. And not just with respect to clothes. Any product of design – be it furniture or buildings or cars or company logos – can look 'modern' for a limited period of time only. Thereafter, any item will begin to look dated or indeed 'old-fashioned'. Yet it's the *same* thing. It hasn't changed. And it's not that it's worn or tatty; it can be in mint condition. So what's going on? Something has guided us to look upon it differently. And the *really* weird thing is that this trait seems to be entirely instinctive. People do not need to spend time analysing what the stars are wearing on TV or in magazines, to gain the appropriate response when they are trying on clothes at the store. Even people who you would not consider as particularly hip or trendy – who you might even label as old-fashioned – still don't look like they've stepped out of the seventies. There's a certain modernism to their outdatedness, if you know what I mean.

It's like there is some kind of social fashion sense – granted, not spread even, but there all the same.

Someone should look into that one day. Might be important.

But I'm blathering. For now it's enough to understand that fashion is massively emotive and therefore important to a lot of people. And so, you've guessed it, there is money to be made. Though you may not realise quite how much. Allow me to enlighten you.

You would probably expect that the revenue of the big-brand clothing manufacturers to be many millions of dollars. And you'd be right. But what might blow you away is that that word 'millions' is not nearly man enough for the job. Put down any hot beverages and read this slowly: the annual revenue of the largest sportswear company in America is ... twenty *billion* dollars. Seriously. As with everything I tell you, look it up. Okay, so now we are getting to the point. How much does this same company spend in endorsements to sports teams and individuals? How much do they pay people to wear their stuff? Right, move well away from that hot beverage and if possible lie down. That single aforementioned company spends somewhere in the order of four billion dollars in endorsements alone. That doesn't even include 'normal' advertising.

Now, I don't just happen to know all these figures. I'm not some savant with a penchant for fashion industry facts and stats. And it is not a domain I have any interest in; or *had* any interest in. Not until I met Karla.

So where does she fit in?

Well the industry big boys are very aware how important it is for cool – preferably famous – people to be seen wearing their gear. That's why they pay them so much to do so. But they are also aware that an awful lot of famous people wear their stuff without having to pay them a penny. And when such an occurrence is captured by the media the executives almost wee themselves with excitement. Be it an official function on the red carpet or a charity bash; or snapped by the pap falling out of a nightclub; or just strolling down Mulholland Drive in sweats. It all adds up to dollars in the pocket for the fashion moguls.

A place like BlueJay in a town like New Meadows plays host to a large number of influential and famous people, just visiting or as guests to private functions. And this is where Karla comes in. She works – covertly – for Igneous Clothing Inc., which as you may be aware is the fastest growing clothing and sportswear company on the planet. They have struck hush-hush deals with a number of establishments like BlueJay, which enables them to tout Karla or one of her peers as just another guest. She schmoozes a little, hones in on a particular person, chats to them, entertains them, makes them feel good about themselves. And then...

'Oh you would look so good in that shirt.'

Or...

'Oh, these sunglasses are just *so* cool.'

Now, when a very vain and wealthy guy is being flirted at by a pretty woman, and that woman says how good he would look in a particular item of apparel, there is only one way this is going to go. He will buy it. Then with any luck he may be snapped wearing it at some point in the future. This is the hope of Karla's employers of course.

Sometimes Karla will suggest, 'we should *so* go shopping tomorrow.' She will of course only recommend items from a certain select set of brands, all of which are owned by the same parent company –

unbeknown to the average punter.

Of course, the strategy is not one hundred percent successful – or anywhere near – but consider two points. One, you can pay an awful lot of Karlas from a slice of four billion bucks. Two, all she has to do is make a few sales, as it were, and she's paid for herself anyway, regardless of whether the mark ever wears the stuff again. It's win-win for the company.

The other benefit of this strategy over the standard model is being able to access the untouchables – the ones that are beyond the reach of multi-million-dollar endorsements because of their occupation or position in society. For sports, music and film stars it's a standard part of their revenue stream. For politicians and high-profile business folk it's not. You may not think that politicians are a desirable target, but they all garner their share of column-inches in the newspapers and that's all that counts.

As an extreme example, when the last president came to power he was the most popular man on the planet and known for his love of the gym and the basketball court. When he was photographed wearing a particular brand of baseball cap, the shareholders could almost feel their wallets getting thicker over night.

Okay, so the likes of the president are not going to be swanning around BlueJay, but senators might be and young trendy CEOs of successful start-ups jetting in from Silicon Valley for a spot of gaming. Unknown to them, they are all fair game – all targets for a surreptitious make-over.

Is it underhand? Yes. Is it devious? Sure. Do I give a crap? Not one bit. I actually quite admire the audacity and subtlety of the strategy. It's a fickle industry messing in the fickle world of celebrity, and they are welcome to each other.

So, that was Karla's world.

At least, that was Karla's world now. I knew her past would harbour darker tales. She was Colombian. And it was impossible to be of that nation and not be touched by suffering and tragedy. It was just a matter of to what degree. Colombia's darker elements are stained deep into the fabric of the country – as well as myself – and just like Lady Macbeth's damned spot, the stain won't come out. I knew this better than most Westerners.

One night we went to see one of the umpteen theatrical extravaganzas New Meadows had to offer. It was some completely insane French Canadian circus thing, with people dressed as pieces of fruit and upside-down bowler hats. The subtlety was completely lost on me. I considered whether this was because I wasn't under the influence of the designated narcotic for the show. Maybe there was some kind of inverse-hallucinogen going around town, which could make this totally crazy shit appear as a paragon of normality. I should have checked in the foyer.

To recover from this torturous ordeal we stopped off at a bar, mercifully bereft of walking headwear, and ordered a bottle of red wine.

I wasn't unaware of the fact that I don't drink red wine. Not unless it's with a meal that is. I would never order it at a bar. Drinking strategy is one of those little things that changes when you spend time with someone. I knew what this meant. It meant I had allowed Karla to change me, or influence me at least. And, as it happened, it didn't trouble me. I was actually okay with it.

We laughed for some time over the ludicrousness of our evening so far, and then conversation turned back to our pasts.

'So how did you get into your line of work?' I asked.

She threw her head back in a wicked wine-fuelled laugh.

'What's funny?'

'That fact that it took you so long to ask. Says something about what you suspect the answer is, yeah? Maybe you think I was a glamour model? Lap-dancer? Hooker?'

'No!' I protested.

Okay, maybe.

'Couldn't be further from it.' She took a long sip of her wine. 'I was a full-on businesswoman. Dress suit, power heels, briefcase, the works.'

'Really?' It didn't actually surprise me as much as she thought it did. She clearly had the capacity. You could cut your finger on her acumen.

'I was a buyer. For one of the big clothes stores. Used to spend a lot of time flying out to the Far East, negotiating deals for clothing lines. I kinda got head-hunted by one of the Igneous high-flyers. It was completely out of the blue. All very clandestine. Someone just rang me up one day at home; wouldn't say a great deal over the phone. The practise they wished to enlist me into was all quite hush-hush obviously. Anyway, to begin with I thought it was a ridiculous idea. But after I considered the prospect for a while it grew more appealing. I was starting to get tired of all the travelling and these guys basically wanted to pay me to go to swanky parties and rub shoulders with influential bigwigs. That was a couple of years back now, and the rest, as they say, is history.' She formed a playful frown. 'Which, thinking about it, is a silly thing to bother saying, because everything is history.' She laughed at herself. She was a little tipsy. It was cute. Her edges had softened. Not that she was overly hard-edged, just kind of precise, you know.

I asked her another question. One that edged onto ground that was potentially much more unstable.

'So, do you have family back in Colombia?'

At the mention of family her eyes dropped and I was quick to offer an escape route.

'You don't have to talk about this if you don't want to.'

'No. It's okay,' she said flatly. 'I'll give you the précis.' Her eyes drifted into the distance as she took a sip of her wine. 'I'm one of four children. Three girls, one boy. We each have a story, each touched by our country's darker culture in one way or another. It started with my elder sister. She met a guy when she was seventeen. He was a member of a local paramilitary group. Mom and dad were not overjoyed, but at the same time they believed the paras were doing the right thing, were just protecting us from the insurgents. Then, one night she went out with her boyfriend and never came back. We found out weeks later that they had both been executed by guerrillas.'

'I'm sorry,' I said. There was nothing else I could say. Karla shrugged in acceptance.

'My brother took it pretty badly. He didn't eat for weeks and hasn't spoken a word since. My other sister reacted differently. She went off the rails. Mixed in with a bad crowd; started doing bad things. We tried to turn a blind eye, but it's hard, you know.'

I nodded and listened patiently.

'I couldn't bear it any longer. Although I loved my family, I had to get away from that mess. The atmosphere reeked of violence. It was contagious and virulent. There was no safe future for me there. When I was eighteen I fled to the US, and I was lucky enough to land on my feet.'

She paused and I sensed that was the end of her story.

'Are you still in touch with your family?'

'My parents and brother, yeah. They are fine. I see them maybe a couple of times a year. But my sister ran away shortly after I left and we haven't heard from her since.'

'That's a pretty bad introduction to the world.'

Karla shrugged. 'Hey, as far as families go, ours is one of the more functional. Our poor neighbour lost all her children in the conflicts and then her husband killed himself. That's Colombia.'

I nodded. I knew.

'Okay,' I said by way of conclusion. 'Let's drink some more.'

I didn't tell her about my experiences of her country. I had vowed never to tell anyone.

After leaving Gemma, when my nature grew darker, I decided I needed to learn more about bad people. So I went somewhere where there was a pretty high hit rate. I stood out like a sore white thumb of course, so I had no choice but to pose as a journalist. It was surprising how accommodating militia members can be. Members on all sides feel they are doing the right thing, fighting for a cause. And they all want their story to be told.

I spent some time living on a rebel camp learning

how they ticked, what drove them. Then it was time to seek out their enemies, the paramilitaries.

It was on a long bus journey to the south that I met Maria, and it was for her that I would feel the most conflicting set of emotions I had ever experienced in my life. And it was *from* her that I would learn my greatest lesson about people.

She was friendly and accommodating and intensely fascinating. I told her I was here to learn about the paras and she offered to introduce me to some people. We spent a lot of time together after that. We spent a lot of time in my hotel room.

If I'm honest, I went off the rails for a bit with her – off into a hedonistic blur. I explored a different side of myself, discovered states I'd never experienced before. And it's fair to say that I took a few risks, but I was only risking myself, and I think I got away with it. I knew I could trust Maria, as I did with everyone.

We had nothing in common, which was no less than thrilling. And she showed nothing but compassion, and indeed, passion toward me. And, I really liked her. But there was something else. A catch. One minor tarnish to her otherwise beautiful nature.

She was an assassin.

I know that sounds crazy but in reality it is not so uncommon in Colombia.

She operated within a private militia. She had killed over forty people. She had shot, decapitated, and disembowelled. She had been party to village-wide massacres. And, within her own mind, she justified it all; justified her actions as a legitimate part of a civil war, as protecting her people from the enemy. And that may have even been valid in the beginning, before I knew her. But not for a long time now. She had grown desensitised to the torture and the killing and in truth she was nothing but a freelance killer.

But here's the ludicrous thing. She wasn't a bad person. However often I say those words it still rings insane, but she was not bad. Not at the core. She wasn't really a person at all anymore. She had been brainwashed. Not by an individual or an extremist group. She had been brainwashed by a culture; by a history. She was a product of her nation. This was just how things were in her world.

And the heartbreaking thing was that I couldn't do anything about it. Her altered state was set too fast. The darkened pathways between her synapses were scored too deep. Even I was powerless to bring her back; to make her understand the meaning of morality and mortality once more; to return the innocence of her childhood.

So it had to end. I knew that. I knew that our worlds could never join.

I lay in a hotel room one morning, thick humid air and a raucous din drifting in from the streets below. I watched Maria in the shower through a gap in the door and was aware of her pistol lying inches from my face on the bedside table. My feelings for her, both loving and loathing were so heavy and conflicting as to make me dizzy and nauseous. And I knew it was time to find my own reality again, away from this madness.

But I didn't lift that gun. Didn't pull that trigger. Just pulled on my clothes and walked away. I didn't say goodbye. Quite simply, I was too scared.

As I made my way up through Latin American I wondered how the conflicts would develop from this point. By this time the narcotics industry was in rapid decline due to the rising popularity of legal highs. Although the drugs trade was the root cause of the troubles throughout this region, without it things were only going to get worse before they got better. Drugs were the lifeblood of this nation – they ran through its veins. They fuelled the economy. They put money in pockets and food on tables.

I wondered mostly what would happen to Maria. When her paying clients dwindled and her work dried up. Where would she go? What would she become? I hoped she would get as far as having to make these choices, but in truth I knew she would most likely be dead before long.

I shed a tear for her and then I moved on. I don't think sleeping with a killer makes you a killer by association, but it made me feel dirty all the same. So I locked away another part of my life in a sealed box, never to be reopened.

That is why I didn't tell Karla about my experience of Colombia.

Later that night we stumbled back to Karla's place and sensibly turned to coffee as our beverage of choice. As we clawed our way back to a drowsy sobriety, I talked a bit more about myself. Not so much the bad stuff – the seeking out of immorals to mess with – but the good stuff, the early stuff. She already knew what I could do. That was why I had approached her in the first place, so we'd had that conversation early on. But I told her a little more about why I did it.

The thing is, what I needed more than anything right now was a distraction, and that was what Karla offered me. But what I also needed was to unburden my soul, and Karla offered me that too. I even told her about Gemma. Some of it.

It was strange that I should feel so comfortable talking to her, considering I felt so out of my depth communicating with someone I couldn't read. I guess it must have helped; in the same way that it's easier to talk to a pet than a person, because you can't see the judgement in their eyes – or the pity, or the anger, or whatever emotion you may be invoking in your listener.

Whatever the reason, Karla became only the second person in my life who knew who I really was. And she was the *only* person in my life that I'd ever opened up to completely. I knew I was making myself vulnerable, but I didn't really care anymore. I needed this release. It was cathartic. I mean in a good way. I wasn't wallowing in self-pity, wasn't acting hard-done-by. I was just talking as the small hours rolled by. And it was good. Everything's relative, but it was good.

Then, after I'd lost my momentum and there had been a silence for a while, Karla asked a question.

'So, why?

'Why what?

'Why are you so bent on figuring out how all this works?' She tapped her temple. 'On getting into people's minds and fixing them?'

I shrugged. 'Because I get a kick out of fixing people?'

She shook her head authoritatively. 'Maybe you do. But that's not what started this obsession is it?'

'Why do you say that?'

'Because you're not that type. I'm sorry to be blunt but you are not the do-gooder charity-worker type. If you wanted to help people then you could just volunteer at a soup kitchen, or give out aid in Africa. Hell, you could have become a doctor with your obsessive-compulsive studying. You would have helped more people that way. So why this?'

I stared straight ahead. As I contemplated the answer I felt my chest begin to tighten. I hadn't allowed these thoughts into my consciousness for some time. My breathing began to grow laboured and I needed to stand. I walked over to the window and placed my coffee cup on the sill before planting my hands either side of it to steady myself.

The first I was aware of Karla's movement was a gentle hand on my shoulder.

'Hey, if you need to talk, then I'm here. If not, that's okay too.'

She stood beside me as I stared out of the window, through my own reflection. After a moment of silence I took a deep sigh and rubbed my face in both my hands to wipe away the dew. Turning to Karla I wanted to speak but nothing came out at first. All I could manage was a pathetic silent movement of my jaw. I tried again and this time the words came. Slowly.

'It was *me* I wanted to fix,' I whispered glumly. 'It's me that's broken.'

Twenty-Five

Uniformity

It felt odd to Conner at first: the uniform, the weight of the equipment hanging at his waist. Being an undercover detective he'd spent most of his career trying to convince people that he *wasn't* a cop, not flaunting the fact. But he quickly got used to it again. He'd forgotten the buzz you get from walking down the street as an icon of justice; rather than skulking in the shadows.

After returning from his trip to the coast he had requested a spell back in uniform. His case on Bigby was indefinitely suspended now the Feds were all over it. The murders were still unsolved and still continuing but there was pressure to chalk them down as turf warfare. Not that this should make murders any more acceptable, but it did seem to. The general population of New Meadows are far too busy being entertained to worry about dealers popping each other off. Announce that there was an unknown serial killer in a black Mercedes shooting people dead on the street and it would be a different matter.

So, Conner wanted out. At least for now. And he wanted to go back to uniform. There was a straight-forwardness to uniformed policing that was particularly alluring to him at this time.

He spent his days in a patrol vehicle with a rather jolly moustached partner, attending incidents of shoplifting and assaults and traffic felonies. Then he filed his reports. Then he went home.

And the crimes did not go home with him.

This was partly due to the short-term nature of the crimes. But it was mostly because he had changed.

Conner didn't know in what way he had changed, but if he'd visited a shrink he might have been told that it was all related to something called dissociation.

Traditionally, medical science tagged dissociation as pathological, in particular that it manifests in the experience of multiple personalities. But, in truth, this 'split-mind' syndrome is just one extreme of a spectrum along which *everyone* lies. Everyone has different personalities inside them, of which one can be brought out to suit the occasion. Just like popping on the gym kit or the Sunday best. Crucially, though, within this *normal* level of dissociation the personalities are not discrete. They are aware of each other; they merge and overlap; they communicate with each other.

This capability is an adaptive function of the human mind. It evolved as a defence mechanism. It allows us to function in extreme situations where otherwise we might be overwhelmed by a barrage of stimuli and the emotions they evoke. It is what enables a surgeon to dispassionately slice open a living person, and yet still be horrified if she witnesses her own son fall and split his lip. A surgeon must be able to emotionally detach such that she does not care for her patient in the way that she does for her child, but in a way that allows her to perform objectively.

Dissociation is what allows the rest of us to carry on about our daily lives, without being emotionally weighed down by the troubles and suffering of the rest of the world. A million people can be dying of starvation on the other side of the world and yet we barely look up from our choco-flakes.

For surgeons, paramedics, soldiers and so on, well-balanced dissociation is imperative. For police detectives the need is not so immediate, yet its absence is just as corrosive over time.

The events of the last few days had allowed Conner to move along his dissociative spectrum, to tease apart his personalities just a little, where before there had been only one.

He had always cared too much, been too emotionally attached to what he was trying to achieve. Now he felt farther removed; more distant. If he didn't resolve everything right away, all by himself, then that was okay. It was all about becoming more objective. Even if there was a life or a livelihood at stake, it wasn't *his* life or *his* livelihood, or any of his family's.

And it was his uniform that served as the wedge that drove his two worlds apart. As soon as the uniform came off, so the killings and the robberies and the parking misdemeanours became nothing more than numbers on a page, lines on a chart. And if the lines went the wrong way one week then they might go the right way next week, and that was what it was all about. He was still going to function in his role but only when he was *playing* that role. It was a clinical approach but it was the only way to maintain any level of sanity.

For the first time in his life, he was learning to detach. And with it he was learning to engage with life once more.

His route home one day took him past a multiplex cinema and he studied the line of billboards to see what was playing. He quickly moved by the latest Sadie Winters flick. By all accounts it was causing quite a stir because her husband had a three second cameo in it. That was all that was needed to get the punters drooling at the entrance and handing over their cash. Either way it was not for him. One film did catch his attention though.

The next day Conner called up Lisa. He apologised for calling her at work and said he needed to borrow a child.

'I know it's not the weekend,' he explained, 'but there's a new Disney film out I want to see. And I need an excuse.'

He could tell she was smiling. 'Sure, tonight is good,' she agreed.

'Great. I'll pick him up after work. Five-thirty?'

'Fine.'

He didn't notice it himself, but the mere fact that the phrase 'after work' existed in his vocabulary, was greatly significant.

He was changing.

Being changed.

It was a good thing.

He arrived at Lisa's doorstep straight from work and pressed the bell. Shortly, he heard Lisa inside, calling up the stairs to their son. Then the door opened.

'Look at you,' she said as she saw Conner standing on the doorstep still in his uniform.

Conner put his arms out by his side to show off his attire.

'Like it?' he said with a smile.

'Takes me back,' she replied. 'What's it all about then?'

Conner gave a little shrug. 'Time for a change.'

They both knew that didn't qualify as an answer, but it didn't need to. At that point their son burst out onto the doorstep.

'Hey Dad.'

'Hey, you ready?'

'Yep.'

'Cool, let's go.'

They set off down the steps as Lisa called after them.

'Back by nine, please. And don't fill him up with popcorn.'

At ten-past-nine Conner duly returned a popcorn-filled child to his mother.

'Go clean your teeth and get ready for bed,' she instructed to their son as she collected him over the threshold and ushered him toward the stairs.

Lisa turned back to Conner as he waited outside the door, this time in his civilian clothes.

'Thanks for letting me do that,' he said with a thin smile.

'No problem,' she nodded. 'So what's really with the move back to uniform?'

Conner paused for a moment, not sure how to answer the question at first. He shrugged.

'Somebody made me realise that there was more to life than investigating the rug trade. That maybe it wasn't even the right thing.'

Lisa nodded slowly, but looked as though she didn't understand. 'And now? Is it the right thing?'

‘Maybe not. But now I get to take my uniform off at the end of the day and then I’m not a cop anymore, so it doesn’t matter.’

Lisa narrowed her eyes with gentle concern.

Conner was waiting to exchange good-nights, but he realised there was something else that needed to be said – had needed to be said for some time. He faltered on his first attempt and Lisa noticed.

‘What is it?’ she asked.

‘I just wanted to say,’ he began eventually. ‘I just wanted to say ... I’m sorry.’

‘For what?’

‘For not being there. Enough. Even when I *was* there.’

Lisa didn’t appear to know what to do with the apology. Conner understood why.

‘I *was* aware. Or maybe I wasn’t, but I am now. Looking back. Those times when we had people around for dinner, and I was supposed to be all social, and I wasn’t really *there*. I would answer questions, but I wouldn’t start conversations. Because I was always somewhere else in my head. Too caught up in some other world out there on the street. It must’ve been pretty bugging.’

She shrugged in confirmation and allowed Conner to continue.

‘I understand now which world is more important and I wonder if it would’ve made a difference if I’d known back then.’

‘Conner, you can’t –’

‘I know,’ he cut in. ‘It wasn’t a question. I know it’s too late. Anyway, sorry is all.’ He stepped away. ‘Good night.’

'Good night,' Lisa returned hesitantly.

Conner turned and started to walk away.

'Conner,' Lisa called after him. He turned and Lisa had stepped out toward him.

'Yes?'

'You will always need to be part of that other world.'

'At the cost of the rest of my life? I really hope not.'

'I know you, Conner. You may be able to take off your uniform at the end of the day, but you will always be wearing that badge.' She reached out and tapped his chest. 'Twenty-four-seven.'

Inside Conner sighed deeply. He didn't argue, but he hoped with all his soul that it wasn't true.

Twenty-Six

Telling Eyes

Karla and I sat on her sofa and I tried to put into words what I never had before. It was three in the morning by this point but I was wide awake. In the end, the statement was quite straightforward.

'The thing is,' I offered gingerly, 'I've ... never experienced happiness.'

'What?'

'I don't mean like I'm constantly sad. Though I am at times of course. I mean, I'm just not capable of that emotion. I can comprehend it; but I can't feel it. I've been on theme park rides and I feel the adrenaline, and it's exciting and fun and a smile appears on my face. And I know that happiness is kind of a subdued but more permanent version of that feeling. But I've never had it. I've never been in that place.'

I paused for a moment, looked away as I dredged up memories from the depths of my past. Then I continued.

'I recognised this at a very early age. I knew when I got a new shiny bike at Christmas I should feel more than a dull, perfunctory satisfaction. But when I didn't, I knew enough to smile at all the right times. And so it continued. It was not until college that I finally decided to see a professional about it. Three in the end, as it happens. But none of them 'got' me. They kept trying to analyse my life and figure out what I needed to change about it to be happy. But there was nothing wrong with my life. I had a stable upbringing, a loving family, a good education, and lots of friends. There was nothing I particularly longed for. It wasn't my *life* that was lacking; it was my *mind*. And none of them understood that. So I had to learn to fix myself. But...'

I gave a deep sigh and then a dry, pathetic laugh at myself, as Karla sat patiently listening.

'The irony is, I became a master at fixing other people but couldn't fix myself.'

'Why?' Karla enquired with a questioning dip of the brow.

'Because that's how it works when I *cure* people – for want of a better word – of their addiction or depression or insomnia or lack of self-confidence. I don't administer any drug. Nor do I give them a soothing neck rub or acupuncture or any kind of physical therapy. There is no actual medicine. I just talk to them. By definition it is a placebo affect – without even the placebo. And because of that, I obviously can't treat myself. It's like I'm the only dentist in town, so I'm the only one with toothache.'

I fell silent and Karla dropped a question into the void.

'How do you describe what you had with Gemma?'

'With Gemma, I found a place I wanted to stay. I cared for her deeply and I *enjoyed* lots of what we shared. But enjoyment is like the excitement on the rollercoaster. It's of-the-moment. It's ascribed to a specific event. It's not an underlying baseline emotion.'

I straightened up and literally shook myself into a

different state.

'Anyway, enough of all that. I am what I am; and I've learnt to deal with it.'

I smiled and it was a genuine smile.

'Good.' Karla nodded, accepting my decision to move the topic on.

'Besides, I picked up some pretty useful skills along the way.'

'Not so useful with me. The reading part at least.' She smiled.

'True. Do you have any idea why that might be?' I was surprised that it had taken me so long to ask this question. I'd known Karla for a couple of weeks by this point. Maybe I was giving myself time to analyse her before I asked. Or maybe I was just enjoying the thrill of her company.

'No,' she replied. 'I had no idea I was any different from anyone else. I think I'm only different to you.'

'I think so too.' If I had been in a suspicious state of mind I would have considered this a remarkable coincidence. But I was too tired to be suspicious.

'It must be a burden. Seeing people the way you do.'

'I guess. I don't really think of it that way. It's just part of me. It's like saying it must be a burden having to breath in and out all of the time.'

'Hmm.' She didn't seem convinced. Rightly so, I guess.

The evening was winding down nicely and I felt more relaxed than I had done for some time. And, as such, I wasn't expecting any considerable bombshells to come whistling in through the window and explode at my feet. Metaphorically or otherwise.

I was, of course, wrong.

I was wrong because then Karla said something that turned my world upside-down. Something that, in a single moment, changed everything...

'Well, even if you don't admit it is a burden, I think it's a good thing that we don't all have your eyes.'

Bang.

'What!?' I turned sharply to her.

'I said –'

'No,' I cut her off impatiently. 'I heard what you said. But...' I was going to ask what she meant. But it was obvious. Now. It should have been obvious for so long. I stood up and began to pace. 'Why didn't I see it that way before?' I was talking to myself. 'Because it makes no sense. But then, it didn't make sense anyway.'

'What are you talking about?' Karla was standing too now.

I stopped jabbering and turned to face Karla. My mind did some super fast processing; realigned certain segments of my brain to the newly-understood facts. And out popped a new plan.

'I need to go to New York,' I concluded.

'Why? When?'

'Now.'

'Now? It's three in the morning.'

'I know. Sun will be up soon.'

I grabbed my coat and headed for the door.

'What's going on?'

At the door I turned to her again.

'She had my eyes, Karla. *Pearle* had my eyes. She could *see* like me.'

Twenty-Seven

Faltering

Conner flicked the TV on to the news as background noise for his morning routine. He was not surprised to be greeted by the faces of super-couple Rubeck and Winters, who had seemingly grown omnipresent in his town over recent weeks – especially since the announcement of their involvement in some massive upcoming event sponsored by the Igneous clothing corporation.

The event was called *Fabrics of Life*, some fair-trade, super-ethical, pseudo-political affair. The hype made it sound like Igneous was promising to feed the hungry, cure the diseased and eradicate poverty across the globe. To save the world. But when a corporate giant was involved it was hard not to be cynical.

Conner headed into the kitchen to prepare his breakfast of black filter coffee and more black filter coffee. He was going to stop there, then remembered that there was no Mila at the office to take care of his mid-morning dietary requirements. That made him a little reminiscent as he threw two slices of half-stale bread into the toaster. He'd heard she was back in town. Back at work in a different department. He figured he should call her up sometime.

As the coffee maker hissed away he could only half hear the news report coming from the next room.

'...There is growing concern over the upcoming event organised by the Igneous clothing company. It is understood that the New Meadows Police Department has received a number of serious threats, verified as genuine using recognised code-words. No official statement has been released as to which specific group is behind the threats, but it is considered most likely to be one of the increasingly militant anti-globalisation movements. Security for such an event is always high, but will be stepped up in light of these concerns. It is believed that the event organisers will be liaising closely with the police force and US secret services. Here now, to discuss the security issues faced by such a high-profile event is...'

Conner zapped the TV off agitatedly. Something about the day had set Conner's mood spiralling off in the wrong direction.

His mood did not improve any on his walk to work as he received a call from Jaz, one of his more irritating informants. Conner was aware that this was not what he needed right now, but figured he had to answer.

'Hey,' Conner began apathetically.

'Got some good info for you,' Jaz enthused.

'Not interested,' Conner responded flatly. 'Not my patch anymore.'

'Not your patch? You live and breathe this patch.'

'Maybe once. Not now. Bye Jaz.'

'Hold up,' Jaz cut in quickly. 'This ain't no two-bit trade. This is bigger.'

'Bigger?'

'Yeah, this is about the killings.'

Conner hung up. Then he turned off his phone.

Getting back involved was way too risky. Psychologically, he had to move on. Physically, he had to not get killed.

He attributed the conversation to a mid-morning hallucination and moved on as if it had not taken place at all.

His day on patrol passed by routinely. He spent most of it distant in his own thoughts. Over recent weeks he'd made a lot of discoveries about himself, come to a lot of conclusions. Ultimately, it meant he knew more now about what he wanted from life than he ever had before. This was a good thing – in general. But the one insight that goes hand-in-hand with realising what you want from life, is recognising that you don't have it. Worse still, recognising that you'd spent a good deal of your life heading along the wrong path. With any luck your trodden path will not be in the opposite direction from where you now want to go. And with any luck there will be a little cut-through, to find your way from one to the other. But maybe not. In Conner's case he wasn't sure which was true.

When he got home, he took a shower and pulled on his civilian clothes. Then he stood in front of the full length mirror in his bedroom – another of those items that a man would never buy himself but quite appreciates when available for use. Lisa had insisted they needed this *particular* mirror. It was from the store she loves in town; the one that specialises in all the pretend old stuff. 'Pretend Old Stuff' did not feature in the store's official marketing material. They preferred phrases like 'classic time-honoured design', which basically meant they could charge a thousand bucks for a wardrobe by calling it an armoire, or inflate the price of anything at all by adding the word apothecary to its title. Lisa had never got around to taking the mirror because it didn't fit in her car, and plus her new place had one fitted already. So Conner found himself studying his reflection in a Rustic Elm Apothecary Floor Mirror.

No longer in uniform. No longer a cop.

He'd learned that lesson. Learned the importance of dissociation, of being able to detach. But as he stood there, his thoughts echoing in an empty room within an empty house, something became all too clear. He had learned the lesson too late. He had nothing to come home to, nothing for that other self to be a part of.

Suddenly, some visceral imperative took hold and Conner found himself leaving the house and heading for Lisa's apartment with no clear objective. It was a Wednesday night and he knew that their son went swimming with a friend on Wednesday nights, so Lisa would be in on her own. It would give them an opportunity to talk, although he wasn't sure what there was to say.

When he arrived he rang the doorbell, but there was no response. She was out. Of course she was out. This was the one night of the week when she could go out. He walked away, but he didn't get very far. Across the street a few doors down there was a little coffee shop, which he decided to patronise. His actions and his thought processes were clipped. They didn't seem his own. He seemed out of sorts. Maybe that was why he was lured into the café. Probably not.

He sat there and drank, and stared, and thought. And he knew why he was there. And the revelation was not welcome. He was spying. Stalking even. And the target was not some criminal, but his wife, the mother of his child. He knew he had crossed a line. But it had been right there to be crossed. And now the line was behind him he couldn't see it anymore.

He didn't know what he expected to see. But eventually, as if this was all part of some orchestrated plan by the man downstairs, he saw it. He saw Lisa return to her apartment and go inside ... with a man.

She had never mentioned a man; never told him that she was seeing someone. But did she have to? Was that his right? It was a grey area for sure. But he decided that their son swung it in his favour. He had a right to know if Lisa was planning to introduce a man into his son's life.

There was no other word to describe Conner's emotion but anger; pure seething anger. Not sadness or envy or regret, or anything else. In a way this response surprised him, but then emotions often do. He seethed for a moment, considering his course of action. He wanted with all his soul to go over there right now and talk to her. He rehearsed over and over in his mind all his arguments, exactly why this was wrong and inappropriate, and why he was being treated so unfairly. He wanted to say these things and even as he walked out of the coffee shop he didn't know which way he was going to turn.

As it happened he crossed the road, heading for her door, got to only feet away ... and then some deeper logic circuitry seized control and steered him off down the street. After a few blocks the anger had changed, thinned out a little, to allow the anticipated despair to seep through to the forefront.

He thought of the last words Lisa had said to him:

'You will always be wearing that badge.' Maybe she was right. Maybe that was all that was left of him.

He walked for a while longer. Then he made the call.

'Jaz? Where are you?'

He met Jaz on a busy street and they walked together. Conner covertly slipped Jaz fifty dollars.

'This is worth twice that man.'

'Whatever it is you've got to say, it's worth fifty bucks. Now spill.'

'Nah, come on man – '

Conner snapped and pushed the informant up against the wall with a hand to the scruff of this neck.

'Listen. I'm not on this case anymore. That money isn't on expenses, it's out of my own pocket. Now you either tell me what you know for fifty or you tell me for nothing, because I've had a really bad day and I'm in no frame of mind to be bartering with pond scum.'

'Okay, okay, take it easy. Jeez, what have you been popping?'

Conner released his grip and started walking again, with Jaz in pursuit.

'Now talk,' Conner instructed. 'What've you got that's so hot?'

'Okay, so as you know there have been a lot of shootings lately. A lot of dead gang members, both Scrips and Sanguins.'

'Of course I know.'

'Well, it's not gang warfare. I can tell you that.' Jaz paused for effect. 'It's a single shooter.'

Conner sighed. 'Yeah, I'd figured that much already. You want to tell me something I don't know? Or you want me to take that fifty back off you?'

'Hold up, hold up. What you don't know is this. The killer used to work for Scrips.'

'A rogue gang member?'

'No, not a member, just a hired hitter.'

'And now who's doing the hiring?'

'Don't know.'

'Who's the hitter?'

'Don't know.'

'You don't know much do you?' Conner stopped. 'Come on, give it back,' he insisted, referring to the money.

'Wait. I've saved the best till last.'

Conner shook his head sceptically. 'I'm sure you have. Excuse me if I don't wet myself with anticipation.' He marched off at a faster pace, one that Jaz found difficult to match without adding a skip every fourth step.

'The killer...' Jaz said to the back of Conner's head. 'The killer ... is a chick.'

Conner stopped dead in his tracks, then turned to face Jaz's crooked grin. He didn't say anything as he started to consolidate facts in his mind. After a moment he took another fifty dollar bill out of this wallet and held it up in front of Jaz.

'This one's not for you. This one's for your kids. Make sure they get fed this month, right?'

'Sure.' Jaz snatched the note and skulked away.

Conner knew that appealing to the conscience of a man who rats on his brother for money was next to useless. But such was his way.

He ran through the facts as he knew them. The New Meadows rug trade was an almost exclusively male domain – equality laws haven't yet filtered all the way down to the streets. Similarly, the Guild of Professional Hitwomen and Thugesses was pretty low on membership. So, the fact that the rug dealer shooter *and* Conner's attacker were both women was too much of a coincidence. They had to be one and the same. So, this seemed to be the state of play. Someone, or some group of people, was trying to stir up trouble between the two rival rug gangs of New Meadows. The same party was not adverse to employing intimidation tactics on the police officers who were investigating the incidents. Yet they were also bright enough not to kill any cops, which would take this thing to a whole other level. It also seemed certain that the same people had managed to set up Bigby, a key link in the rug trade supply chain and who freelanced for both Sanguins and Scrips.

To achieve all this meant the guilty party had some serious resources behind them, particularly to frame Bigby and to pull off the stunt with Mila in the lock-up.

As Conner rounded a corner in one of the glitziest, most bedazzling sections of the Strip, an advertisement caught his eye, in the way that an advertisement does when it's flashing out from a one hundred and seventy foot video screen. Predictably it showed the immaculate forms of Rubeck and Winters plugging the forthcoming Igneous event. But this time it didn't draw Conner's attention. His mind was locked on the puzzle.

Some party wanted to mess with Scrips and Sanguins and didn't want a little thing like the law getting in the way. Indeed, they actively wanted to discourage the law from playing any part in it. All facts considered, it was as if there was a third rug trading gang operating on this turf. One that was immensely resourceful and powerful, and yet so well hidden or disguised that they could conduct their business under the noses of the police and remain completely unknown. They could sell directly to the public and yet rouse no suspicion.

Conner began inspecting every face on the street with distrust.

A third gang.

Trading on this very street.

Placing goods in the hands of knowing or unknowing consumers in exchange for cash.

So much cash that the gang would resort to extreme tactics to protect their market.

Whoever they were, they were ingenious.

And then Conner stopped dead as if he'd walked into an invisible wall, causing several cursing pedestrians to almost pile into the back of him. But he was aware of no one.

Sometimes the best place to hide is in plain sight.

He turned slowly. And looked up. And there was the answer, staring him in the face, flashing out at him from a one hundred and seventy foot video screen.

It was not a gang selling counterfeit gear.

It was a gang selling the real thing. The biggest gang of them all.

This was big, Conner concluded.

Too big for him alone.

PART FOUR

Answers

Twenty-Eight

Old Friend

Something about being back in New York set my disposition on edge. I stood apprehensively on the doorstep of the apartment, trying to summon the courage to announce my presence. It was not forthcoming. Eventually, more through fatigue than courage, I managed to raise a nervous finger to the doorbell.

There was some movement from inside, then the door opened. I let the moment bed in for a while before I released my feeble offering of an opening syllable.

'Hi.'

She didn't speak straight away. Still trying to shift herself into the right context. A context that I fitted into. Then finally she spoke.

'There's a face I didn't expect to see again.'

'Is it a face you're going to slam the door in?'

She shrugged. 'I don't think you're a bad person Aaron. Relationships break down. I understand that. I'm not going to judge.'

She was judging, of course, but it was nice of her to say that. Felicity was Gemma's best friend, a teacher at the same school. I knew her and her husband quite well back then. We used to spend time together. Meals and drinks and all that couply stuff.

I liked Felicity, she was a good sort. But then I would expect no less from a friend of Gemma; she had high standards – generally. I knew Felicity from the Gemma period of my life, post-death you might say. So when she saw me standing there it wasn't like she was seeing a ghost, but almost as good as. I hadn't seen her for the best part of ten years so I knew it would still be quite unexpected. But if there was anyone that could answer my questions it would be Felicity. She was there when I was not; when I left. Gemma would have confided in her.

'Do you mind if I come in? I need to talk to you about something.'

Felicity beckoned me in and shut the door behind us. She did the whole hospitable offering of hot beverages but I declined; just wanted to get on with it. But I wasn't so rude as not to do the small-talk bit. Actually, that's being overly-harsh on myself. I was genuinely interested.

'How's Trent?'

'He's good. He'll be sorry he missed you.'

I smiled. I studied the family portrait on the mantelpiece: Felicity, Trent and two young children. 'Two little ones then?' I enquired.

'Not so little now; five and seven. Jim and Beth.'

It genuinely made me feel good to know they were doing well.

'So, what's going on?' Felicity put to me as she took her place on the sofa.

I sat down in an armchair facing her.

'It's about Pearle.'

'*Pearle*?' Felicity was taken aback a little by this. She wouldn't have expected me to know anything about

Pearle. 'What about her?'

'I'm not entirely sure yet. What can you tell me about her?'

'Well, she wasn't planned. The guy she was with was a bit of a jerk and he soon vanished when Gemma fell pregnant.' Felicity's eyes darted off to one side in recollection. 'Pearle was ... different.'

'How so?'

'Well, to begin with, when she was very young, it seemed like she was a bit withdrawn or slow or something. But it wasn't that at all. She was confused.'

'At what?'

'At why we were lying to her.'

'Lying?'

'In the way adults do when kids are first getting to grips with language. Virtually everything adults say is nonsense. Most of it is either fiction or downright lies. Like "Oh, do you think teddy is hungry?". And all the tooth fairy and Easter bunny and Santa Claus stuff. Anyway, this confused Pearle, even at the age of three. Not because she knew this stuff wasn't real, but because she knew we were lying to her.'

I listened silently.

'After a while it got better. By the time she was five, she understood the subtle difference between fiction and lies. She understood the role played by fairytales and make-believe. That's what five-year-olds are good at after all. So she played along, and things were much easier. But one thing was still true...'

'What?'

'You couldn't ever fool her.'

This was all sounding familiar.

'But you want to know what the weirdest thing was?'

'Go on.'

'Gemma said she took after you.'

I didn't look as surprised as Felicity expected me to. I didn't understand it but I'd seen this coming. I nodded slowly. What I'd just heard had utterly confirmed one thing: I had no clue what was going on.

'This was what you'd come to hear wasn't it?' Felicity asked. 'How did you know?'

It was my turn to speak.

'When Gemma and Pearle got the virus I came to see her. I spoke to her just before she lost consciousness. She said that Pearle had my eyes. She seemed really concerned that I knew this fact, but I didn't know why. I didn't realise this was what she meant.' I thought for a moment before my next question. 'Did she have any idea as to how this could make any sense?'

Felicity shook her head. 'No. At least, not as far as I know. Eventually, she went to one of those new-fangled companies that sequence people's genomes. She spoke to someone there, but I don't know what she found out. It was just before ... you know.'

'Do you know who she spoke to?'

'Well, she emailed me a link to the company website one day. Hold on, I'll dig it out.'

Felicity stood up and left the room. A few minutes later she returned with a print-out.

'Here. This was the place, GenieTec. And this was the guy she spoke to, Dr Venton.'

'Thanks.' I studied the print-out quickly. The GenieTec office was in New York.

'I guess you know where you're going next.'

I stood. 'Yeah, guess I do.'

'Say hi to Trent for me,' I said as we walked to the

door. Then I turned to Felicity, feeling that I owed her something. A lot in fact. 'Listen ... I'm glad you were ... you know ... there for her. I...'

Felicity saw me struggling. 'Ten years have passed Aaron. There's nothing more to say.'

I nodded, feeling like I'd failed, but being relieved all the same. She was right; there was nothing I could say. I turned to leave and it was Felicity's turn to speak up.

'Aaron.'

I stopped and turned back.

'You talk about Gemma like she's dead.'

She was right. But it was just my fucked-up way of dealing with things.

'She's in a coma. Her doctors say it's unlikely she'll ever wake up. And if she does, she'll probably have severe brain damage. So in every other sense of the word she *is* dead. She's not part of this world any more. I just hope she's part of a better one.'

And I left.

I didn't waste any time in heading over to the GenieTec sales office – the New York transportation system took care of wasting it for me. The office was on the ninth floor of a Manhattan sky-rise. I took the elevator up and as I pushed through the frosted glass doors of the office I was almost dazzled by the gleaming perfection of its interior. Anything that couldn't be made out of glass was coloured white, including the sharp-lined attire of the woman behind the desk. I felt like I'd soiled the place just by being there in my non-white garments. This image was presumably intended to imbue a sense of purity and wholesomeness. Maybe they felt that decking it out like the Pearly Gates would allay any fears of potential customers who were concerned that using this technology was acting against God's very will. I didn't let God's will trouble me overly. I had my own agenda.

The neatly turned out woman was the only person in the room. She didn't wait for me to approach but came around to greet me with a shake of the hand.

'Hello sir. How can I help?' she asked, showing off her remarkably white teeth.

'I need to speak to Dr Venton.'

'Are you a current client?'

'No.'

'Would you like me to go through the levels of service we provide?' She turned toward her desk and indicated for me to take a seat.

'No,' I said firmly, not moving. Clearly, she was the well-polished sales interface to this firm and I didn't have time to parry her sound-bites all day. 'Listen,' I said sternly. 'This is in connection with the death of a previous client. I can't say any more. I'm sure you wouldn't wish me to say any more. Unless you want to go on record for the company?' I leaned forward. 'I really think it's best if I speak directly with Dr Venton.'

'Umm, this is just a sales office,' she explained apologetically. 'All of our experts work out of our labs in Mountain View, California.'

Silicon Valley, how clichéd of this most modern of companies.

'And, I'm afraid,' she continued worryingly, 'Dr Venton himself is at conferences in Europe all this week and next.'

I sighed. I was willing to travel to the west coast but I wasn't going on a geneticist hunt across the Atlantic.

'Have you got a mobile number for him?'

'Err...'

She did, of course, but I knew she wouldn't be allowed to dish it out willy-nilly.

'Email address, maybe?' I offered in a bout of benevolence, not bearing to watch her squirm any longer. She perked up a little. She fetched a business card from her desk and handed it over. It was semi-opaque plastic with the funky little logo you'd expect from a start-up genetics company; plus the name and email address of Dr Venton.

'Thanks for your help,' I said with a smile and turned to leave. Then stopped. 'Oh, almost forgot,' I said as I began fumbling in my pockets. 'Can you put these on ice or whatever it is you need to do with them; and forward them to Dr Venton.' I pulled out two plastic containers and held them to her. 'Sorry, I don't know how this thing works so I did one of each.'

The poor woman looked unsure what to say as I offered her two small pots containing samples of my blood and urine. Eventually, she managed one word.

'Spit.'

'Pardon?'

She collected herself. 'Sorry, I mean, saliva. We just need a sample of your saliva.'

'Oh, I see. Well, I'm sure these will do.' I dumped them in her hands and started to walk away.

'Are they your samples?'

'Yes,' I said over my shoulder.

'I thought this was about an existing client,' she called after me. 'Do you want to be sequenced too?'

'I'll explain in my email to the doctor. Just make sure he gets them. Thanks.'

And I was gone.

I got a plane back to New Meadows. During the flight, whilst the guy next to me slept on my shoulder, I became aware of just how complicated things were becoming, especially for a guy that really should have such a simple life. I felt that by this stage everything should be coming together nicely, but everything really wasn't. In fact, everything was diverging at an alarming rate. I had now collected another insurmountable conundrum. Gemma's daughter seemed to exhibit at least some of my skills. This was entirely implausible for two very considerable reasons.

Firstly, Pearle was not my daughter. Trust me, this was an impossibility of gestation.

Secondly, my skills are self-taught through years of obsessive study and practice. So it's not like anyone could inherit them anyway.

If there is one lesson I have learnt during my life that's worth remembering it is this: if a whole bunch of weird things happen, then they are usually all related. After all, weird things, by definition, are not run-of-the-mill. They are rare, uncommon. Two weird things might just be a coincidence. But the more that occur, the more likely it becomes that they all stem from the same cause. I'd lost count of how many weird things had now happened.

Whilst I waited for Venton's return, there wasn't anything else to do but head back to New Meadows. It's curious in a way that I actually left with the intention of returning. Normally, when I needed or decided to travel somewhere, I just moved on; but this time I didn't even check out of my hotel room.

I knew why this was. There was someone in New Meadows who I could talk to about all this shit. And at the same time there was someone who offered me a distraction when I needed it. I was indulging myself, it was true. It totally violated my rules of conduct, my modus operandi. But maybe I was just tired of playing that game.

Twenty-Nine

Intentions

Karla and I took a trip to Spain – it's about halfway up the New Meadows Strip, on the left. There aren't many really nice places to hang out in New Meadows, but out the back of this hotel it was quite pleasant. I'm no expert in Spanish history but as far as attention to detail goes, it appears the creators of this resort really went to town – well, a mock Catalonian village, in fact.

There was a chapel, a green, some aged knotted trees, and a set of gravelly boules courts, bustling with old men. Overseeing the proceedings were further elderly gentlemen sitting on a fake-old stone wall under the shade of a eucalyptus tree. They had golden leathery faces and gnarled walking sticks, and looked like they'd been sitting there a hundred years. I know from a previous encounter that these men didn't even speak English, and they cast suspicious eyes over passers-by, just like *real* locals. In fact, they seemed so authentic I'm pretty certain they weren't tourists at all but stooges shipped in from Spain by the resort owners – or deepest Central America at least.

On the far side of the square there was a whitewashed stone building that served as a local tapas bar. Inside the bar the walls were bare stone with random splotches of green paint. Irregular wooden benches were surrounded by chairs that were nothing more than lumps of tree trunk. Yet another great stab at authenticity. Hell, it wouldn't surprise me to discover that the owners had shipped the whole village in from Spain – brick-by-brick, person-by-person. That's how much money was behind these places.

We got ourselves a drink from the bar and ordered a number of dishes, then made our way to a table outside. Karla seemed a little uneasy, on-edge, though I admit I still found it difficult to judge with her.

The food came presented on plates and dishes carved from wood, and was lovingly doused in artery-narrowing quantities of salt. The dishes consisted largely of seafood. The kind of seafood with more legs than I usually like my fish to boast, but which Karla seemed to prefer. The wine, though, we both enjoyed equally as we sipped it from white ceramic bowls.

Karla was quiet and as we ate in silence I casually glanced around the setting, studying people as is my wont. After we'd polished off most of the food and two carafes of sangria, Karla spoke up.

'Hey, you know what I found out when you were away? Something that might interest you.'

'What?'

'I shouldn't really tell you. It's a bit hush-hush.'

'Go on. You've got to now.'

She leaned in conspiratorially.

'Well, my employer, Igneous, want to start a campaign to make counterfeiting anti-social and get establishments to ban it. Like smoking is anti-social in every other state, here they want to make wearing fake goods anti-social.'

I snorted incredulously.

'You may laugh, but they don't pay your wages.'

'Fair comment. So how do they intend to enforce that?'

'Well, I got talking to someone quite high up in the company after a seminar they made us go to this week. He's supposedly an expert in anti-counterfeiting measures. He was saying that whatever method they devise to ensure the authenticity of an item, the counterfeiters soon catch up. Whether it's holograms in the label, or fabric watermarking, or electronic ID tags. The crooks are never far behind. They're just too good. So, he was saying, there's only one way forward. There is only one foolproof method of identifying whether a garment is fake. A method the counterfeiters can never foil.'

'And what is that?'

'Ask the person who's wearing it.'

'Huh?'

'The industry is totally locked down these days. The stores don't sell the fake stuff. So if you buy it, you know about it. It's always cheap, and it's always on the street.'

'Sure, the owners know what they're wearing, but they don't shout about it. That would cancel out the street cred effect.'

'Right. That's why I thought you'd be interested.'

'Go on,' I said with suspicious eyes.

Karla did a quick double take of her surroundings to ensure no one was in earshot.

'Okay, so the idea is to get establishments like BlueJay on board and ban fake goods. Make it just another part of the dress code. That would mean that anyone trying to pass through the doors covertly flouting the rule is going to be self-conscious about it. So, all they need is some mechanism for detecting this. Preferably, remotely and non-intrusively.'

She was right. I was starting to get interested.

'If they could get this off the ground,' she continued, 'and the idea spreads, then imagine the impact. If you know you might set off alarm bells by strolling into your favourite restaurant with your knock-off Gucci handbag, then...'

'Then you might just have to buy an *actual* Gucci handbag.'

'Right. It could kill the rug trade dead. But it all hinges on implementing a successful detection system. Such a system would be worth literally billions of dollars to these companies.'

'And do they know how to create such a system?'

'No.' She sipped from her glass with a twinkle in her eye. 'But I know a man who could help.' She smiled broadly at me.

She was right of course. In fact, somewhere buried deep in the internet was the encrypted source code for a system that was a long way toward the goal they sought – the Hide system that I had been instrumental in developing ... and destroying.

I didn't say anything to Karla, and her reciprocated silence was a conspicuous departure from her usual chatty self. She excused herself from the table to visit the bathroom and I watched as she walked away. I couldn't read her, not like other people. She didn't exhibit micro-expressions; her skin didn't flush when she lied or was embarrassed; she showed no involuntary responses to my prompts. But on a larger scale, I could see she was behaving differently. She seemed withdrawn: less eager to talk, yet less comfortable in silence. Only during the last conversation did she become animated.

Something was beginning to fall into place in my mind, though I hadn't been aware anything was out of place. I tapped my finger slowly on the edge of the table as if timing the revolutions of my thoughts.

And then ... bang.

It dropped.

As subtly as from the Eiffel Tower through the Crystal Palace, the penny dropped and it smashed my world to pieces.

I could avoid the nature of the facts no longer. Whatever innocent context I tried to bludgeon them into they just wouldn't fit. There was no escaping the reality. Suddenly this sunny day had turned dark and I had a feeling things weren't going to get brighter anytime soon. My mind raced. There was no winner so it just kept on racing. Trying to reach the finish line. Trying to fathom how everything fitted together.

As Karla returned, I stood up, clumsily knocking my chair over backwards. I stumbled back a couple of paces. Heads darted in my direction but I was looking only at Karla's face, a mixture of stricken guilt and terror. For a moment our eyes met in a knowing embrace and then I fled. It was time to walk away once more. But this time I knew that what I was leaving behind I could never hope to find again.

The sun beat down casting a short shadow beneath me. It was the kind of stagnant heat that you only find inland. It was like swimming through warm treacle. My feet scuffed the sandy path as I trudged along, my mind burning with anguished thoughts. Everything was falling into place.

A voice called from behind me.

'If you keep walking, you'll never know.'

I stopped, my head stooped, a tear rolling down my cheek. I didn't want this. I heard footsteps rush up behind me and felt a hand on my shoulder.

'*I* didn't know,' Karla said softly but with urgency.

I shrugged off her hand and turned around angrily. 'What do you mean you didn't know?' I shouted. 'How could you not know?'

Karla spoke with exigency.

'They didn't tell me, not till last week, when you were away. However they figured out that you couldn't read me, they did it without me knowing. They couldn't risk telling me anything, because if they were wrong you'd know as soon as you met me.'

She took a small step toward me and softened her tone.

'Listen. I *do* work for Igneous, and BlueJay is my patch. That's the truth. Somehow they knew that you wouldn't be able to read me and somehow they got you there. But I don't know how. They knew that if they were right you'd spot me and be intrigued by me and want to know me.' She let out a deep breath. 'They watched us for weeks until they were sure that it was safe to approach me.'

My mind was still too fuzzed to understand whether that made any difference.

'And *then* you deceived me!' I snapped with crisp anger.

Karla said nothing for a moment, her face showing guilt and sadness.

'They offered me something I couldn't refuse,' she said softly with a saddening of her eyes.

And as I wondered what sum of money that might have been, what remuneration package it might have included, I wasn't expecting to hear her next word.

'You.'

She saw the perplexity woven into my brow. 'Don't be so surprised,' she continued, as simultaneously a tear rolled down her cheek and she gave an amused smile. 'God, for the most fascinating guy I've ever met you've got a damned low opinion of yourself.'

I was confused. I didn't know what to say, didn't know what to think. Whatever she said, could I trust her now? I shook my head and threw my arms in the air in frustration.

'How the hell am I supposed to trust someone who's in bed with my enemy?'

'Fucking hell Aaron. You know what these people can be like. I was scared of them. I'm sorry,' she pleaded. 'All I wanted was to be with you.' She grabbed my wrists and held them by my side.

I shook my head in disbelief. I paused, trying to assimilate this new knowledge with all the puzzles of my past.

'But, they –'

What started as a shout tailed off into nothing, as a chain of fireworks started to go off in my head. I pulled myself from Karla's grasp. I stumbled to a nearby wall, sat and hung my head in my hands.

The line of hundred-year-old men sitting at the other end of the wall gazed with mere quiet intrigue, nothing more. They'd seen a lot in their time. A slightly insane foreigner was hardly going to interest them if they'd seen wars come and go.

I had to think this one through. My brain was throbbing so hard it felt like it was going to burst out of my skull.

There was more to this. Much more.

I took a moment to focus and decided I needed to play at being on her side; needed to ask more questions. I wouldn't know whether her answers were the truth, but I'd know what they were and that might be useful enough.

'So, is anyone watching us?'

'No, I don't think so. Too risky. They wouldn't want to chance you spotting them.'

'And this whole story about wanting to detect people wearing fake goods. Is that true?'

'As far as I know, I really think it is.'

'And what is your brief?'

'To recruit you, basically.'

'And to the best of your knowledge, who are you working for?'

She shrugged. 'Igneous, like I say. Why?'

I declined to answer. The information bus had just turned down a one way street.

'Okay, Karla. I don't see that we have any choice but to play along, until I can figure a way out of this.'

'Why do you always need a way out?'

'Trust me, we need a way out.'

I took her hand and led her out of Hotel España. 'Come on, big smile.'

Of course, I could just disappear again. But that would leave Karla in a very dicey situation. Having failed her mission, having blown her cover, she was no longer of any use. That didn't sound like a good thing to be, with the guys she was dealing with. Big Business could be just as nasty as Big Crime.

But it wasn't just Karla.

I was starting to get mighty pissed off with there being so many questions and so few answers. Every fact uncovered seemed to bring with it three more mysteries.

The latest one being: how did Igneous know about me? And how come I ended up exactly where they needed me?

I knew exactly where the answer lay: at the bottom of a bottle of beer, or maybe the second bottle ... or the eighth.

Outside the hotel we parted company. Karla headed for the shops; I headed off the Strip for the darkest, quietest bar I could find. I knew I'd hit the jackpot when I found a sign pointing down a flight of steps to a basement entrance. No windows was exactly how many I needed right now.

When I stepped through the door I was somewhat surprised by the ambience on the other side. It wasn't quite the flea pit I had imagined. It was actually quite pleasant. It was just a no-messing joint. No gimmicks, no themes. Not for the tourists. The locals had to have somewhere to drink without having to remortgage their house for each round.

I got myself a beer and took a booth in the corner. I was already slightly under the influence of lunchtime sangria, but I was thinking clear enough.

Have you ever noticed that you think differently at different times of the day? Have you ever had a really big decision to make and noticed that in the morning you'll always fall on one side of the fence – the safer, easier, less scary side – and last thing at night you'll think the opposite? That's because inside you there is more than just one person. You have multiple personalities that manifest themselves under different circumstances. Mostly, the belief systems of these different yous are reasonably well aligned. They are variations on a theme. If you need to make a decision then it's best to tap into them all to get a consensus. But if you need to execute a specific task, then you need to enlist the right one for the job. Getting *in the zone* is what they call it.

My specific task right now was puzzle solving. For this I needed clear wits and focused acumen. In short, I needed to be *sober*. With this in mind non-alcoholic beverages were the order of the day.

But I was also really hacked off, so I just got a slice of lime with my beer and hoped that would equate.

I started to locate all the pieces of the puzzle and laid them about at the front of my mind. I knew I didn't have all the pieces but I hoped I had enough. I had to take this thing back to basics. Look at things logically.

Fact number one: someone wanted my skills.

There were really only three people that knew about my skills. Properly knew.

One was in a coma, so I figured she didn't have anything to do with this.

The second was Karla. She claimed that Igneous had manipulated her and orchestrated our meeting; and however many questions this threw up, I felt I had no choice but to believe her. The alternative was to believe that the only person in the world I couldn't read – the only person who could probe me for information – just happened to work for a company that desperately wanted to develop a system just like Hide. That was too much of a coincidence.

So that left the third alternative, the third entity that knew all about me: my previous employers. And one person in particular who had the necessary resources and bitterness to put me through all this. The man I'd screwed over. The man I'd died to hide from. Zack Bayliss.

To the best of my knowledge to-date I was invisible to Bayliss. Even if he didn't buy that I was dead, I assumed he had long since lost track of me. It made me feel nauseous just considering that this might not be the case. But as I reluctantly allowed myself to accept this conclusion, one big chunk of the conundrum fell into place.

At this point, if you're keeping up, you should be wondering how Zack Bayliss, a deputy director of national intelligence, is in any way associated with high fashion? That's because you don't know what I know. Not about Bayliss, just about the intelligence service in general. Let me give you some background.

When I was inside, it was well known that the agency set up and ran lots of businesses as fronts, such as garages, shops, cafés and so forth. It was often easier to get these places into the flow of underground knowledge than an individual agent. It was easier to convince the underworld that these businesses were legitimately illegitimate if you see what I mean.

It was also well known that some of these fronts became successful businesses in their own right. They actually turned a decent profit, paid for themselves. This was not surprising considering the power of their backers. There were indeed fairly well accepted rumours that some of these businesses were now large corporations being run by the agency to fund its own operations.

It was all entirely plausible.

And now something seemed undoubtable.

BlueJay, one of the trendiest bar chains in the world, was a wholly-owned subsidiary of the US secret services. Why BlueJay and not Igneous itself? Well, I'll get to that later.

I traced my mind back over the events of recent weeks to figure out how they'd led me here. There were some subtleties I was missing, I knew that, but one thing was abundantly clear. I was part of such an audacious display of human manipulation that I might almost have been impressed – if I weren't so busy being extremely ticked off.

I realised now that I'd always been a little complacent – conceited even – about the fact that I could not be influenced. I was always confident that if anyone tried to con me face-to-face, I'd know about it. But I underestimated the lengths to which some people might go when a lot of money was involved; or maybe just for kicks.

So ... how was I brought here?

The bits I know are as follows. Someone in New Meadows was arrested for Pearle's murder to draw me out. Burch was set up for this purpose and of course did not know why. So when I spoke to him I wouldn't learn anything. A meeting was set up at BlueJay between Burch and some rug dealers – who also knew nothing about what was really going on. Then, once I was there, Karla just had to be sat down in front of me to see if I took the bait; see if their theory was right about her – that I couldn't read her.

And that was one of the two things that was troubling me most right now. How had they known that Karla was someone who I wouldn't be able to read? Even if they had a theory about how to *make* someone unreadable, how had they tested it?

The other major hole in my theory was that Bayliss never knew that Gemma, and so Pearle, was connected to me. If he had he would have shown up at our door much sooner – after I'd gone AWOL.

I finished up my beer and headed out onto the street, not knowing where I was going next. I didn't want to tell Karla who I thought was behind all of this. Just in case. If things got dicey he could easily terminate both of us. Though he'd probably spare me. Like he always had done. Who knows how many times he had found me before; how many times he had tried to manipulate me into helping his cause?

Maybe he didn't actually want my help per se. Maybe he wanted me to know he was getting close, to see if the Hide system was still about; make me paranoid enough to go dig it out of the internet and move it someplace else.

As I was following this line of internal questioning, my thoughts got rudely interrupted by the annoying tones of a mobile phone erupting. After silently cursing the kind of idiots who enjoy excessively loud phone alerts so much that they don't even bother to act on them, I decided to answer it. Still wasn't used to that happening.

I examined the now silent phone. It was a message from our friendly geneticist Dr Venton. He was back in town.

This town.

Thirty

Fragments

An hour later I was in a departmental common room at New Meadows University.

'Thanks for coming here,' I said as I shook the geneticist's hand.

'No trouble,' he said. 'I am affiliated with the college here, so I need to pay the occasional visit. Besides, I really wanted to speak to you.'

'That sounds ... intriguing'.

Dr Venton was not one of those eccentric boffin types with limited personal skills and even more limited dress sense. He was one of those kinds of boffins with astute business nous; who sets up spin-off companies, plays tennis at the weekends and is worth an absolute mint.

He wore chinos and a blue shirt open at the collar, and sported a trendy pair of frameless spectacles. He was balding, but knew how to wear it – in such a way to accompany his neatly clipped silver-black beard. In short, he was the kind of old guy I wanted to be when I grew up.

After sourcing mugs of coffee, we took up comfy seats set by a large full-height window, looking out over a campus lawn, as neatly clipped as Venton's beard. Then it was time to get down to the nitty-gritty.

'You'd like to know why Gemma came to see us?'

Venton enquired.

'I would.'

He nodded slowly. 'Normally, of course, we wouldn't divulge any information about another client. But this is ... a special case. This is a case about which ... I think you ought to know.'

'Good. That makes things ... easier.'

He smoothed his beard as if contemplating where to begin. Finally, he figured it out. 'You may be aware of the service offered by GenieTec. That is, to advise our clients of their relative risks with respect to a range of genetically-determined diseases, such that they might adjust their lifestyle accordingly. This is what people normally seek from us. Gemma, however, visited us for a rather different reason. She came to us with a specific puzzle to solve.' He took a sip from his mug. 'And in fact, she was turned away at first by one of our more closed-minded associates. But fortunately he told me about her and I got in contact.'

'Why was she turned away?'

'Because what she was suggesting just wasn't within the realms of possibility according to my associate. According to science as we know it, even.'

'But it was possible to you?'

'The thing about the logical minds of most scientists is their desire to fit things into boxes. But nature just doesn't fit into boxes. Our current simplistic understanding of anything is only ever a best guess until we uncover a whole other layer of complexity that we just aren't expecting. Time and time again, throughout history, this has proven to be the case. Things,' he paused for effect, 'are never as simple as they appear. More coffee?'

'No. Thanks.'

Venton crossed the room to the coffee jug simmering on a hotplate.

'Allow me to digress for a moment,' he said as he topped up his mug, 'and tell you a little story that illustrates the point. A completely true story. Back in the nineties a woman, who we shall call Sara, needed a kidney transplant. Her family was tested to see if they were suitable donors. Sara was hoping for good news, but what she received was something entirely unbelievable instead. She was told that two of her three sons were *not her children*. Two of her sons shared no genetic material with their mother, even though she conceived them naturally with her husband, who was confirmed as the father.'

I thought about the logistics of this for a moment as Venton retook his seat opposite me.

'That's impossible, surely?' I concluded.

'Exactly how most experts saw it at the time. One specialist even suggested that Sara had sneaked off for secret fertility treatment with donor eggs; as this seemed more plausible than accepting there were things he did not understand. Fortunately, a more open-minded doctor vowed to solve the conundrum and after two years' hard graft she finally cracked it.'

'Go on.'

'It turned out that Sara was what we call a chimera, a mixture of two different people; two non-identical twins that had fused in the womb and grown into a single individual. As a result she had two distinct sets of genes.'

'Fascinating,' I said genuinely. 'But how does this relate to Gemma?'

'Well, the first point of the story is that things are not always as straightforward as high-school biology lessons might make out. And the case of Sara is actually not so weird compared to some of the other stuff that's happened during our evolution.'

Venton stood up and moved over to a whiteboard on the wall.

'You've heard of Darwin's tree of life, right?'

He started sketching a tree, root at the top and branching into two at each level down.

'This is the nice neat way it's supposed to work. Species splitting off to form neat branches like this. But sometimes life has other ideas.'

He labelled one of the bottom leaf nodes 'cow' and another 'snake'. Then he switched pens to red and drew a line between the two in a sweeping motion across the board.

'Every cow on this planet has a fragment of DNA inherited from the snake family; a fragment which didn't exist until long after any common ancestor.' He circled the common ancestor in red as he said it.

'How?' I asked as I knew I was supposed to.

'No one really knows for sure. Quite possibly a virus. Viruses are shovelling genetic material between species all the time, which makes a complete mess of this tree. In fact it makes it not a tree at all.' He rapidly drew lines criss-crossing between the branches. 'But let's get back to you. The point is, DNA moves in mysterious ways ... sometimes.'

Venton topped up his coffee mug just to be sure it didn't run dangerously low and then sat down again, leaning forward this time.

'You probably know what I'm going to say,' he put to

me.

'Say it anyway.'

'When we analysed Pearle's genetic makeup, we identified a fragment of genetic material that did not come from her mother or her father. And thanks to your recent visit, I can now confirm –'

'That it comes from me.'

'Right.'

'But how?'

'Well, like the case with Sara, this is where the weird stuff comes in.'

'Hit me.'

'It had us stumped for quite some time. I enlisted the insights of a friend of mine and we pored over Gemma's medical history. As you well know, there was one very significant medical event she experienced in her past, and this was what helped us finally crack it. It's all related to a phenomenon called microchimerism.'

I looked at him blankly.

'Apologies for the crash course in genetics, but you kind of need to know.'

'Don't worry, I can take it.'

'Good. During pregnancy, a mother and child's biological systems are theoretically separate, but some rogue cells do pass between both, and can survive for many years in the other person. This is called microchimerism. It's a more dilute version of Sara who we talked about earlier. But there's one remarkable and beautiful twist to this natural feature of pregnancy.'

'Go on.'

'It was shown in a number of experiments – on mice of course – that during severe trauma, stem cells from the foetus can be employed to repair damage to the *mother's* brain. There's no reason to assume that this doesn't happen in humans also.'

He let me think about this for a moment. The significant medical event in Gemma's history Venton had referred to was when she almost died carrying our child. I started to realise where this was going.

'What are you saying?' I asked.

'I'm saying that when Gemma was fighting for her life, pregnant with your child; when blood was draining from her body and millions of brain cells were dying by the second; an ancient survival mechanism kicked in. Stem cells from the unborn child were pumped into Gemma's body to repair her brain. The child you lost ... sacrificed her own life to save her mother's. So that's how your genetic material was still present in Gemma when Pearle was born.'

I stood and walked to the window. I'm a smart guy and I understood all this, but my mind was on the verge of exploding, which was unfortunate considering what was still to come.

'So, that's all remarkable and exciting stuff. It's maybe a million-to-one, maybe unique. But my guess is that it's one of those things that happens quite a lot, like with Sara, but no one ever really notices. Why would they? Normally it would not manifest in any noticeable way. And that brings us to the next bit. As I'm sure you are already starting to realise, the next bit is twilight zone. Or it's a Nobel prize waiting to be won.' Venton twinkled. That explained why he was so keen to see me.

Okay, timeout for a moment. What Venton had just explained to me was, at least, very unlikely. What he was about to explain was extremely unlikely. The fact that they came together and occurred to me was therefore, who knows, billions-to-one. This may be leading you to doubt the credibility of my story, but don't forget that there are seven billion people on the planet, and the reason you are reading *my* story is because something incredible happened to *me*. If you read a story about someone who hit the lottery jackpot *twice* then you may say it was ridiculous. But let me tell you, this actually happened too. Not only that, but the lucky couple in question, after playing for seventeen years, managed to hit the jackpot of two different lotto games on the *same* day. The odds? A mere twenty-four-trillion-to-one. Look it up.

The point is this, crazy shit happens. Take it from me. Just don't bet on it.

Venton continued with his story. 'It was quite fortunate that Gemma chose our company to visit. Else this may never have been uncovered.'

'Why?'

'Because the rogue fragment of DNA we found, the one that came from you, contains no recognised genes.'

'I don't follow.'

'Only two percent of human DNA is considered to do anything useful – the remaining, often called junk DNA. This two percent is made up of discrete sections – or genes – which each play some role in determining an individual's traits: height, eye colour, flappy earlobes and so on. Companies like ours only analyse a client's genes. In fact, they generally only analyse a small subset of genes; those known to play a role in certain diseases. People don't generally need to get their DNA sequenced to discover their eye colour. They have mirrors for that.'

'So, how are you different?'

'Well, the normal service we offer is not. But part of

our research is to identify new gene candidates amongst the junk DNA. We do that by comparing sections of human DNA to that found in animals with common ancestors. If we discover that a particular fragment of DNA is present in both humans and say orang-utans, then it is likely that it has been preserved for a reason – that it performs some function, either now or in our recent history. So, when Gemma came along with her little conundrum we took a look at these gene candidates as well. That's how we discovered a variant that hadn't come from either of her parents. But there was something else significant as well.'

'What was that?'

'These new genes in Pearle were active – at least that's my guess.'

'Active?'

'Yes. We contain in our makeup a whole bunch of archaic genetic material, accumulated throughout our entire evolutionary history. In every cell of your body you still harbour genetic coding for all the features of your ancestors – fins, scales, tails, everything. As you've probably noticed you don't have fins and that's because these genes were deactivated long ago – and many of them are now degraded beyond any use. Sometimes they get reactivated accidentally, resulting in babies born with tails or webbed fingers or body fur. They are known as atavisms. And sometimes they are reactivated on purpose. Nothing you do in your life can ever affect your genes, but you *can* alter their expression – turn them on and off. And what's more, this alteration can persist over generations.'

Venton paused as if to check I was keeping up.

'Still with you,' I confirmed.

'Good, because this has mind-blowing potential that few people are aware of. Environmental conditions experienced by a parent can affect the expression of genes in their offspring. The significance would be lost on most, but what we are talking about here is non-genetic evolution; dare I say it, non-*Darwinian* evolution. And it's very real. For example, it has been shown, that even the *grand*children of malnourished wartime mothers tended to be smaller than average, even if they were healthy and well fed. The malnourished mother altered the expression of the genes she passed on so that her descendents would be smaller and so more likely to survive in times of short food supply.

'Admittedly, there is no known mechanism for such a thing to occur between *father* and child, but, hell, it has, so let's ignore that for a moment. The point is this: something happened to *you* over your life that has affected the expression of a number of your genes. And through some almost-miracle, this was passed on to Pearle.' He paused for a change in gear. 'Gemma recognised some trait in Pearle that she was sure came from you. That was why she came to us. That was her conundrum. Do you know what that trait was?'

I was caught slightly off-guard by the question.

'Do you not?' I was getting so used to him knowing so much about me that I was surprised when his knowledge ran dry.

'Gemma didn't want to tell me.'

I nodded. She was a good girl.

I decided not to tell him either.

I thanked the good doctor and said I would be in touch. He wasn't so keen to see me leave before agreeing to assist in his research, but right now academic discovery was not top of my agenda. A stiff drink was.

I thought about what Venton had told me, particularly the last bit. My obsessive behaviour had actually affected the expression of some of my genes. As I gather, *this* was not so remarkable – it's an established mechanism. What was interesting, though, was that the genes in question existed at all.

Although, deep down, I think I had known this all along. I was not aware of the mechanism, but I had always felt that through my learning I was reawakening an ancient skill. The fact is that before humans developed spoken language we had communicated for millennia by other means; by body language and facial expressions and scent. I had found the key to turn this skill back on. The pertinent question was why it was ever switched off.

As luck would have it, I have a theory about this that I prepared earlier. I'd thought about it many times before. It goes something like this. When humans surpassed a certain level of intelligence, when complex societies and cultures began to form, there was one ability that rapidly became essential to their continued success: deception. Whether you wish to accept it or not, deception is an integral and necessary part of our world. Lies are requisite to harmonious existence. Not to mention all our relationships, as they are built not on trust but on private thoughts and well-intentioned, well-judged fibs.

Consider a woman working on the reception of a large corporation. She has recently split up with her long-term boyfriend and as a result is desperately unhappy and confused. A client arrives at her desk. How should the woman greet him? By pouring her heart out all over his business suit? Or with a cheery good-morning and the exchange of meaningless pleasantries?

Masking our true emotions at appropriate times is fundamental to the success of a complex, civilised culture. Deception greases the wheels of our society.

That is why it was imperative to discard any ability to see through it.

To offer a documented proof of principle, it has been shown that people with a certain unsightly skin disorder are less able to identify subtle signs of disgust in other people. This is a specific adaptation in people with the disease to protect their emotions from hurtful reactions to their appearance. It is an extreme example of the general evolutional trend to mute our abilities to read other people. The trend that I had personally reversed.

As my mind reeled, I was suddenly aware that I was now holding the final piece of the puzzle. The picture was now complete, and it was this final piece that bore the greatest revelation. Such a monumental revelation that I was in no doubt that from this point forward my life would never be the same.

It was now obvious.

Pearle was still alive.

Thirty-One

Reclaimed Innocence

I knocked on the door and Karla opened it. I didn't even wait to be inside. I drew a photograph from my inside pocket and held it up to her.

'Do you recognise this girl?' I asked.

Karla studied the picture I was holding.

'Yes, actually,' she proclaimed eventually. 'Yes, I do. Who is it?'

I stepped into the apartment and Karla closed the door behind me.

'She is who they used to test you.'

Karla looked confused. I looked at her straight and shared with her my recent monumental revelation.

It was a revelation that put a whole new spin on one specific detail that I had not considered relevant before: Gemma's illness. She contracted a variant of something called encephalitis lethargica. Most people will never have heard of it and I have a pretty hard time saying it. It is a devastating disease that swept through the world in the 1920s, resulting in the deaths of millions of people. The illness was commonly known as "sleepy sickness" because those that survived remained forever in a strange statue-like state. There have been no epidemics since, although there have been some very isolated cases.

Why is all this pertinent? Well, at the time, when I found out about Gemma, I did a lot of research into the illness, as you would expect of me. And now something from that research pinged back into my mind. When the US biological warfare programme ended back in the sixties, a viral form of encephalitis was revealed as one of the standardized biological weapons it had developed.

That was a different era. But the point is that the symptoms of encephalitis lethargica are desirable as a weapon. Maybe less so for mass warfare and more so for covert operations; for assassination or just incapacitation. What this led me to wonder was whether Gemma's illness was no accident after all. Rather that somebody just needed her out of the way for a few days to orchestrate Pearle's supposed death of the same disease, which presumably was all smoke and mirrors, all faked medical records after the fact. They didn't care how ill Gemma became; whether she lived or died even. They just needed it to look like no foul play was at hand, even to medical professionals, and especially to me when I came sniffing around. Otherwise, the game was over.

I didn't know how they found out about Pearle, or how they knew she was connected to me, but I figured I'd get to that bit sooner or later. Meanwhile I was agitated and fired up. I looked Karla in the eyes.

'Where did you meet her?'

'In Washington a few months ago. I was sent there on a course by my company.'

'I bet you were.'

Everything was pretty much cast iron now. I punched the wall with the base of my fist.

'God damn manipulating, murdering scumbags. This

ends now. It's time for someone else to be alive again. Me.'

I marched toward the door.

'Where are you going?'

'To get Pearle back.'

'No, Aaron, please.' She grabbed my arm. 'When they find out you know they'll have no use for me any more. I'm dead.' Her eyes were wide with fear.

She was right of course. I turned to her and took both her hands. Adrenalin was pumping through me fiercely, but I tried to calm myself for her sake.

'Listen, I'll be back by tomorrow. Get some things, go somewhere, and hang tight.'

'And then what? Be like you? Hide in the shadows for the rest of my life? I can't do that.'

'You won't need to. It's time for me to step out of the shadows. I have a plan. Trust me. Okay?'

I kissed her on the cheek. She attempted a nod. That was good enough for me.

Okay, so the plan was quite nascent. The objectives were very clear; it was just the method of getting to them that was a bit sketchy. Still, I was fairly confident it would come together when it needed to. I know from experience that as long as the requirements are unambiguous then the implementation will follow naturally.

First objective: Pearle.

I had a hunch as to where she might be. She was too valuable not to be somewhere secure. She would have to be within one of the agency's facilities. The only one I knew of within the vicinity of the DARPA offices was an unofficial medical research facility a few blocks down the street from the HQ. This place has a number of permanent residents, for various reasons I won't go into. Suffice to say it has living quarters. Its purpose also nicely aligned with what they would be doing with Pearle. So it seemed like a good bet. But at the same time it was kind of a rash assumption.

What I should have done – what I'd *always* done before – was stand back, take some time, and figure this one out without making a scene; without rippling the pond. But I was done with that. My anger had manifested into acute impatience. From this point forward, every obstacle standing in my way was going to be swiftly addressed with a twenty-pound sledgehammer.

Aaron Braunn was back on the map.

And he didn't care who knew about it.

In line with this newly-endorsed no-messing approach, I had a cunning plan for confirming whether Pearle really was at the aforementioned medical facility...

I was going to walk in and take a look.

Those of you that have watched too many spy films will be under the impression that these high security establishments use fingerprints and retinal scans and the like to control access. Well on the most part they don't. They use contactless security passes like pretty much any office in the world these days. Security passes that hang conveniently about the body of their owner, even when they are out in the street.

It was nearing the end of the working day when I started loitering – expertly of course – down the street from the facility, and soon people began filing out through the security gates. I eye-balled a couple of guys who were heavily engrossed in conversation and who looked pretty senior – well they had grey hair which was good enough.

Sliding one of their passes out of its little holder as I brushed past them in the street was like taking candy from a baby – a sleeping baby, that didn't even like candy. In fact, it was so easy I picked a few more up over the next twenty minutes or so. I didn't want to spend any longer because I needed to crack on before any of my targets noticed and actually bothered to report their badge stolen.

Casually, I walked up to the front gate and with a soft beep walked straight through. Ditto for the doors at the main entrance. The passes would all have different levels of access, allowing passage through different parts of the building. I didn't want to be seen fumbling with them at every door, but fortunately, as they employed radio ID tags, I could just stack them all together and wave them past each sensor nonchalantly.

I wasn't sure exactly where I was heading, but I was pretty sure I needed to get to the west side of the complex. I didn't want to hang around in the lobby too long, so I headed right, through some turnstiles with Perspex barriers that swished apart at the presentation of my card stack.

The corridor I found myself in led to a dead-end with a few elevators in it. I called an elevator and when it arrived some passengers stepped out. I flashed my best I-belong-here smile and stepped in to replace them.

I went to the second floor, stepped out and headed right. The corridor was flanked by offices and labs filled with people looking important. I kept my eyes forward and my walk brisk. At the end of the corridor it went two ways. I picked one but it didn't take me anywhere useful so I doubled back and headed the other way.

I'd only been here once before, a long time ago, but something felt right. I passed through a couple more restricted doors with my passes then hit another. This one was different. This one decided to be an awkward bugger and beeped a red light at me – if that was possible. I tried again to the same response. None of my passes had access to this area.

The door sported a small obfuscated window with a grid of reinforcing wires. I didn't know what was behind it but the mere fact that this was a door that didn't want to let me past meant it was a door I wanted to be on the other side of. Me being rather like a cat in that respect. And rather like a cat was exactly how I was going to get through it.

I didn't want to look conspicuous fumbling at the door so I turned around and headed back the other way. This was a big place, with lots of people working in it. I was banking on the fact that everybody did not know everybody else.

I noticed an empty office, stepped in and grabbed a selection of large files off the shelf. Then I found somewhere a couple of doors down to lurk; a small kitchen facility. I busied myself pretending to make a coffee and with every person that passed by I stuck my head out to see if they were heading for my door. After a few minutes I spied a likely candidate – a youngish guy in fairly trendy gear. Quickly, I put one of my pilfered identity cards in my mouth and bundled the large pile of files into my arms. I trotted up behind the potential door opener, scuffing my feet a little to alert him to my presence.

When the man reached the door he was only too pleased to hold it open for me. I thanked him as best I could through pursed lips and made a conscious choice to head whichever way he wasn't; left, if you're interested.

The thing about human nature is that on the most part we strive to avoid confrontation and we hate to offend strangers. This is especially true in the US I have found. As such, even in a high security building you will almost never be challenged, as long as you seem to fit in. Consequently you can tailgate through a door 95 percent of the time, unharassed.

I was getting close now. This wing was less officey and more labby. There were examination rooms and hospital beds. I kept on walking. Eventually, I came to another security door, but this time I was on the inside. There was no detector to swipe a pass in front of, just a release button.

I knew that if I went through this door I wouldn't be able to come back the same way; not without doing the cat thing again. But it was past core hours now and people were thinning out. I had no choice. I just had to keep covering ground until I reached what I was looking for. I pressed the button and pushed the door open for a quick look. The corridor beyond was carpeted rather than tiled. It had a different smell about it. This was it.

I walked through and let the door click shut behind me. I could have jammed it open but that would have set off an alarm after a short time. And I didn't want any alarms going off. Not yet.

I was getting close now; I could sense it. I walked with greater purpose; glancing sideways through every open door. There was a large kitchen, a lounge room with a TV; a recreation room with a pool table. Then there was a slightly more open-plan area, followed by another corridor flanked with closed doors. The sleeping quarters.

There were a few people around, but not too many. They were here for different reasons. Some were night staff for the subjects next door; some were subjects themselves. I just had to find one in particular.

Suddenly, I was nervous, terrified. Not of being caught, but of meeting Pearle. I hadn't really considered before what a terrible ordeal she must have been through. Her mum falling ill, then herself being snatched away to live in this clinical place; prodded and probed by creepy scientists. And now another strange man was going to burst in and take her away again. I hadn't really realised that this could be the biggest hurdle of all. Screaming children were a real nightmare to conceal when escaping from high-security government establishments. That was a hurdle I wasn't going to be able to deal with by sledgehammer. I was just going to have to handle it when I got to it; which was suddenly very close.

As I rounded the corner there was the noise of a TV. The sound had that frantic high pitched quality of children's entertainment. It was coming from a room with its door slightly ajar. The door had a child's drawing taped to it featuring the stick-figures and rainbow of a typical child's masterpiece. I stopped walking. I took a quiet step forward and peeked through the gap in the door. The room was decked out like a nursery. Brightly muralled walls, mounds of cuddly toys. The TV was on the far side, cartoon images casting a colourful glow into the room.

And there in the middle, perched crossed-legged on a large red beanbag, was a young girl with fair hair.

I steeled myself. How not to become the bogeyman. I took a deep silent breath through my nostrils then pushed the door open. It made a tiny sound. The girl didn't jump; she just turned her head.

'Hi,' I said in a soft voice almost lost in the sounds from the TV.

I remained outside the door as the girl studied me for a moment. Then she wiggled herself free of the beanbag, placing the teddy she had been hugging back to continue watching TV, and walked toward me.

'Hello,' she said.

I crouched down to her level and regarded her face. It was flat and emotionless but I could see Gemma in every muscle. My eyes welled up heavily. This was almost too hard to take.

'This is...' I tried to talk smoothly, but my voice crackled. 'This is hard to explain. You don't know who I am but...' I wasn't sure how to finish the sentence.

I didn't need to.

'I trust you,' said Pearle. 'You're a good man.' And with that she threw her arms around my neck. I took her up into my arms and hugged her tight; and it felt like I'd suddenly found a part of me I never knew was missing. I cried a little; I took in the moment. Then it was back to business. It had to be.

'It's time to go,' I said. 'We don't have much time.' I dropped Pearle to the ground. 'Do you have any things you need to bring?'

Pearle rushed back into the room and scooped up teddy and squished him lovingly into a pink rucksack, then scooted round the room gathering a few more pieces. Just as she was ready to go she stopped and turned.

'Oh, I need to leave a note.'

She tore a piece of paper from a scrap book on the floor and selected a crayon from a tin; then she started to write in slow considered letters: 'Thank you Miss Polly xxx'. When she was done she dropped the crayon and ran to the door.

'Who's Miss Polly?' I asked.

'She's a good lady,' said Pearle.

It was time to get out. There was almost certainly a quicker way out than the way I'd come in but I didn't know what it was and I couldn't risk getting stuck anywhere. I figured that the best plan was to retrace my steps. I knew the route and there was only one door I couldn't get through – and I could deal with that.

We approached the TV room. There was one guy in there alone. I crouched down to Pearle and whispered.

'Go wait for me by the door,' I said pointing down the corridor, and she skipped off silently.

I entered the TV room.

'Hey man,' I said casually. The guy looked up. 'I've gone and left my pass in the lab.' I hoiked a thumb over my shoulder. 'Don't suppose I could grab yours for a minute?'

'Umm,' pointed out the man eloquently and narrowed his eyes. 'Do you...'

Oh enough already with the cross-examination, I thought, and I punched him in the face and grabbed his pass. I had given him ample opportunity to be helpful.

I legged it down the corridor, grabbed Pearle's hand and barged through the door.

'Okay,' I said to Pearle, 'we need to be brisk without

running.' My brisk was slightly faster than hers and she ended up being dragged along beside me.

Fortunately, the hospital area was quiet, as this was the place where Pearle was most likely to be recognised. We got through there; out the other side; along all the corridors; past all the offices; down the elevator.

Sure we got a whole host of strange looks; mostly because people didn't expect to see a kid in their workplace. They knew something didn't quite sit right. But they were all off home to their other-halves and widescreen TVs, and they really didn't want to make it their problem.

Then, in the lobby, just as we were about to exit the last door, there was a voice from behind us.

'Hey,' it called.

I turned. I was a packet of nerves on the inside but wrapped in a perfectly-composed exterior. The owner of the voice was a portly older man with grey thinning hair.

'Hey, you dropped your pass.'

Time froze. It was lying on the floor about a third of the way from him to me. Don't be a nice guy, I prayed, but it was too late. He was already stooping down to retrieve it for me.

I stepped quickly toward him and reached out a hand as he came up. He smiled at me, looked me straight in the eye, and handed over the pass without even glancing at it.

'Thanks,' I said with a smile.

He ruffled the hair of Pearle on his way past and was gone. I looked down at the pass in my hand. Jane Harleson. Long blonde hair. I wouldn't have pulled it off.

I took Pearle by the hand and we were out. We got to

my rental car and hit the road, speeding out of the state, marginally below the speed limit.

The next part of the plan couldn't involve Pearle, but equally I wasn't ready to say goodbye to her again so soon, for however brief a time. So, just as soon as we were out of the state, I treated her to a milkshake at a roadside diner. I'm pretty partial to a vanilla shake myself.

We got a seat near the window and Pearle pulled her teddy out of her bag and sat him up on the table.

'So, what's your bear's name?' I asked.

'Brown,' she said. 'Mummy named him.'

I nodded and smiled for a moment. 'I like that name,' I said, and not just because etiquette dictated.

'Why?' Pearle asked.

I wasn't expecting the question, but then, of course, she knew I had a reason for liking the name, other than just courtesy.

'It's my name too,' I explained. 'My last name means Brown in a different language.'

She seemed to like this answer. She reached up and held the bear's hand out to me.

'Brown, meet Mr Brown.' She giggled as I shook the little stuffed paw.

'Nice to meet you Brown. Thanks for taking care of Miss Pearle for me.' Then I leaned toward Pearle and cupped a hand beside my mouth. 'We forgot to get him a milkshake,' I whispered to her with mock concern.

'It's okay,' she whispered back as she prodded his belly softly. 'He's on a diet.'

We shared a laugh at Brown's calorific expense, and I was relieved to see that the girl seemed remarkably emotionally-intact considering her ordeal.

I glanced around the diner and my mind suddenly leapt back to the day Gemma and I were reunited after I'd gone into hiding. Pearle was studying me and she stopped slurping her drink to ask a question.

'Why are you sad?'

My instinct was to respond by saying I wasn't sad. That's what one is supposed to do with a six-year-old kid. But not with this one. The rules didn't apply. I had to answer straight. I suddenly realised how annoying I must be to other people sometimes.

'I miss your mum,' I said honestly. I'd explained about her mum on the drive here. It was the first topic we covered. It wasn't one that I was going to be able to avoid.

Pearle's eyes fell to the table glumly. 'Me too.'

'I know,' I said without promising that everything would be okay, and I reached across and put a hand on hers. How *are* you supposed to reassure a kid you can't lie to? This, in case you were in any doubt, sucked big time.

As the poor kid began to cry she hopped down from her chair, ran around the table and threw her arms around me. I pulled her up onto my lap, brought teddy Brown into the embrace and we held each other until it was time to go.

A few hours later I dropped Pearle off with surrogate auntie Felicity. I hadn't expected to be back there so soon. I gave her some money to take Pearle to the mall to get some new clothes and stuff; and I apologised profusely for not being able to stick around.

I kissed Pearle on the forehead and told her I'd be back. She knew I wasn't certain about this fact but she didn't say anything.

It was time for the next part of the plan.

I didn't know what it was yet.

But it was probably dangerous.

Thirty-Two

Sleep

I stepped off the plane in New Meadows feeling better than I had in a long, long time. Things were coming together. I knew I still had a long way to go to end this thing, but for the first time it felt feasible.

But, just as I was emerging from the departure gate in what could almost be considered a Good Mood, I realised something terrifying. It leapt up at me so unexpectedly that I actually blasphemed out loud.

The thing is, I'd become too accustomed to looking out for myself, the invisible man. It was easy for me to walk away from trouble. But now I was responsible for someone else. Multiple someone elses. Pearle was as safe with Felicity as I could make her right now. At the very least I knew she was too valuable for any harm to come to her.

Someone else was not.

I pulled out my phone hastily, almost sending it toppling to the ground. I punched a few buttons to make a call, and eventually it began to ring. And ring. After an excruciating period of time – like almost three rings – Karla picked up.

'Where are you?' I barked over her greeting.

'How specific do you want me to be?'

'Very specific and very quick.' I was racing through

the airport terminal by this point, barging impolitely past anything in my way. Most of those things happened to be children or old people, but it couldn't be helped.

'I'm in the lobby of the Cairo Hotel,' Karla replied.

'Good. Noticed any suspicious guys lurking around, checking you out?'

'Aaron, I don't mean to offend your gender, but there's always guys checking me out. That's what they do.'

I'd never thought of that before. How do women know when they're being tailed? I made a mental note to think about it another time, if I needed to.

'Okay, fair point. Listen carefully.'

'What's going on?'

'Just drive.' I'd reached the exit of the airport and was stealing a cab off an innocent family. The driver wasn't too keen on queue jumpers but I'd snapped at him with enough menace to get him moving.

'What?' said Karla.

'Not you,' I said to her. 'The Strip,' I barked at the driver. 'Not you,' I said to Karla again. 'Right, listen.'

'Me?'

'Yes. Start moving. Get somewhere with a lot of people. The hotel casino will do. You moving?'

'Yes, I'm moving. What's going on?'

I ignored the question for a second time. 'I'm going to hang up in a minute, so listen carefully to what you have to do. First, take a note of my number, then dump your phone. No, better still, plant it on someone. In their pocket or bag or whatever. Got that?'

'Yes, but...'

'Then get the hell out of there, as far away as possible, but stay where there's lots of people. Then get hold of another phone. Steal one, borrow one, buy one if you must. Whatever you're comfortable with, but do it quick. Then call me. Okay?'

'No, not really. What's happening?'

'Just a precaution. I'm hanging up now. Know what you're doing?'

'Yes.'

'Good. Do it.'

Click.

This was more than a precaution. It was a necessity. I just hoped it was enough. I didn't wish to impugn Karla's talents, of which she had many, but she was worthless to them now – to Zack Bayliss or whoever was running this show – now that I'd blown her cover. And that meant she was a corndog within 24 hours, unless we could hide her. I hoped she was right in believing that she wasn't under constant surveillance. The fact that she was still alive supported this. But if she was hanging onto her cell phone it wouldn't be long before they pin-pointed her.

I hung around on the Strip waiting for a call. I wished I'd arranged a back-up rendezvous, so I'd know where to head next, but there hadn't been time for that.

It was 45 minutes before my phone leapt into life and I thrust it to my ear.

'Karla?'

'Aaron.' She sounded out of breath and scared.

'What's happening?'

'I was in a store getting a phone. It took quite a while and there was this guy in there hanging around and when I left he left at the same time.' Her words were rushed and falling into each other.

'Is he still behind you?'

'I don't ... think so.' Her voice was laboured. It sounded like she was running.

'Where are you?'

'I'm on Henson Street, just off –' there was a pause '– just off Eighth Avenue.'

'I told you to stay with the crowds.' I started running.

'I know.' She sounded like she was about to break down. 'But there were so many people. I couldn't move fast enough. I just wanted to get away.' She started to sob.

'That's okay,' I reassured. But it wasn't. 'You did a good job. Stay on the phone.'

People scattered as I barged through them. Those that didn't scatter quick enough got helped along by me. It was slow going. Running through a crowd of tourists is like running through ... well nothing else. Nothing is as frustrating as trying to get somewhere quick through a dense throng of contrary sightseers.

I needed to make it across the highway – six lanes of traffic. The nearside was almost stationary so I weaved through it to a tune of angry horns.

As luck would have it this stretch of road had a barrier between the carriageways to stop idiots like me trying to cross the street. I vaulted it clumsily and tumbled headlong into the next carriageway. A taxi screeched almost to a halt but I was gone before the driver's fist was even out of the window.

Now there were more people to plough through. I decided I preferred cars. I made a bunch more enemies as I shoved them aside one-by-one. When I was through the worst of it I brought my phone back to my ear.

'Karla? You okay?'

'I think there's a man behind me now.' She was

crying with fear. 'I'm scared Aaron.'

'I know. I'm coming. Just keep moving. Try to head back to the Strip.'

'Okay, I'm taking Ninth.'

I was almost at Seventh, two blocks away – two blocks of milling idiots in my way.

'Good. When you get to the end, head south, okay? That's left. Take a left onto the Strip. I'm coming the other way.'

I had to make a snap calculation as to whether it would be quicker to head up Seventh, along Henson, and back down Ninth. But I figured I wouldn't make it there before Karla popped out on the Strip and then I'd lose her in the crowd. But I was making really bad progress as it was. There was only one thing for it. I jumped into the road. I was heading up the right-hand side of the road, so the traffic was going my way, only slightly faster than walking pace, but much quicker than threading myself through the tourists.

Car horns blared from behind me but I zoned them out and just kept running. Three minutes later I was on the corner of Ninth Avenue. I spun round looking for Karla.

'Where are you?' I shouted down the phone.

'I'm inside.'

'Inside where?'

'I saw someone coming out of a building so ducked inside. There's a keypad on the door so I thought it would be safer than out there.'

I didn't express my concern that she'd caged herself. I just started to race up Ninth.

'Karla, which building?'

'I'm going to take the elevator up now.'

'No, wait! Karla? Which building? Which door?'

Silence.

The signal couldn't make it out the elevator shaft.

Damn it to hell.

I desperately looked up at every building, but it could've been any one. I stopped mid-way along the street and waited for the call to re-connect.

Then ... in a way that in no respect aided my predicament ... I got shot in the arm.

That was really bloody annoying, to be frank.

The phone in my hand flew out of my grip and went clattering across the paving slabs. Instinctively, I grabbed my busted arm, before the training kicked in and I went for my gun instead. But before I had even begun to turn around the shooter was on my back – literally. He'd been ordered not to kill me. I knew that because I was still alive. This was classed as me lucking out.

As we toppled to the floor I threw my head backwards catching him on the nose. Then I launched an elbow into his stomach and arched my back to throw him off me.

He may have had more recent training on his side, but I had something else. I was driven. And not by anger, by something stronger. Fear. Fear for someone else's life.

The man on the floor went for the gun he had naïvely re-holstered for his non-lethal attack. I kicked his wrist as hard as I could, then with my one good arm I grabbed his collar and pulled him to a sitting position and slammed him against the wall. Then I stood back and pulled my weapon.

I agonised for what seemed like an age over whether to put a bullet through his head; whether he'd become page one of my People I've Killed scrapbook. But I managed to suppress the urge, to temper my rage. After all, he was not the bad guy. He was just another puppet.

'You're not worth it,' I proclaimed and shot him lower down instead. 'Arm for an arm,' I added and left him sobbing. Wimp.

I scooped up his firearm and then my phone. The casing of the latter was cracked but it seemed to be functioning.

'Karla?' I shouted into it.

'I'm on the fifth floor of the cream-coloured apartment building.' It was a hushed voice now. She wasn't moving anymore.

I looked up. I could see it ahead.

'Stay there,' I instructed.

Then a terrifying thought struck me. My assailant had come from behind me. Karla was being chased from the other direction.

There was another man.

He must be in the building.

'Karla, don't say another word. Hide best you can. I'm coming up.'

When I got to the entrance I punched the call button for every apartment in the block. After a few seconds I got about three incoherent responses at once.

'Police. Open the door. This is an emergency.'

The door buzzed and I pushed through it.

I put the phone to my ear. I could hear breathing. That was good. Breathing is an attribute I like in all my favourite people.

I couldn't take the lift. It would not afford me the covert entrance I desired; what with the big glowing number counting down my arrival; not to mention the irritating voice announcements.

With one arm straight by my side and the other holding a phone to my ear, progress was slow.

Too slow.

When I got to the second floor I heard a muffled noise from the earpiece which sounded like it came from Karla; then a noise that sound like her phone being dropped, followed by some talking that I couldn't make out.

Then there was a noise I didn't need a phone for.

Two bangs.

Very loud bangs of unmistakeable nature.

Then...

Silence.

My heart leapt into my throat then sank through the pit of my stomach. I snapped the phone shut and pounded up the remaining steps.

As I lurched round the corner at the bottom of one flight of steps there was a woman coming the other way and I almost crashed straight through her. But a last minute lurch minimised the impact to a glance. And although physically I didn't even break step, for the briefest of moments my mind was in a different place and time. Somewhere distant and fragrant. Somewhere calm. But then, just as quickly, I was back, pounding up the steps.

All thoughts of a covert entry discarded, I burst onto the fifth floor and pelted around the corridor.

Then a sight I didn't want to see.

Two bodies on the floor.

And lots of blood.

I rushed toward them. A quick assessment of the gunman determined that he was no longer a threat. A gun lay on the floor which I kicked away. Then I collapsed to my knees in front of Karla, lying in an ever-growing pool of blood from a gunshot wound to her stomach.

'Karla!' I shouted.

She was still alive and conscious.

A couple of people were now standing shocked in the hallway, looking on.

'Call nine-one-one,' I instructed aggressively. 'Now!'

I turned to Karla. She was lying awkwardly, but I didn't want to move her too much. I rested her head on my knee and pressed down on her wound with my hand. She didn't complain. In fact, she looked at me and smiled.

'Can you hear me, Karla?'

'Yes,' she said. 'I'm ... fine.' And she smiled again. 'Tired, but fine.'

She wasn't fine. She was experiencing a sense of euphoria due to the lack of oxygen.

'Good,' I said. 'We'll have you sorted soon.'

'I need to tell you something, Aaron. Before I go to sleep.'

'No sleep,' I said sternly.

She made a relaxed groaning sound like someone who'd just slipped into a comfy bed.

'No sleep,' I repeated. 'What did you need to tell me?'

She seemed to have a wave of alertness wash over her. She began to talk more lucidly.

'I need to tell you something. Something that you're too dumb to figure out for yourself. In case I don't get another chance.'

'Shhh, you will.'

'No, just listen. I care for you, Aaron. And I wish things could've been different. But we both know the truth. There has only ever been one person in this world for you. One person you will ever love.'

'Don't. She's ... she's gone.' I stopped and bowed my head.

'Aaron, listen.' She took two deep breaths. 'You have spent ... your entire life ... learning to communicate with people subconsciously.' Her voice was laboured again. Each word was a challenge. She swallowed and a trickle of blood seeped out of her nose. 'If there is anyone ... anyone in this world ... anyone who can bring her back ... it is ... *you*.'

'No,' I said crying and shaking my head. 'No.'

'Yes.' Karla insisted. She was finding it increasingly difficult to form her words now. But she had a determination to finish what she'd started. To say what she had to say to me. 'Aaron ... she's been waiting for you ... waiting for you to wake her up.' She was panting now as if she'd just run up a flight of stairs. 'Don't leave her there ... all alone in her bed.' She coughed a little and took a struggled breath which gargled and rasped. Then she looked at me with dewy eyes. And it was a look I recognised from years before; one that would accompany her final words. 'Go wake her up, Aaron,' she whispered almost imperceptibly. 'For me.' And she closed her eyes.

'No!' I screamed.

A large group of people were gathered around us now, staring in horror. I checked her pulse and breathing. Neither were present.

With one good arm and one busted, I attempted to administer CPR. But my mind was fuzzy. I couldn't remember the ratios of compressions to ventilation. Was it ten-to-one? Fifteen-to-two? I couldn't remember!

Someone placed a hand on my shoulder to pull me away, to take over, but I shrugged them off. I wiped the streaming tears from my face with my sleeve, and started pumping her chest and breathing into her lungs.

Compress. Breathe.

Compress. Breathe.

'Where's the goddamn ambulance?' I cried out as I kept fighting for her.

Compress. Breathe.

Compress. Breathe.

Kept trying to kiss life into her lungs; pump life through her veins. For just long enough. Just until the paramedics arrived. To bring her back.

Compress. Breathe.

Compress. Breathe.

I couldn't feel the pain in my arm. Only in my heart. A deep dark fissure opening up.

Compress. Breathe.

Compress. Breathe.

Finally, the paramedics arrived. They fought through the crowd of bystanders. At first they were gentle with me, but I wasn't going to stop. Like a possessed metronome, I kept on with my rhythmic routine...

Compress. Breathe.

Compress. Breathe.

After a moment one of the paramedics forcefully dragged me off her.

'No,' I cried, and reached out before slumping back against a wall. I'd lost a lot more of my own blood than I'd realised. And as the pain came flooding in, I collapsed unconscious to the floor.

With Karla.

We both went to sleep. Both let dreams take us away from the nightmares of this world.

But only one of us woke up again.

Thirty-Three

Last Respect

I sat in the secluded corner of a bar nursing my n^{th} shot of local rum of the morning; my head drooped, my eyes bloodshot and my stubble into its eighth day of growth. I was numb.

Somewhere it had gone wrong.

I was supposed to *help* people. Make things *better*. Save the world. Clearly, I had messed up. This was evident in the fact that I was drinking rum at ten in the morning waiting for the funeral of yet another woman I had let down.

I took a deep breath and drew in the aromatic Colombian air. As I did I realised this was where my mind had been for that fleeting, and apparently portentous, moment a week ago, when I was rushing up the building to save Karla. A smell from somewhere had reminded me of this place. And now, here I was.

And I was seriously considering where my life was going from here. After this day. The puppeteers in this play were still pulling their strings. Manipulating and killing for the sake of their pockets. There was still an assassin walking the streets of New Meadows who I was increasingly sure was all Bayliss' doing as well.

That was the big picture. And I could live with that, if

I had to. If it was just me who had to. But Pearle changed everything. It was not just me any more. She was still with Felicity. I'd called her up every day and sent her postcards too. But I was acutely aware that she would not be safe there forever. In fact, would not be safe there for very much longer at all. But I was also aware that I could not hide both of us. Especially because I still didn't understand how Bayliss had known I was still alive; how he had known how to get to me.

Somehow, this had to end. I had to end it. Increasingly, it was looking like there was only one way to do that.

But first, I had to pay my last respects.

The shade of the tree I stood beneath offered little relief from the heat as I stood back and I watched the ceremony from afar. None of the mourners knew me. And I didn't much want to introduce myself.

It was a small gathering, everyone clad in black from head to toe, standing motionless like a flock of grieving ravens. I couldn't hear the words, just murmurs carried on the sticky air. They wouldn't mean anything to me anyway. Not for the language, but for the sentiment. I am not a religious man. I knew there was no onward journey for Karla now. She had reached the end of the road. She was gone. That was that.

This was another moment in my life when I wished I could *believe*; when I longed for a sign. But none was forthcoming. So, I just stood and mourned patiently in the starkness of my atheistic reality.

Eventually, the service drew to a close and the mourners began to drift away, into a different version of the world from the one they knew before; one with one less person in it.

As I watched, waiting for my moment to step forward, I realised I was not alone in my detached role. I was not the only person observing these proceedings from afar. There was another. A woman, half obscured by a broad tree trunk some way away. She was too distant for me to make out her face, but somehow I was drawn to her. Maybe it was her scent, carried on the tropical air. The woman looked up and saw that I was studying her, and she turned away casually.

I started walking after her briskly. I didn't know why, but I knew I had to. As I got close enough for her to sense me, she neither quickened her pace nor turned to face me. She just kept walking.

When I was within arm's reach, I put a hand out to touch her shoulder but then I pulled back. Instead I just uttered one word as we walked almost side-by-side.

'Hello?'

The woman stopped. I stopped.

And slowly she turned.

And when her eyes met mine, I froze. My heart raced and my breath quickened, but I couldn't move. She didn't speak. She gave me the time I needed, and eventually, I uttered her name.

'Maria.'

The suggestion of a smile flickered at the corner of her mouth.

'Hi.'

The feelings that coursed through my body were beyond intense, in the way that Jupiter is beyond the end of the road. My emotions for Maria at the time were so deep and conflicting as to make me dizzy, but now I had to try to fit her and all of that intensity into now, into my current reality, and my brain was melting at the prospect. The pieces that my mind was attempting to synchronise were chaotically orbiting my head, but eventually one fell into view.

'You...' I began with minimal eloquence '...were there last week. It was you I passed in the stairwell.' I took a step back. 'You killed Karla.'

Maria didn't respond. She was always somewhat reserved.

It answered a question from a long time ago. Where do assassins of the drug trade go when the drug trade is no more? They go in search of its successor.

But it raised a lot more questions. Firstly, the obvious one, why was she here? Assassins don't generally attend the funerals of their victims. The question manifested on my brow and Maria instinctively interpreted it.

'Karla,' she said flatly, 'was my sister'.

I felt my jaw drop open, my eyes grow wide. This wasn't possible. Karla and Maria were two streams of my life that were entirely unconnected. Or so I thought.

'There's something I'm missing,' I said as I felt my own eyes narrow.

'Yes, there is,' she confirmed and then followed it with a word I wasn't expecting. 'Aaron.'

She knew my name, my real name. But when did she know it?

Maria began to walk away.

'I don't have to answer to you,' she said as I chased after her. 'You walked out on me. I'm just doing what I do. Being what I am. What my country made me. I can't be anything else.'

'You work for Bayliss, right?' I probed.

'I don't know who I work for. They're not so careless

as to let me know.'

'But you're hired to kill rug dealers right? On both sides. Both gangs.'

She shrugged. It was a yes.

'Then let me tell you something. You are working for US intelligence, sponsored by the big corp clothing industry.'

'Money's just as green, wherever it comes from.'

She stopped walking, bowed her head and released a big sigh. Her whole demeanour changed. Her hard shell softened a little as if she could no longer maintain the pretence of nonchalance. Then she looked up at me with sad eyes.

'I missed you when you went,' she said softly, just as I'd remembered her. 'I knew you wouldn't stay, but I missed you all the same. And...'

I saw her compassion trying to break out, but it was sealed in too deep, beneath the thick callus that had formed to protect her raw emotions. It is hard to believe that people like Maria can exist in the world, a blend of such extreme traits. But they do exist. Places that are as messed up as this, give rise to messed up people. It's sad. As I watched her I began to feel my own conflicting emotions bubbling inside again

'I didn't kill Karla,' she said. 'I was trying to *save* her. My employers are not so dumb as to hire me to kill my own sister. They sent a couple of goons instead. I tried to save her but I didn't get there in time. I don't really know what happened. It was a blur. There were two shots. Then there were two people on the floor and I wasn't one of them. I just had to get out of there as quick as I could.'

Most people looking at her face would have seen a

stony expression, hardened through many years of horrific sights. But her face wasn't completely empty of emotion. Not to me.

'I'm sorry I got you messed up in all of this,' she said.

'Got me messed up in it?'

This was the bit I was missing. Maria took a seat on a nearby bench and I sat down next to her. We were silent for a while, as if allowing the ripples in the universe to settle again. Finally, she spoke.

'Okay, it makes no odds now. You may as well know.' She turned toward me just a little. 'You remember that night soon after we met, you wanted to try some cocaine?'

'Remember? I didn't remember anything for two days after that night.'

'No, I figured as much. You were out of it. You told me a lot of things about yourself.'

'What things?'

'Your real name. Who you were running away from. Why you were in Colombia.'

'Oh shit.' I dropped my head into my hands.

I knew that when I had visited this country, I had been at my lowest ebb. I had been reckless. I didn't much care for the world and I only had myself to risk. But I always believed I'd got away with it.

I came here to seek out bad people and make them ... not bad. Make them dead. But meeting Maria had made me realise that even if you think you are doing it for the right reasons – like she had to begin with – taking a life changes you. You cross a threshold and you can never cross back; never return to who you were. And in the end you just end up adding another bad person to the world.

I was surprised that after she had learnt about my purpose in her country – in her bed – it hadn't changed her attitude toward me. If it had, I would have seen it. But she was a complex character.

I was conceited and complacent back then. I over-estimated my abilities. It was dumb to believe I wouldn't be affected by mind-altering drugs just like everyone else. And when I came out the other side I figured I had got away with it. I was too short-sighted to imagine there could exist a person who lived so much for the moment that discovering her lover had sought her out as a victim barely fazed her. If it had I would have known.

'When my contracts dried up here,' Maria continued, 'I went to the US. I had every intention of getting out of this game. I went to New Meadows to get in touch with Karla. I actually got as far as standing outside her apartment block on more than one occasion, but I just couldn't go through with it in the end. To cut a long story short, I ended up getting involved with a bad crowd again, Scrips. Started doing some work for them. My sister was working for the real McCoy and I was working for the fakers. There was an ironic symmetry to that which summed up our entire relationship.'

Maria sat quietly for a moment, seemingly lost in her own sombre thoughts. I was still no nearer understanding how all this fitted together, but I gave Maria the time she needed and eventually she continued.

'Unfortunately, female assassins are not as commonplace in the US as they are down here, so I kind of stood out. And one day, thanks to some idiot gang member, I got arrested. I was looking at some serious time or even the chair so I had to cut a deal. I didn't want to grass any of my current clients so all I could think of was you. I mentioned your name and who you had worked for and the next thing I know a smart suit turns up called Smith. They're all called Smith I think. They got me off and then I had to do what they said.' She shrugged. 'But it paid well.'

'And what did you tell them about me?'

'Not a lot really. Told them you were alive. I think that was enough. I don't know how they found you or drew you out. Apart from getting orders to do their dirty work, including messing with some cops, the next I heard was that they wanted to know about Karla. I didn't even know they knew who my sister was, but these guys have very big databases.'

'Yeah,' I confirmed, 'they do.'

'They asked me all sorts of odd questions about what she was like as a child and stuff. I don't know what that was about, but I was in their hands. I couldn't say no.'

We sat in silence for some time after that, until we both concluded that there was no more to say.

'Thanks for talking,' I said.

'No worries – anything I can do to help shut them down. I don't hold any allegiance to them now, not after Karla, and they know that. It's not safe for me back there any more.'

I stood to leave. 'Sorry for your loss,' I said, forgetting that loss of life to her was like loss of car keys. I hoped that for her sister at least she would feel something more.

'Thanks,' she said, and I think she did.

It may seem odd that I was walking away. This woman had been killing rug dealers for money on the streets of New Meadows on a weekly basis. But in all honesty, I just didn't know what else to do. However hard I tried I just couldn't ever think of Maria as anything other than a victim.

After a few steps, I turned back to her.

'Just one more question.'

'Sure.'

'That night, when you found out why I had come here. Why didn't you kill me?'

She didn't need to consider the question.

'I hadn't been paid to,' she stated matter-of-factly.

I nodded and walked away. As well as mourning Karla that day, I mourned Maria's soul, which had been taken from her at such a young age.

Maybe it would be my turn to be mourned next.

It was time to face the music.

Thirty-Four

Uninvited

As I stood at the beginning of a long gravel driveway, contemplating my walk along it, I knew one thing. When the driveway ran out, so did my plan. When I reached the doorbell, everything from that point forward was improv.

A couple of days ago, I'd got in touch with an old hacker friend of mine who thought I was dead. After he was past the initial shock I asked him for a favour; asked him to dig out an address for me. He came through.

The address was that of Zack Bayliss. This was his nice little house in the suburbs. This was where the ending started. One way or another.

I tapped my holster and started walking.

The chime of the doorbell rang regally in the expanses of the house. Shortly, I heard footsteps. I studied the rhythm. It was a woman approaching. So, first improvised course of action: silence this person without any fuss.

Within a split second of the door being opened, the occupant was facing the other way with a hand clamped firmly over her mouth and a gun barrel pressed against her temple.

'Not a sound or things turn bad,' I whispered.

Another split second and she was cable-tied to a chair in the hall with duct tape over her mouth. Only then did I stand back and study my victim. Only then did I allow myself to acknowledge who this woman was. And I must admit I was shocked.

It appeared all those rumours back when I was at the agency were spot on. Ms Tanya Scarlett, Personal Assistant, was indeed providing some *very* personal assistance. As I briefly observed her struggles and grunts I noted that there was still something about her. Something that repulsed and attracted me at the same time. It was an indefinable quality and one I really didn't have time to try to pin down right now.

All I had to recognise was that Tanya being here did not change anything. I headed through the house feeling my way stealthily toward the lounge. Then there was a voice.

'Who is it honey?' it called. And I followed.

It was a big lounge. You could have had a decent sized game of lacrosse in the expanses between the furniture. It was decked out in white. A tasteful hide of something dead lay in front of a fireplace of grey-striated marble. And there in the centre was Bayliss, loafing on a white leather sofa the size of a family saloon with a scotch-on-the-rocks in one hand and a folded broadsheet in the other. The pleasure at meeting me in person for the first time was immediately evident in his greeting.

'What the fuck!' He sat up and pushed himself back into his chair as I strode across the room with a gun targeted at his ample forehead.

'Language!' I reproached as I stopped a few feet in front of him, revelling amid the fear in his eyes. 'Now, this ends here. And it ends in one of two ways. Either it ends with a high-velocity projectile and a long day scrubbing brain out of shag pile for your maid. Or it ends in a nice friendly chat. The choice is yours.'

And then he said something I really wasn't expecting. I mean, it totally knocked me for six.

'Who are you?' he asked.

'*What*?'

'Who the fuck are you?' He slowed it down this time to make sure I got it.

The really annoying thing was he wasn't lying. He really had no clue as to who I was, which was rather worrying because someone who had put so much effort into playing me over the last year or so, really should remember me.

I thought quickly – threw this new nugget of truth into the mix. I couldn't possibly have this all wrong, surely? All the pieces fitted together. It had to be right. There was no one else who knew about me from the start; knew about the Hide system. No one that had the power to fake deaths, kidnap children, frame murderers. There was no one else who could have played me like this, other than the very someone who was sitting right here in front of me.

Or someone sitting very close to him.

Then it came to me. And it should have come to me sooner, since uncovering the chief assassin in this game. In fact, my whole eye-opening experience with Maria should have taught me not to be so chauvinistically short-sighted in general.

'Stay there,' I said as I backed out of the room.

I poked my head into the corridor, looked at the woman tied helpless to a chair, and the pair of eyes that looked back told me everything.

The thing about PAs is that they have an awful lot of power, by proxy that is. They filter all communications, they pp signatures, they send out emails and letters on behalf of their superior. They can, if they are devious enough, take on the persona of whomever they are assisting, to their own ends. To make deals and issue commands. The extent to which this can be pulled off is probably severely limited in normal business, but ironically in the business of national security it is a different story. The nature of the commands issued by a man like Bayliss, do not get openly talked about at cocktail parties. So if Ms Scarlett wanted someone arrested, no questions asked; then no questions would be asked. Having said that, it was an extremely dangerous game, requiring nothing short of a mastermind.

A moment later we had a cosy little threesome in the living room. So to speak.

Now I was pointing the gun at Scarlett, and she was pointing her seething eyes back at me, and they had a depth of intelligence that was suddenly all too apparent.

'Want to tell the boss what you've been up to?' I suggested. She didn't like the suggestion; just kept those eyes trained on me.

'What the hell is going on here?' Bayliss piped up impatiently.

This new dynamic was all news to me and I hadn't had time to process it. I did some quick mental processing. Bayliss would definitely have known about the Hide system at the time; and whatever dodgy intentions were earmarked for it. He would also certainly know about BlueJay – that it was controlled by his agency. He may even know about the close underhand ties forged with Igneous. But it appeared he knew nothing about the recent meddlings in my life.

'You won't kill us,' Scarlett spat with vehemence.

'Why ever not?'

'You'd be on death row before you could spit at the judge.'

'A price worth paying just to ruin your sofa to be honest.'

'Why?' chipped in Bayliss as he leaned for his scotch with a not quite successful stab at nonchalance. My stab at kicking his wrist was wholly more successful. He winced and retracted his arm.

'Because she killed a friend of mine for a start. And she comatised my girlfriend.'

The accused thought about this for a moment, obviously coming to the same conclusion as me in that she wasn't touchable for so much as parking in the mother-and-child space at the grocery store.

'Your *ex*-girlfriend,' she quipped. 'You left her, remember?'

I slapped my forehead with my free hand. 'You're right. *Ex*-girlfriend. Well that's okay then. I'll get my coat.' Then I thrust the gun six-inches closer to her face and returned the menace to my tone. 'No fucking difference. They are both ex-people now and that's your doing.' I held my firm pose for a long moment then I eased off. I loosened my gun-touting wrist a little and nodded my head slowly. 'But you are right. Killing you wouldn't get me too far. I have other plans.' I didn't actually, but I was sure I would soon. 'First, though, as we're on such good terms, I want some answers.' I perched myself on the edge of the armchair opposite them both and leaned forward. 'How did you know I was alive?' I knew the answer to this of course, so it was a good control question.

Bayliss remained quiet. Odd considering what he was discovering about his mistress's handiwork. She didn't seem overly keen on responding either.

'Come on Tanya. Be nice. This shiny thing in my hand doesn't really give you an option.' I brought the gun in-line with her kneecap. 'And how far am I going to get with the information you give me, after I walk out of here and you press the panic button? A mile? Less? And who am I going to tell if I get further? You run the country. I don't even exist.' I leaned in. 'So, tell me, how did you know I was alive?'

She sighed. 'Okay, one of your former associates ID-ed you in an Indian Reservation casino.'

'Wrong.' Well-educated suggestion though. 'Stop testing my patience.'

She made an aggravated exhalation, but it was all for show. I got the clear impression that now her cover was busted she was actually quite ready to brag about her clever little deeds.

'Fine,' she began after an exaggerated pause. 'You'd actually done a pretty good job. We didn't know you were still alive. Not until the FBI contacted us, saying they had someone in custody with information about one of our former agents.'

'Who did the FBI have?' I knew this too of course but didn't want to show my hand.

'Colombian woman called Maria who you apparently had a fling with. Should learn to be more careful with the pillow talk when you're sleeping around.'

At that remark I raised my gun-holding hand instinctively to bring it across someone's face but I stopped myself.

'God, I wish *he'd* said that,' I seethed.

'Why?' Bayliss queried.

'Because I feel like punching someone.' I calmed a little. 'You knew nothing about this. Why are you not flipping out?'

He shrugged.

Then Scarlett smoothed a hand down his thigh.

'Oh, he won't flip out,' she said confidently.

And suddenly I realised. This was not a case of a PA abusing her position. It was her who ran the show. He was just a figurehead.

I returned to the story. Just needed to confirm I had it straight. 'So, what did Maria tell you?'

'She told us that you'd run away with a girl called Gemma. It didn't take us long to find out which one and where she was.'

Tanya dried up again. This was taking too long. I had to start feeding her.

'Keep talking god damn it. Pearle?'

'We knew that Gemma had visited a gene-sequencing company. Our agency is quite interested in the data these companies collect, so our boys at NSA regularly siphon it off.' She gave a proud wink. Every movement was starting to grate. 'So, when a snippet of your DNA showed in Gemma's daughter, alarm bells rang. Obviously, we assumed she was your daughter. And from what her mother said on the GenieTec reports the kid had some interesting abilities. That made her very attractive to us.'

'So you decided to incapacitate her mother, so you could snatch her and research her abilities. And ultimately you did something to Karla to make her unreadable by me, such that you could manipulate me indirectly?'

'That's about the size of it.'

'So what did you do to Karla to make her that way?'

'Ah, well I'm not going to reveal all of our secrets am I now.'

Damn – she didn't know. She wasn't the boffin. Either way, I didn't have time to push her on that one. I continued the story.

'Then you put Jackson Burch in jail for the murder of Pearle to draw me out and lead me to Karla.'

Bayliss was clearly getting bored of not hearing his own voice and piped up again.

'You're getting good at this. Maybe soon you could fuck off and talk to yourself someplace else.'

'Hmmm.' I thought about this for a moment, considered it a reasonable suggestion, then kicked Bayliss squarely on the side of his head. He was out cold. I felt much better.

'You did all this because you're in the pocket of Igneous. You wanted to know if I still had a copy of the Hide system; or you wanted me to develop a new one. To detect people wearing fake clothes. Seems so trivial.'

'When there's billions of dollars at stake, nothing's trivial.'

'So I am learning. They also paid you to destabilize the rug trade in New Meadows? Carry out a few killings; start a turf war? Scare off the cops?'

She didn't answer. But it was a yes anyway.

'And that's why you chose to set-up Burch for the killings, because he was a key link man on the street.' I was talking to myself now as much as anyone. 'Boy, fashion sure does corrupt.'

I knew a lot of this because I'd done my homework;

done a little digging with the cops.

'Anyway, enough chit-chat. Time to get what I came for.'

'And what is that?'

'I want out. Out for good.'

Scarlett laughed out loud at this suggestion. 'Aaron, my dear boy. You know there's no out. Not from how far in you are. Like a little tick screwed into flesh, you're not coming out alive. You're with us or you're dead. That's how it is. We like our employment contracts simple – keeps HR off our backs.' It takes something to make jokes at the wrong end of a gun barrel. You can't know how much until you've been there. 'You can keep disappearing if you like. But it will get harder every time. And when we need you, we'll come find you again.'

'Well maybe you'll think differently when you consider what I'm about to know about you.'

She flashed me a frown. '*About* to know about me? What are you talking about?'

I smiled and shook my head in mock disbelief.

'Have you forgotten who I am?' I dropped the gun to my side and looked her sternly in the eyes. She was beginning to realise what I meant. And as soon as she did it would be too late. For as soon as you're aware there is something you don't want to think about, there it is, right slap bang in the middle of your head.

'Is there something you don't want me to know about, Tanya?'

For the first time she lost her composure. She began to glisten with perspiration. Her eyes were locked onto mine, but they quivered ever so slightly. She was desperately trying not to look away; trying not to look at something. If she were straining so hard it must almost be in her line of sight. I looked over my shoulder. Then I stood up and walked over to the mantelpiece.

'Oh yes,' I said. 'I've heard about this.'

An hour later, it was time to get the hell out of Dodge. Bayliss was immobilised in the corner, with tape and a few sedatives. Tanya was sitting upright in a dining chair in the centre of the room.

'All done. Time to go,' I announced. I holstered my gun and walked to the door. At the last moment I turned back.

'Oh, I almost forgot.'

'What?' said Tanya with a distant look in her eye.

'There's a contract out on your life. Well, his actually,' I said, nodding at the sleeping Bayliss. 'I've hired a really good assassin. You might be familiar with her work.' I smiled. 'If she doesn't hear from me this evening, then ... well, you get the idea.'

I left the room. Then I legged it from the Bayliss residence, my feet making satisfying gravel-grinding sounds as they slammed into the driveway. I was pleased at fleeing in such an un-stealth-like manner, like sticking up my mid-digit, only far more productive. Strangely, my mood improved still further when the first bullet whistled past me, kicking up a plume of dust as it impacted the ground.

I had not left my hosts too incapacitated because I'd not wanted them to have to be found by someone else. So I knew the heavies would be turning up sooner or later. Just hadn't thought it would be this soon. I had been belting down a footpath between the well-manicured gardens of large houses, when the unmistakeable sound of a car screeching to an angry halt came from behind. I dealt with this new information in a rather unconventional manner.

I stopped and I turned around. I don't know why, and I don't know why a smile formed on my lips as I watched two burly men pounding towards me, emptying bullets into the air like they had shares in a munitions factory. They didn't appear to be getting any closer. Time seemed to have slowed.

I had clearly spent too much of my life moulding my brain to the shape of a Hollywood movie, because then a banging rock track kicked off in my head. It was one of my favourite tunes of all time. One of those songs that makes you feel invincible. That when you put it on the car stereo you just keep reaching for that volume knob until you feel so powerful that the laws of reality just don't apply to you anymore, and you can throw the car into that bend at whatever speed seems most fun. I nodded my head and tapped my feet to the drum beat as it picked up, and as I watched the men it felt like I could almost see the bullets whizz past me; that I could will them to miss.

Then time skipped a beat and the men were bearing down on me like rabid butchers. It was time to drive. Yet I was still peculiarly untroubled. I just reached for that volume knob and put the pedal to the metal.

An attractive terracotta lion figurine exploded in front of me but I was already shielding my face. My forearm was peppered with shards of pottery but I felt no pain. I just felt good. I pelted along the suburban streets, faster and faster, leaving the two men panting in my wake. And I kept running flat out for the two straight miles to where I'd dropped my car.

It was only as I recovered my breath that I realised why every one of those bullets – from the guns of trained marksmen – had whistled past me. It's because they weren't trying to hit me. They just wanted me to stop running. Tanya Scarlett wanted me alive – to call off the contract. That was the idea. So, it was true, I had no telekinetic powers over speeding projectiles, which was a bummer because that could have come in handy. But I allowed myself to be smug over the running bit anyway. That was all me.

It was too soon to say it was almost over.

But for the first time I thought that it might not always be too soon.

Thirty-Five

Heroes

As I waited for my associate to arrive, my mind drifted back to when I was fourteen years old; to when a superhero died. A *real* one, I mean. It's not that I'm some kind of delusional comic book nerd. I don't quote my personal moral code by reference to Marvel back-issues. You know that by now.

However, like most people, I do know the basic superhero concepts. All superheroes have a super power, obviously. And they all have a weakness too. They *can* be harmed. But, most importantly, they always recover. They always find a way to fight back and save the day. But *he* didn't – not this day.

The man himself was actually a film actor known for his portrayal of a popular superhero character. But for many people – adults and children alike – it was hard to distinguish the formidable figure from the alter ego he played on screen. So when he was thrown from a horse and broke his neck so severely that he would never walk again, the world was shocked and saddened. I was too, but in my naive childish way I saw it differently. It seemed apparent to me that this was the first scene of his next adventure. A touch of silver-screen magic had leaked into real-life, and this was the superhero's next calling. I was totally sure that he would rise to this new challenge. He would fight his way back. He had the fame and the fortune to attract the research that was required in the field of spinal injuries. He *would* walk again, I was certain of that. And in so doing he would save the world – the real one this time. In this respect, I was quite excited.

And sure enough, the chapters unfolded. After some years there was a breakthrough and against all odds he began to regain feeling and some movement in his body. It is impossible to imagine the elation of once again feeling a wife's hug, where there had been nothing but numbness for eight years. I know this sounds like movie pap, but it's all true. And so is the next bit; the bit when, suddenly, he was dead. Blood poisoning from bed sores. This really wasn't in the script.

It affected me a lot more than most. At my adolescent age I had spent all of my recent years uncovering one-by-one the dull reality behind each of the childhood fantasies doled upon me by a grown-up world; coming to terms with the fact that they were little more than lies. So with the death of this hero came the death of my last remaining fantasy. And that settled it. There was no magic in the world. No greater guiding purpose. Bad things happen to good people, and good things happen to bad people. That's the way it is.

However, this experience did allow me to realise something quite fundamental, even at that young age. It made me realise just how desperate the world is for a superhero. I don't just mean those of the comic books. For there is an inexhaustible supply of would-be superheroes throughout history and across the globe. From the legends of King Arthur and Robin Hood, to the

Gods of a thousand religions. From Santa Claus to Peter Pan to a myriad other folklore characters. Monsters from the Lochs. Spirits from the other side. Aliens from distant planets.

The world longs for something ... something *else*. Something powerful and exciting. A little bit of magic.

But there's one tiny flaw with every one of these revered characters. That's just what they are, *characters*. They are all make-believe. Or at least, none of them are tangibly real; not as far as my own personal belief system is concerned. Only the deluded or slightly peculiar can take comfort from the existence of any of them. And, in a way, these believers are the lucky ones. Religion, for example, is a very powerful placebo. If you *can* believe in a God, then invariably He *will* help you. Alas, the rest of us are left wanting.

All of this leads to an interesting philosophical question. If any one of such mystical characters could be proven to be real, which would bring greatest good to our world?

It was clear to me that Jesus was not a contender. I was sure his timely reappearance would not result in peace on Earth to all mankind. Indeed, it would probably result in the bloodiest period of holy warfare the planet had ever borne witness to. The fundamentalists would finally have someone *real* to fight over. Heaven forbid.

Similarly, if aliens turned up on our doorstep, it would scare the living crap out of most people, even if the little green fellas did insist they came in peace. We've experienced racism before, but the display that would ensue from this event would cast a planetary shadow over any that preceded it.

The answer, of course, is *None of the Above*. What

we really want are the everyday heroes. The bystander that throws himself on the tube lines to save a stranger. The pilot who expertly lands a stricken plane in the ocean, then wades up-and-down the sinking craft, waist deep in water, to save his passengers before himself.

But the miraculous events that give rise to these heroes are few and far between. Or maybe it's that these brave souls are rare in themselves. Either way we find ourselves obliged to revere a different class of hero. Some would say a less worthy class of hero.

The celebrity role models.

The superstars of stage, screen and sports field.

In an increasingly post-faith world, *these* are the Gods that we idolise irrationally. These are the deities that impressionable adolescents worship fanatically, and pilgrimage toward, and post effigies of on their bedroom walls.

They are the ones who teach us how to act, how to look, how to *be*. And so they wield an alarming degree of power over the collective psyche of our world. We should channel it wisely ... if we have the opportunity.

Consider Danny Rubeck, the retired football player from England. He caught the attention of the media early in his career when he was romantically linked with a member of the royal family. From then on he never looked back. In his sporting career he reached the top of his game, captaining his nation's team and playing for them in over one hundred games. This alone would have been enough to secure his name in history, for him to become an ambassador for his sport and a hero for his nation.

But, if anything, he sparkled *off* the field even more than on it. He had that certain indefinable quality, the Xfactor. He drove fashion. Not just for clothes or hair. His image became the very definition of good-looking, in a very literal sense. He was, basically, just plain cool.

But if all this wasn't enough to make him one of the most admired people on the planet, he managed to trump the lot by marrying one of Hollywood's most popular A-listers.

Sadie Winters was an undeniably good catch. Raised on the wrong side of the tracks, she strived tirelessly for the stardom she longed for. She was the very epitome of the American dream. She was beautiful, but also a very talented actress. No Oscars on the family mantelpiece yet, but it was only a matter of time.

The pairing of these two individuals – a British sporting icon and a beloved American actress – was like manna from heaven for the global media. And what makes them still the hottest couple on the block is that they appear almost squeaky clean, still together after ten years of marriage and three adorable children.

They are nothing short of a symbol for the people of the world. A symbol of success, integrity and family values. Of course, this means one thing. They are marketing dynamite and the advertisers know it. Consequently, they are obscenely wealthy. But maybe in this case it is justified. The existence of an entity like Rubeck-and-Winters has an immeasurable affect on the world. A few snaps of the couple on a red carpet can do more to lift the spirits of the populous in bad times than a hundred world leaders shaking hands over a new international trade agreement or nuclear disarmament treaty.

Of course, continual gratuitous coverage of media sweethearts is enough to make a manly man like me –

ahem – almost want to hurl. But in a world of people drowning in a constant tide of dark news, it would be remiss of me to overlook their power to heal.

I ruminated over these ideas as I sipped my beer and I was so lost in myself that I didn't notice the man approach me.

'You look like shit,' he said.

'Thanks,' I responded.

Thirty-Six

Finale

The façade of the Rock Hotel was fully Igneous-branded for the occasion, adorned with large flickering flames, courtesy of some technical wizardry, and two eight-story high images of the stars of the show, Rubeck and Winters.

As the Fabrics of Life event had approached over recent weeks, details as to its nature had slowly leaked into the public domain. Though it was increasingly difficult to tease apart the truth from the speculation. In essence, most eager onlookers believed that the Igneous clothing firm had generously sponsored an economic think-tank to study the ethical dilemmas faced by large multinational corporations in the modern world. And the result ... was a solution. A solution to how a consumer-driven 'globalised' world could, well, *work*. No more was known than that. It seemed far-fetched, but the fact that ultra-ethical couple Rubeck and Winters had bought into whatever the plan was added significant credibility to the occasion.

Although, not everyone was so ecstatic. Or so it would seem, given the recent serious threats against the event received by the police and verified as genuine. Due to the threats, the cordon around the hotel extended for one block in each direction, such that the immediate vicinity was uncharacteristically quiet. Beyond the barriers, a street away, was a different story. Thousands of excited fans jostled for position, staring up at the huge video screens. Around the world people would be doing likewise in their own living rooms. This was a big event. A big event with no known fundamental substance, yet engendering a sense of unparalleled significance. Such is the glittering magic of celebrity.

A reporter shouted into a camera with the screaming crowd as a backdrop.

'I'm talking to you live from outside the Rock Hotel, venue for the Igneous Fabrics of Life event. The launch of a campaign that has been billed as one that could change the world.'

An event that would change the world.

'As you can see behind me there is huge excitement as it nears, and we'll be with you live throughout the proceedings.'

Inside, the atmosphere was similar in a more reserved fashion, although was sure to change as the champagne flowed. The audience was studded with so many stars as to make the night sky jealous. These were the elite invitation-only guests. Considering the security concerns surrounding the occasion only those with a very long history of not shooting people were on the list.

The venue was vast, as to be expected from a convention hall in New Meadows. It was decked out like an awards ceremony, with guests grouped around circular tables.

From the stage at the front, a catwalk jutted into the audience. This was a fashion show of sorts, after all. Though no one knew really what to expect.

No one knew what to expect.

As the chattering onlookers grew steadily more excited with anticipation and champagne bubbles, there was one group of individuals that were slightly less relaxed. Those charged with preserving the security of this event. Despite the potential for this to be nothing more than a massive publicity stunt, in everyone's hearts and minds it was much more than that. And certainly in the minds of the New Meadows officials this was a fundamentally crucial occasion. As such, no risks could be taken. It was decided that no private security firm would be involved in the operation and even the regular venue staff were all off-duty. The only people in the room who were not A-listers were either secret service agents or long-serving police. The heads of security were determined that any threats would remain firmly outside, that any demonstrations – be they anti-globalisation or anti- anything else – would be restricted to the streets. So far there had been only a few limited scuffles with police.

A thirty-foot tall number '10' illuminated above the stage and began to count down. The audience accompaniment grew louder with every second that ticked down, until by the time it reached '4' the whole room was chanting the numbers.

No one knew what to expect when the countdown hit zero, but they assumed it would be wonderfully dramatic. And they weren't disappointed.

The music that had been building as a crescendo cut to silence, and the room fell to darkness. The only illumination that remained was from the white lights that beaded the edge of the catwalk, twinkling through the dry ice fog that flowed over them.

There was a tantalising pause, then bang: a wall of sound. Then, a beat later, two spotlights burst into life. And there they were, Rubeck and Winters, standing on either side of the stage. The crowd erupted into a standing ovation.

The two stars beamed radiant smiles and waved at the crowd, soaking up the adulation as only stars know how. After a perfectly orchestrated period of time, in sync with the music, the couple walked toward centre stage and joined in the middle with a kiss. And as their lips met, flames burst from the stage behind them and the Igneous insignia shimmered into view.

The couple turned and started their journey down the catwalk. They were both dressed in white. Rubeck in a suit; Winters in an elegant dress. Not the usual apparel associated with Igneous clothing, but more than fitting for the occasion.

They walked hand-in-hand, each waving their free arm at the crowd as they passed. This was a royal visit, in all but name.

Everyone in the venue was thoroughly in-the-moment. Despite all the concerns, nobody felt the least bit uneasy that something unscripted may occur. Nobody, except maybe one ... or two.

As the couple reached half-way along the catwalk they stopped, and in a choreographed skit they played-acted a little quarrel. Then in time with a beat in the music they tore at each other's garments and in a split second their haute couture was in tatters on the floor and they were standing there showing off the other star of the show: consumer fashion.

The onlookers whooped with appreciation as Rubeck struck a pose, now wearing jeans and a checked-shirt with torn-off sleeves; his arm around the slender waist of his wife, now wearing a little summer dress with a slim leather belt.

They held their pose for a moment before continuing their journey; one confident stride after the next. With each footstep a thousand flashbulbs fired, capturing another moment in time, another moment in the life of the camera's quarry. With each pace forward the music cranked up a notch, the lights shone brighter, the beaming smiles got wider and the audience grew louder and louder, forgetting their place, their inhibitions.

And as the iconic couple reached the end of the catwalk, the cacophony peaked, everyone solidifying into a shared moment of adulation. All attention aimed toward one point in space and time, as if right here, right now, these two people were the centre of the universe.

That was when the two gunshots rang out.

Both bullets were on target.

What followed was screaming mayhem. Only a few in the right place would have known at that point what had just occurred. Those that had turned in the right direction would have seen a waiter standing in an aisle between the tables, facing the stage. They would have seen him standing in a pool of champagne and broken glass. And they would have seen him holding firmly above his head a silver platter, perpendicular to the ground. What they might not have seen was the two freshly-formed dents in the centre of the platter.

This image existed only for a split second. Then the chaos ensued. Bodyguards surrounded the shell-shocked celebrity couple within seconds and man-handled them off the stage. At the same moment, at the back of the room, a number of special agents were over-powering a woman with a gun.

The guests were not sure which way to run for the best, but were running all the same.

Only one man inside the building knew what was going down. The waiter with the platter. And he just, well, waited. He stood amidst the enveloping melee enjoying his own inner tranquillity. Of course, he was not a waiter at all. Just like all the other catering staff at the event, he was a cop. He knew that very soon he would be whisked away, by people who were rapidly trying to piece together what had happened here. Not that they would wholly succeed because what had happened here could not have happened. It was impossible. That was entirely the point.

Outside, the initial mood of hysterical terror transitioned to something quite different. When, slowly, details began to emerge, the raucous crowd died down to a point where they were virtually silent, staring up at the video screens. Each and every one of them felt they had witnessed something truly remarkable.

Inside the cordon where only members of the press were allowed, a reporter talked animatedly into a camera.

'I'm standing outside Rock Hotel, New Meadows, which only moments...' She was flustered and faltering as the events unfolded around her. '...which only moments ago was host to a remarkable scene. Information so far indicates that a woman fired two shots at the celebrity couple Rubeck and Winters. It appears from initial reports that tragedy was avoided in the most astonishing fashion.'

Scurrying reporters and camera operators bumped

past the reporter, who was visibly ruffled. Holding a hand to her earpiece to block out the growing din behind her, she continued.

'We understand that an undercover policeman, posing as a waiter, blocked the bullets with a silver champagne platter. The whole event was broadcast live across the world. Footage is being analysed to further elaborate details of the events witnessed here, but at this early stage it does appear that the assassination of Danny Rubeck and Sadie Winters was prevented by a policeman blocking the gunshots with a silver platter.'

The expected equanimity of her voice, instilled through years of training, had been overturned, replaced by disbelief and wonder. The camera she was addressing panned around to show the crowds as the reporter took a moment to collect herself. Then she continued.

'The many thousands of fans who have been waiting here to wish the couple well are standing stunned but chattering excitedly. Many are already hailing this a miracle; an act of God.'

The reporter was distracted momentarily by a message in her ear and then started moving toward the hotel entrance.

'I'm just hearing that the unnamed hero is about to leave the hotel now.'

A gaggle of reporters rushed to surround the entrance of the hotel and shortly afterwards a group of heavy suited men exited the building shielding another man dressed in a waiter's uniform. The suited men formed a circle around the man and attempted to usher him to a waiting car, as reporters bombarded the new star with questions.

'People are calling this an act of God. What do you

say to that?'

Conner smiled at the suggestion but didn't respond. He'd sooner believe in an act of silverware than an act of God, but he figured that was not what the nation was waiting to hear.

'People are hailing you a hero,' shouted another questioner. 'How do you feel about that?'

Conner shrugged coyly as he was jostled along.

'Can you explain what happened?' came another question as a microphone was thrust in his direction. This time his entourage had stalled momentarily and he had time to turn to the questioner with a knowing glint in his eye.

'Magic,' he beamed.

As Conner was bustled down the sweeping flight of steps outside the Rock Hotel he happened to look out over the heads of the throng in front of him. Across the street he saw a man he recognised, sitting on a wall. The two men exchanged smiles. Then the moment was gone.

'Do you have anything to say to the viewers watching?' called one reporter as Conner passed by.

Conner considered this for a moment and decided that this was one question he needed to answer. He shook free from the grip of the bodyguards and stepped back toward the reporter who had put the question to him. One of the suits put a firm hand on Conner's shoulder, but he shook it off. Orders from above must have allowed Conner his moment because the hand didn't return and instead the heavies formed a neat barrier around Conner in his new position.

'Yes I do,' Conner said to the reporter, in a raised voice to carry over the din. He turned to look into the lens of the accompanying camera. It was a message for everyone, but in his mind he was only talking to one person. And he hoped she understood.

'The greatest lesson to learn from all of this,' he began, 'is that fashion is not worth losing a life over. And it is not worth living your life *by*.'

As Conner spoke, the frenzied swarm of onlookers in the distance grew too much for the law enforcement. The barriers finally came down. The horde pushed through the cordon of police and flooded toward the hotel entrance.

Conner tugged at his shirt. 'These labels we are supposed to bear, these *brands* we are supposed to flaunt, they are just that; as if burnt into our skin from the branding irons wielded by our would-be owners – the corporations that want to tell us who to be. And when we succumb, what we are left standing in is nothing but another restrictive uniform. Like the one we wear to work, consumer fashion is nothing but a uniform for our leisure time –'

The bodyguards spotted the impending danger of the manic crowd rushing toward them and started to manhandle Conner away. As he was jerked backwards he reached into his jacket pocket and pulled something out. He shouted back to the camera as he was dragged off.

'Sometimes we have to take off the uniform that dictates who we are. We have to take off our uniform to allow our other self to see the light again.' And with that, just as he was bundled into the back of a black car, he threw his police badge high in the air.

It was time to allow his other self to see the light again.

Thirty-Seven

Magic

I watched with some pride from across the street from the Rock Hotel, having sweet-talked my way into the press area. I'd met Conner some weeks ago in BlueJay. He needed my help and I took him on as a project. Although, I couldn't possibly have imagined all of this would follow.

The plan fell into place when I was at the Bayliss residence. I needed the Zack and Tanya show to end once and for all. Tanya Scarlett in particular was using her power for her own titillation, as well as being on the bung from corporate sponsors.

I saw her invitation for the Igneous event on the mantelpiece and knew it offered the perfect opportunity to bring Tanya Scarlett's reign to a spectacular close. So I told her in no uncertain terms that bad things were going to happen at the event. I told her that I was going to be there, dressed as a waiter and that I was going to shoot Rubeck and Winters. And she knew I could do it. She knew if there was anyone on the planet that could get in there with a gun, it was me.

Scarlett was deeply in the neatly-styled pocket of Igneous Clothing and they were looking to her to protect this gig at all costs. So I knew she'd be there and I knew she'd be on edge. I also knew that although she wouldn't be allowed in with a gun – being officially only a PA – she would arrange to get hold of one inside from one of her agents.

So, then it all came down to my exquisite knack of persuasion.

I hesitate to use the word 'hypnosis' here because this term no more describes a specific method than the term 'magic' does. Consider the variation between a performer making someone act like a chicken on stage, and a therapist helping someone overcome agoraphobia. Nevertheless, the word's brevity serves a purpose.

You will have heard that you cannot hypnotise someone to do something against their will, something that they don't want to do. This is not strictly true. As you will also have heard of sane normal individuals being brainwashed by cult leaders and religious fundamentalists to commit suicide and murder innocent people. And brainwashing is just another form of hypnosis.

It *is* true though that this sort of extreme behaviour cannot be induced during a mere stage performance, or during an hour in somebody's living room. So how did I get Tanya Scarlett to fire a gun at Rubeck and Winters? And how did I orchestrate the whole thing so perfectly? Well it really wasn't that hard.

Things are not always quite what they seem. Some things, in fact, are quite the opposite. You have to look at things from a different point of view; flip things on their head. Ask yourself, which is cause and which is effect?

Amidst all the pandemonium following the incensed gunshot attack and the divine silverware intervention, there was one crucial point that everyone missed; and will forever miss. When Scarlett fired her gun at Rubeck and Winters, she was not aiming at *them*.

She was aiming at the *platter*.

When I was in Bayliss's living room – whilst the man himself was still accommodatingly blood-staining his upholstery without complaint – I spent a little time with Scarlett. Using as a prop the silver tray bearing Bayliss's scotch, I embedded what some might call a post-hypnotic suggestion, though she was never in the trance-like state that people associate with hypnosis. She was too resistant for that. But there was no need for it. The intense confrontational nature of the encounter lent itself nicely to my cause: associating that silver platter with me, with my promise to destroy her big day; defining it as a marker of things turning bad for her. For once, I won't explain the details. Let's just say I got inside her head.

On the day, all Conner had to do was stumble into her path, make a little commotion and thrust the tray into the air; and Scarlett would be popping bullets into it before even she knew what was happening. And because Conner was in a line between her and the stage, to everyone else it looked like she was aiming for the stars and that the waiter had somehow stopped the bullets with some divine inspiration.

Why was all this so necessary? Why could I not just have dealt with Scarlett on a smaller scale? Because I had an ulterior motive...

To solve a bigger problem.

It was a problem that had troubled me ever since the beginning. A problem that was very personal to me, but one that was affecting everyone on the planet to an ever greater degree. Although few were aware, it was undeniable that the world was suffering from the greatest pandemic it had ever had to face. One so damaging that if it could not be cured then the entirety of our race's achievements would count for nothing.

This disease to which I refer is: unhappiness.

It wasn't just me. I may be a special case, but despite all the riches of the developed world, people are less content now than they have been at any point in history. And if, with all our ingenious advancements, we are less content in our lives than the animals around us, then what was the point of our millennia of evolution? What was the point of coming down from the trees in the first place?

To answer this question you need to understand how it can be so, that the haves of the first world are no more content than the have-nots of the third world; how the haves of today are no happier than the have-nots of the post-war era.

How can this be so?

Consider this.

If a happy person gets paralysed in an accident then they become a happy person in a wheelchair – eventually. And if an *unhappy* person wins the lottery then they just become an unhappy millionaire.

This is true. I've seen it. The point you may take from this is that whatever happens to you, you never really change; after a period of adjustment you return to whoever you were before. This is true, if left unchecked.

But there's a more fundamental point, and it is simply this: happiness is state of *mind*; not a state of material.

It's not about what you have; it's about how you *think*. And states of mind *can* be altered. People *can* change. I've seen this too. I know how to do it. I know how to make the world smile. If just for a day.

So I figured the world needed a hero today.

And a little bit of magic.

Because that can be enough to change a person, for the better.

Yet despite the fanfare that would ring out from this moment, I knew it was a mere token.

I knew that one hero could not cure the world.

I knew that *I* could not cure the world.

That's *your* job. It's your turn now.

Know that you don't have to be trapped in the person you are today.

Tomorrow you can be a different person.

Decide who you want that person to be.

Exploit your many selves.

Harness your altered states.

And change.

Believe. Strive. Live.

Most of all ... live.

It was my turn to live again.

That's why when I knew the world needed a hero today, I figured it didn't need to be me. I didn't need the acclaim. I was happy to slip back into the shadows. I've been in them so long I think they'd miss me anyway.

Shaking myself from my reverie I was just about to move from the wall I'd been perched upon when a twist to my story presented itself that I really wasn't expecting.

'So, do I get the exclusive?'

The voice came from beside me. I turned to see a young woman standing there.

'I think you've missed him,' I said, nodding across the street.

'No,' she said shaking her head. 'No, I haven't.' And she hopped up beside me onto the wall where I was still sitting.

I turned and looked at her face. I didn't recognise her, but at the same time she wasn't totally unfamiliar. Somewhere deep in my memory her face registered a chord.

'Do I know you?' I asked, figuring that was a good way to address the conundrum.

'Not as well as I know you.'

Her words were not threatening. I struggled a bit longer to tap my memories, but then she put me out of my misery.

'A long time ago, there was a girl in a bar, drinking with her college friends. She wanted to become a journalist, but she was lacking in self-confidence. Then a mysterious man starts talking to her. Makes her see things differently. Changes her outlook. Changes *her*. Just a little.'

I remembered her now. It was a long time ago. She was a nice girl then and had grown in to a pleasant woman now. Otherwise I might have been more concerned. But I was still perplexed. How was she here now? I expressed my confusion with a deeply puzzled brow and asked the question.

'How ... do you know who I am? How have you managed to track me down? The US intelligence couldn't even do that. Not for a long time anyway.'

'Ah, well, *they* weren't looking for the right thing.'

'How do you mean?'

'They were looking for the pebble. I was looking for the ripples.'

'Go on.'

'Someone who touches so many lives as you, leaves their trace in those people's thoughts. And thoughts aren't so private these days. A couple of decades back it would've been different, but today many wish their lives and thoughts to be public domain. Not you, of course, but some of the people you've helped. That day, after meeting you, what do you think I did?'

I shrugged. 'Tell me.'

'I wrote about it in great detail in my online journal. I figured that if this is what you did with your life, mine wouldn't be the only anecdote buried in the web. It was pretty tough tracking any down, because there was no common theme, until I recalled your opening question, and that was the link I needed. So I managed to track a few people down, asked them a few questions, found out a little about you, figured out a little about your movements.'

'You should be a detective.'

'Ha, I am now. After six years as an investigative journalist I became a straight investigator. Don't worry; I don't really know much about you at all. Just something happened recently which made me realise you were in New Meadows. I have no idea what just happened in there.' She nodded to the Rock Hotel. 'But when I saw you here, I figured *you* might.'

She smiled at me with a wink and I smiled back knowingly.

'I don't really expect an exclusive. I know you're not the media-darling type. I just wanted you to know ... just wanted you to let one person say it to you ...'

'Say what?'

'You *are* a hero.'

I paused for a moment, staring ahead.

'Thanks,' I said as I hopped off the wall. 'I appreciate it.'

Then I walked away. But after a few paces I realised something. I realised that I wasn't that person any more. I didn't need to be the person who walked away. I turned around and took a few steps back toward her.

'Aaron,' I said as I offered a hand.

'Mila,' she replied, refusing the hand and opting to give me a hug instead. It was good to be back in the real world.

I scribbled some details on the back of one of my various fake business cards and handed it over.

'Here. Give me a call and I'll give you your story. Just not right now. I have someone to go see.'

Thirty-Eight
Cure

Once again I found myself standing at the entrance to the hospital ward. Only this time it was different. In many ways. Firstly, it was different because I was not alone. The small hand of a young girl was pressed firmly into mine.

I'd had more time to get to know that girl. I'd learnt that she had only inherited my skill to read people, as this was the only one that was a reawakened latent ability. Not my abilities to change people. So I was still the only dentist in town. But I didn't think that mattered. I felt that I would find my cure here anyway.

No doubt I would have stood at the entrance much longer with apprehension. But not everything was under my control these days.

Pearle tugged me forward impatiently.

'Come on, come on,' she said, in the way kids do when adults need bringing into line.

Her eagerness was understandable. She hadn't seen her mother since she'd been taken from her. I'd told Felicity that it wouldn't be safe to bring her here until I'd done what I'd needed to.

We reached Gemma's bedside and Pearle climbed up onto the chair beside it to put an arm across her mum's chest and kiss her on the cheek.

'Hello mommy,' she said softly. She looked up at me. She wasn't sad or concerned. I'd told her what to expect and I'd told her everything would be okay. And she knew I meant it ... of course.

I pulled up a chair on the other side of the bed to Pearle and leaned in to Gemma's ear.

'Thanks for waiting,' I whispered. 'It's time for you to wake up now.'

As I pulled away I looked at Gemma's peaceful face. It was completely flat and emotionless to everyone, but I caught the tiniest of muscle movements and I knew what it was. It was a smile from deep inside.

Nobody else would have seen it. But *I* did.

I always do.

Epilogue

Buried

www.**pauljnewell**.com
/**altered**states
/**epilogue**

learn more...

www.pauljnewell.com

author@pauljnewell.com

VIRNATION

www.virnation.com

appian publishing

www.appianpublishing.com

red states altered states altered states altered states altered states altered states altered states
just this book just this book just this book just this book just this book just this book just this
and philosophy and philosophy and philosophy and philosophy and philosophy and philosophy and philos
sorts about allsorts about allsorts about allsorts about allsorts about allsorts about allsorts abou
u and me and you and me and you and me and you and me and you and me and you and me and you and me a
a double helix a double helix a double helix a double helix a double helix a double helix a double h
in ways I have in ways I have in way I have kin way I have kin way I have kin way I have kin way I h
sons become reasons become reason become treason become treason become treason become treason become
ats more than hats more than hat more than chat more than chat more than chat more than chat more th
all we have in all we have in all we have in all we have in all we have in all we have in all we hav
alters the sum alters the sum alter the sum falter the sum falter the sum falter the sum falter the
afts of their rafts of their raft of their craft of their craft of their craft of their craft of the
in your hearts in your hearts in you hearts win you hearts win you hearts win you hearts win you hea
the start from the start from the start from the start from the start from the start from the start
chapter one to chapter one to chapter one to chapter one to chapter one to chapter one to chapter o
very end of it very end of it very end of it very end of it very end of it very end of it very end o
one now I know one now I know one now I know on now I know son now I know son now I know son now I
is it a puzzle is it a puzzle is it a puzzle is it a puzzle is it a puzzle is it a puzzle is it a pu
u know don't you know don't you know don't you know don't you know don't you know don't you know don
remember its u remember its u remember its u remember its u remember its u remember its u remember i
land happiness land happiness land happiness land happiness lan happiness plan happiness plan happi
he and it is a he and it is a he and it is a he and it is a he and i is a she and i is a she and i i
fit of for benefit of for benefit of for benefit of for benefit of for benefit of for benefit of for
ate our mind state our mind state our mind state our mind state our min state your min state your mi
errors of mine errors of mine errors of mine errors of mine error of mine terror of mine terror of m
lone never be alone never be alone never be alone never be alone never be alone never be alone never
cure the world cure the world cure the world cure the world cure the world cure the world cure the w
our life live your life live your life live your life live your life live your life live your life l
pajone twitter pajone twitter pajone twitter pajone twitter pajone twitter pajone twitter pajone twi